Last Light

Also by M. Pierce

Night Owl

Last Light

M. Pierce

St. Martin's Griffin New York

LASTLIGHT. Copyright © 2014 by M. Pierce.
All rights reserved. Printed in the United States of America.
For information, address St. Martin's Press,
175 Fifth Avenue, New York, N.Y. 10010.

www.stmartins.com

Library of Congress Cataloging-in-Publication Data

Pierce, M.
    Last light / M. Pierce.—First edition.
        pages cm.—(The night owl trilogy ; 2)
    ISBN 978-1-250-05836-2 (trade paperback)
    ISBN 978-1-4668-6253-1 (e-book)
    1. Authors—Fiction.   2. Absence and presumption of
death—Fiction.   3. Electronic books—Fiction.   4. Brothers—
Fiction.   I. Title.
    PS3616.I355L37 2014
    813'.6—dc23

                                              2014030942

St. Martin's Griffin books may be purchased for educational, business, or promotional use. For information on bulk purchases, please contact the Macmillan Corporate and Premium Sales Department at 1-800-221-7945, extension 5442, or write to specialmarkets@macmillan.com.

First Edition: November 2014

10 9 8 7 6 5 4 3 2 1

For Anna, again

For one white singing hour of peace
Count many a year of strife well lost.
—SARA TEASDALE, *"Barter"*

Last Light

PROLOGUE

December is the cruelest month to die in.

Sheer wind gusts across the Narrows. The wind is white with spindrift. I can't see an inch in any direction, but I know the Trough—six hundred vertical feet of ice—hangs below me.

This is where I die.

I crouch against the face of the mountain. My arm bleeds into my jacket. When I tip my sleeve like a cup, blood spills into the wind.

I know what this will look like: like I underestimated a technical climb, or the cold and altitude overwhelmed me.

But I never underestimate a climb.

I begin to descend, the teeth of my crampons catching in the ice, the pick of my axe lodged against a rock. Hand over hand, foot over foot. Slow going in the bitter cold.

When a blast of wind tears at my pack, I hug the mountain and swear.

Another gale dislodges my boot. My leg swings out. I am exposed, and the wind rips over me. I flip my axe and drive the spike into the ice. *Too late.*

With a snap of breaking ice, I come loose from the mountainside.

I am in the air, thrashing. I fall and tumble. My helmet dings a knob of ice.

The white world wheels around me, and I land with a crack.

Then stillness.

I feel no pain through my screaming panic. I roll onto my back and wheeze. *I'm alive.* My goggles are broken, a shard of lens in my cheek. I taste the ferric tang of blood.

But I am breathing. I can see. I can move.

I need help.

"Help . . ."

The word is a tatter of air.

There is no one here to help me. My blood and I are the last heat on this mountain.

I think of Hannah. The thought of her comes with a current of feeling, which grows and deepens until my chest aches. She is long gone, and I can't sleep now.

I can't sleep now . . .

Chapter 1

HANNAH

I remember the book signing—I always will—when so much else is forgotten.

I helped convince Matt to do it, along with Pam and his editor. *People know who you are,* we told him. *The secret is out; you have nothing to lose. Do this, at least, for your local fans. Think about how they've supported you.*

And Matt agreed, after weeks of resistance. One signing. A stand-alone event, lightly publicized, to be held at his favorite independent bookstore—Flight of Ideas.

That Saturday afternoon in December, the crowd filled the store and a line formed down the street. Readers drove in from surrounding states. An Arizona local, unprepared for the Denver cold, collapsed in line and brought a screaming ambulance to the chaos. News stations deployed their vans. Reporters and photographers clamored for a word with Matt, flashing their press passes as if they meant anything.

A modest stock of Matt's books sold out within an hour.

The store manager and employees moved through the mob, wringing their hands.

And I stood beside Matt, watching the madness. What had we done?

Matt sat at a small table with Pam to his left and me to his right. We brought water, coffee, tea, cookies—but he touched nothing. Empty displays loomed around us. A printout dangled from the table, half torn: M. PIERCE EXCLUSIVE BOOK SIGNING.

Readers came bearing multiple copies of his books, hardcover and paperback, various editions. They chattered at Matt as he dashed off his signature. Their stories were variations on a theme of adoration. *I read* Ten Thousand Nights *in high school. I've read all your books. I've reread this book so many times. I can't wait for your next book.*

Matt met each fan with a stomach-level stare. He looked grim and determined.

When his pen died, he slid it across the table to Pam.

"The pen," he whispered.

About twenty minutes into the signing, Matt rose and disappeared into the crowd.

I found him in a storage room.

He stood facing a shelf of boxes, a hand covering his face.

"Matt?" I touched his back. He didn't move. I slid my fingers up his spine and kissed his shoulder blade. "Hey, that's a lot of people out there, huh?"

Matt's silence frightened me—always. We'd been living together for just a month and a half. Matt spent most of his time writing. My job at the agency absorbed me. In so many ways, we were still strangers, circling the mystery of one another. And when I was alone with Matt, as I was in the storage room that afternoon, I sensed I was alone with something volatile.

Finally he said, "Do you think my editor did this?"

"Did what?" I moved to get a look at his face.

Another long silence.

I waited it out.

"You don't know what it meant to me," he said.

Matt pulled me in for a quick hug and walked out of the storage room.

The signing ran for another half hour, during which Matt sat with his hand half covering his face. Pam gave me a few puzzled looks. I shrugged.

Matt said I didn't know *what it meant to him.* He was right. I didn't know what *it* meant. I didn't know what the hell *it* was.

But now I know. It was his privacy. And now I know how he valued his privacy. Above me, above his family, above everything.

Two months after the book signing, I stood in a phone booth in New Jersey, just outside my motel.

I listened to the ringtone on the line. I listened to the rain, a steady frigid patter.

What I am doing, I thought, *is wicked. How can I?*

And then I pictured Matt.

The scenes of our last days together were surreal.

Matt moving money into the wall safe in our condo.

Matt pacing, talking excitedly about freedom and his writing.

Matt vanishing onto a snow-choked trail in the mountains.

Watching him go—watching him smile back at me. Real fear in my heart. Confusion. And now this: a facsimile of grief that I would present to Matt's family. Who had I become?

"Hannah?"

The voice sounded far off. I crushed the phone against my ear.

"Matt . . . hi."

"Hannah. Are you okay? I miss you. Fuck, I miss you."

My eyes began to sting.

"No, I'm not okay. How can I be? How can I be okay?"

"Listen, Hannah. This is as hard as it gets. Everything will get easier after this."

"No." I clenched my teeth. "I don't think so."

"It will. Baby bird, trust me. I don't even want you there. Why are you going? Tell Nate you can't go. Call him now and tell him."

"No. I'm going. I deserve this."

"Hannah . . ."

I swallowed thickly and closed my eyes. A car passed, crunching over old ice and snow.

"It doesn't matter," I whispered. "If I seem guilty or sad, if I can't look your family in the eye . . . however it goes. Maybe that's what grief looks like. I don't even fucking know. I don't know anything. I don't know why I agreed to this."

"Is that how it is?" Matt's voice chilled. "Then tell them I'm alive."

"Matt, no. I—"

"No, go on. Tell everyone the truth. I won't do this. I won't be made to feel like I've conned you into this, like I'm manipulating you. Mm, I know . . . it was all well and good when we were together, but you get away from me for a few weeks and suddenly you can't remember why you did this? I thought you wanted this for me."

"I did. I do. Stop it. You can't get—"

"What can't I get? Angry? I'm not angry, Hannah. Do whatever you want. I told you not to go out there. I told you to stay away from it all."

I stayed quiet then and so did Matt. He was right. He told me not to get involved with his family. He knew how it would hurt and how guilty I would feel. And I, a self-saboteur of the first degree, did it anyway.

I helped my lover fake his death.

I lied to my family, Pam, the police.

Now I would lie to Matt's family. I would show them my phony grief. I would watch their sincere suffering. I would go to Matt Sky's memorial.

"This is crazy," I whispered. "I feel sick every day. I'm lonely. I have a z-zillion questions. Are you okay? Do you have enough food? The book . . . I mean, did anyone—"

"Hannah, I miss you so fucking much. Please . . ."

Simple longing filled Matt's voice, and just like that, the tension between us faded.

"I have to see you," he said. "Soon. I'm fine. Food's fine. No word on *Night Owl*. I put out some feelers, posted questions on forums. No replies."

"When I'm back, I'll drive out."

"Yeah, when you're back. Soon as you can. It's been so fucking long. I'm going crazy, bird." Matt's breath quickened. He hesitated, and then went on in a rush. "I want to be with you. I want to be inside you. For hours. Here, by the fire. I need you like that . . ."

The cold of the phone booth disappeared. I pictured Matt in nothing but his skin, and I could practically feel his breath on my lips.

"I need you, too." I lowered my voice. "Like that. In . . . inside me."

"God, you're so good. So good to me. *Hannah . . .*"

Matt was probably touching himself. I heated at the thought. How unfair, his unimpeded access to that beautiful body. And how strange that our romance reverted to this: furtive phone calls, lonely nights, waiting, touching ourselves.

Were we moving backward, or was this new and exciting?

"How . . ." he said. "This thing with us—how is it still so—"

"Intense," I murmured.

A car door slammed.

I lingered a moment over my vision of Matt—his body draped across the couch, his back arching and hips seeking mine as he played with himself—and then I opened my eyes. The morning light stung.

"Shit," I hissed.

A silver Cadillac sedan was parked across the street, and striding toward my phone booth was Nathaniel Sky.

Chapter 2

MATT

I gazed at the cabin's vaulted ceiling. Thick stained beams formed a truss from wall to wall and they gleamed in the firelight.

I needed Hannah on top of me, riding me hard.

My dick rose against the fabric of my lounge pants.

"Intense," I repeated. "Mm . . . say that again. Talk, I want to hear your voice. Tell me what you want. Are you alone?"

I strained to catch the sound of Hannah's breath.

I lay on my back on the couch, my fingertips skating up and down my stomach.

"Shit," Hannah said.

My hand paused. "What's up?"

"Nate's here."

"God, I don't care," I said, and for a moment, I didn't.

I sneered and sat up. My T-shirt flopped into place.

"I have to go," she said.

"I know. Fine. Good luck."

"Don't be angry, Matt."

"I'm not. Are you? Is he listening?"

"No, he's waiting outside the phone booth."

"The phone booth? What the fuck, Hannah?"

"I can handle it. Gotta go. Bye."

"Fuck." I dragged a hand through my hair. "Fine. All right. I love you . . ."

"Yeah. Bye."

The call ended with a loud click.

I frowned and flipped my TracFone shut.

"Goddamn it," I whispered.

That was my first conversation with Hannah in three weeks. We spoke a few times before that—when she told me she planned to attend the memorial, when *Night Owl* happened, and of course when I first got to the cabin. I was in bad shape then.

"I love you," I said again. The wind answered, pressing against the cabin. Hannah would have told me she loved me, but Nate was watching. I understood that.

I tried to picture them together: Hannah and my brother somewhere in New Jersey. Hannah in a phone booth. Nate waiting outside.

Jealousy rose like bile in my throat.

Oh, Nate and his grand house and his do-gooder job and his happy fucking family . . . he always swooped in when I checked out. He would comfort Hannah. He would hug her. His arms would be around her, not mine.

I pocketed my phone and began to pace the main floor of the cabin. I kept the place terrifically hot, the thermostat at seventy and a fire always burning in the grate. I would have kept it cooler if Laurence were with me, but the lucky bastard got to stay with Hannah. His absence would raise suspicion. Missing Matt, missing Laurence—doesn't add up.

Though technically I was *dead* Matt, not missing Matt.

I had a mountain lion to thank for that.

Finally I plopped down at the desk, which I had positioned in front of the deck. The sliding door gave view to pines and mountains caked with snow.

Kevin must have paid a pretty penny for this place. The cabin sat far back on four acres. The nearest neighbors were a mile up the road, and they weren't around.

I was alone.

As far as Kevin knew, I was dead.

Hannah called Kevin a week after my "disappearance." He was a mutual friend with a conveniently remote cabin.

She fed him the lines I fed her. *Can I stay at the cabin? I need to get away. I want to be closer to the search. If Matt's out there, I want to be out there. But I don't want to impose. I understand if . . .*

Kevin offered the cabin without hesitation, as I knew he would. He was in Miami anyway. I felt a twinge of guilt as I surveyed the Rocky Mountains, and I shrugged it off.

I had to remember, I was driven to this.

The media, the public, my editor, even Pam—they drove me to this. I couldn't write in the public eye, and what could I do if I couldn't write? But they wouldn't understand.

I flipped open my notebook and studied the first line of my new story.

December is the cruelest month to die in.

I smiled and slouched in my chair. I couldn't go wrong, riffing on Eliot.

I thumbed my way to chapter one and began to write. A cup of cold coffee stood by my laptop. I sipped it as I worked.

I wrote for three hours, stopping only to laugh or gaze out at the mountains. Once I walked through the cabin. Then I returned to the desk. As long as I was in the story, I wasn't aching for Hannah. As long as I was in the story, I wasn't worrying about Hannah on the East Coast with my family.

I burned out around two in the afternoon. My stomach growled. The fire was dead.

Middle of the fucking day.

I booted up my laptop and connected to the Internet, the dial-up ringing and grating.

I drummed my fingers on the desk as my e-mail loaded.

I had a new e-mail account and a new laptop, bought with cash. New clothes, a new prepaid cell, nothing taken from the condo. The scope of the search for me didn't inspire confidence in

Colorado law enforcement, but I knew my finances would be checked, the condo searched, and phone records reviewed. Standard missing persons protocol. I covered my bases.

A new e-mail appeared in my in-box:

YOU HAVE RECEIVED A PRIVATE MESSAGE ON THEMYSTICTAVERN
.COM FORUM

My God. I sat forward.
Was this it?

I navigated to the forum and swore as I waited for the page to load. Fucking dial-up, fucking dial-up . . .

First I checked my forum post. It had forty-seven views and no replies.

SUBJECT: From one NIGHT OWL to another
by nightowl on Wednesday, January 29, 2014
Message me. I want to talk. You're not in trouble. I'm not angry. I'm intrigued.

I had one new private message. I clicked the little envelope icon and scanned the sender details. The user name, icarusonfire, was unfamiliar.

The message was four words long.

SUBJECT: [no subject]
by icarusonfire on Saturday, February 8, 2014
What do you want?

I replied immediately.

SUBJECT: Re: [no subject]
by nightowl on Saturday, February 8, 2014
You know what I want. I want to talk. You're not in trouble, I promise. Call me.

I included my new phone number below the message.

And I waited.

Ten minutes passed without incident. Anxiety began to coil up inside me. Had I scared him away? Him . . . her? I checked the profile info for icarusonfire. It was a brand-new forum account, made that same day, with no post history. I smirked. Clever . . . and careful.

I checked my phone. It was fully charged and had decent signal. I set the volume to high.

"Call me," I muttered. "Call me, fucking call me."

I browsed the forum as I waited.

That site felt haunted—as much as any digital space can feel haunted—and memories needled at me as I perused the forum.

There was my post in early June 2013: NIGHT OWL SEEKING WRITING PARTNER. I laughed as I reread it. My God, I was such a snob. *Please know how to spell. I expect timely replies. I reserve the right to drop you at any time.*

It was Hannah Catalano who took the bait.

I know how to spell, she replied, *and I can handle being dropped. Can you?*

That was the beginning. That was the start of our story, and it was a good story.

The heat whirred on and I jumped.

Fuck, what was I waiting for? A call that wouldn't come. I slid my phone across the desk and moved to restart the fire. I needed a shower. I needed to chop more wood.

Hell, I needed to eat—and to take stock of my food situation.

I was halfway to the cellar when my phone began to ring.

Chapter 3

HANNAH

I stumbled out of the phone booth and stood staring at Nate, who stood staring at me, his expression unreadable.

"N-Nate . . . hi."

Nate looked paler than I remembered him, his black hair a shock of darkness against the sky. He wore an elegant black suit and tie and a wool coat that reached his knees. Sleepless smudges stained the skin beneath his eyes.

I was running on little sleep, too. My flight from Colorado to New Jersey had landed at seven that morning. Nate wanted to pick me up at the airport, but I insisted on taking a cab.

Then he begged me to accept a ride from my motel to his house, and I gave in because part of me missed Nate. We hadn't seen one another since October of last year, and that was during Matt's meltdown. And even then, Nate made a good impression. Fiercely loyal to his brother. Forgiving. Gracious. *Handsome.*

I blinked rapidly, clearing that thought.

"Hello, Hannah," Nate said. He opened his arms and I went to him automatically. We didn't quite hug. He gripped my elbows and pressed a kiss to my cheek, and then he drew back and searched my face.

I began to shiver.

What could Nate see on my face? He took his time looking at me. His dark, impenetrable eyes swept my expression, the search so thorough it felt intimate, and at last he smiled and said, "It's good to see you."

"It's good to see you, too."

"What are you doing out here?" He nodded toward the pay phone.

"Oh, my phone . . ." I shifted my purse. "My phone died. I wanted to call my mom. She's been really supportive. I needed to hear her voice."

I hated myself for lying. The guilt was acid.

Nate glanced at the run-down Motel 6 behind me. He cocked his head. As always, he reminded me of a hawk. "I take it your accommodations are without phone service?"

"Ah, no. Er, yes, of course." *Fuck.* "Phones . . . they have phones. I was just on my way to—" I looked across the street, where only one establishment stood. SMOKEY'S TOBACCO SHOP. *Seriously?* I flushed. "Um . . . buy a pack of cigarettes. So. The pay phone was on my way." I looked at my boots.

"Cigarettes," Nate said.

"Yes, cigarettes."

"I didn't know you smoked."

"Well, I didn't. But I do now." I lifted my chin. "And I know it's bad for me, and I'd rather not hear some doctory spiel about it. Matt used to smoke. Sometimes."

"I'm aware. One of his many healthy habits. Shall we, then?" Nate turned on a heel and headed for the tobacco shop. I trailed after him.

Fucking Matt, look what you've gotten me into now.

The shop was full of pipes and incense, blown glass, rolling papers, and Rasta clothes. I tried to hold my breath. A gray-haired man with a spindly beard—Smokey, I presumed—sat at the check-out counter.

Nate hovered as I asked for a pack of Marb Reds and picked

out a lighter. I didn't protest when he intervened to pay. My face was on fire.

I waited in the shop while Nate brought the car around. The rain had turned to slush.

He dashed out and got the door.

As I buckled my seat belt, I remembered the last time—the first time—I was in Nate's car. It wasn't so long ago. Then, we were going to rescue Matt.

"I know what you're thinking," said Nate.

I glanced at him. God, he was nearly Matt. Matt's dark-haired brother, at home in his car the way Matt only ever looked in his Lexus: A prince in his purring, expensive machine.

Nate tipped his head against the headrest.

"But there's no Matt now, is there? No drive to Geneva. No boy to save." A wistful smile played on his lips. He rolled his head toward me. I stared at the cigarettes and lighter in my hand. "Go ahead, Hannah."

"What?" I swallowed.

"I don't mind if you smoke one in the car."

"Oh . . . no, it's okay, I—"

"Please," he said. "And you should have offered me one by now."

Nate plucked the cigarettes from my hand and neatly peeled off the plastic. He rapped the box against the heel of his hand.

"I didn't think," I mumbled. "You're . . . a doctor."

"Yes, that's right. I'll have one for my brother."

We lit our cigarettes and lowered our windows a sliver.

I took thin drags and exhaled fast. Soon I was dizzy. The smoke made my eyes water. Perfect—false tears.

When I looked at Nate, though, I saw very real tears standing in his eyes.

"It's all right," he said. "It's okay. I don't know—it makes no sense. Is my brother dead? I can't say it." He reached for me, found my hand, and held it tight.

Nate didn't cry, but I began to think I might. I couldn't stand to see his grief.

We finished our cigarettes and Nate pulled me over for a hug. His long fingers curled at the back of my neck. I pressed my face against his coat and breathed in the scent of cologne and smoke. I let myself imagine he was Matt.

"It's all right," Nate said again, and I knew he said it for himself.

We pulled up to Nate's house at noon. We had an hour to kill before the service.

Mounds of graying snow lined the drive and a half-melted snowman stood by the front steps. Still, the home was magnificent. Yellow light shone in the windows. A large winter wreath hung on the door.

A few cars were parked along the street, and I recognized a catering van.

"Home sweet home," said Nate. "I really wish you'd agreed to stay with us, Hannah. That motel . . ." His nose wrinkled. Classic Sky disdain, barely disguised.

"I wanted to, Nate. It's just, this house . . ." I stumbled over my excuse.

"Too many memories?"

"Yeah." I climbed out of the car before Nate could get my door.

He rounded on me, blocking the sidewalk.

"Hannah," he said. He sounded cautious. "A few items, nothing major. Val—she's quite upset." He gestured to the house. "Owen, we haven't explained it to him. He's too young, you see? But Madison knows, and she understands."

"Okay, got it." I felt a Pam-esque urge to say: Will you be coming to your point in 2014? Something more was on Nate's mind, clearly.

"Good, good." He tugged off his gloves. "No one gives a damn about the book, of course. Don't worry about that."

My stomach dropped.

The book.

Night Owl.

The book Matt started in Denver and finished in Kevin's cabin. The book that somehow leaked onto the Internet and got published as an e-book by "W. Pierce."

Matt swore he had no part in it—no part beyond writing it, that is. I believed him. After all, *Night Owl* chronicled our romance in aching detail. No way would Matt, Mr. Privacy Above All Else, publish that book for the world to see.

But who did, and why?

I remembered when I first heard about *Night Owl*. Pam got wind of the e-book in late January. Just weeks after appearing, it was viral. Half a thousand reviews on Amazon. Pirated copies all over the web. The text posted on forums, blogs, Facebook.

And *my* name was in it, Matt's name, the whole story.

I sat up late that night reading the book, by turns horrified and aroused. And livid.

I called Matt in the early morning. I was shaking, shouting into my cell. "How could you put it online? How could you publish that book without asking me?"

"What?" he said. "What book, what fucking book? Where?" Panic bled into his voice. *My God,* I realized then, *he has no idea.*

"Hannah?" Nate waved a hand before my eyes.

"Huh? Sorry. Uh, the book. It's . . . just so disturbing. So embarrassing."

"I can only imagine." Nate was suddenly upbeat, talking hurriedly. "The audacity. It's absolute filth. Dragging my brother's name through the mud, and yours. You know, it follows the whole episode in Geneva with alarming accuracy. Matt had a local friend there, at a farm up the road. Could be her. Who knows what he told people when he was in that frame of mind? Whoever it is, they know about my house, my family, our—"

"Excuse me? Could be . . . who?"

"The woman at the farm. She could be the author." Nate nodded. "Someone close to him, definitely. His psychiatrist? That's almost too sick to consider, but who knows? People are so depraved, so desperate for money. They'll take advantage of anyone, Hannah. Predators."

Nate took my shoulder and steered me toward the house.

"Don't worry, though," he went on. "I've invited Shapiro. Ah, George Shapiro. Have I mentioned him? I'm sure Matt did. The family—"

"Lawyer," I said. My voice shrank with dread. "The family lawyer."

"Yes, that's right. It's libel, that book. Defamation . . . whatever they call it. Shapiro is prepared to bury the author. I know you'll talk to him." Nate squeezed my shoulder. "Yours is the strongest case. Never mind the expense, this is important. For you, for Matt's legacy."

We were stalled at the front door. Nate held me by both shoulders and gazed earnestly at me, confident in my compliance. What could I say? *Actually, Nate, Matt wrote* Night Owl. *He's been chilling at our friend's cabin, pretending to be dead. Sorry about that.*

Fuck.

I gathered a breath and opened my mouth. *Say something! Stop this ridiculous manhunt for "the author." For Matt.* "I—Nate, it's so soon after Matt's passing—"

The front door swung open.

The odor of potpourri and seasonal candles hit me.

"This must be the infamous little bird," said a voice thick with cynicism.

I looked up, and up, at the tall figure standing in the doorway. We had never met, but he was unmistakable.

The middle brother.

Seth Sky.

Chapter 4

MATT

I sprinted up the cellar steps and rushed to my phone. I quickly checked the caller's number. It wasn't Hannah.

"Hello?" I let out a shaking breath. "Hello?"

Nothing. And yet I knew someone was there, sentience in the silence on the line.

"Please, don't hang up," I said. "I told you, you're not in trouble. Talk to me." I began to pace. "Come on. Icarus on fire, right? Clever name. I'm glad you called."

I waited then, because I had said enough. I even smiled. Life is stranger than fiction.

"So, you're alive," said a voice. It was a female voice, smooth and cultured.

I paused in front of the fireplace. As I watched, a castle of cinders collapsed.

"Excuse me?"

"You're alive," she said.

You're alive. The words should have worried me, but I felt safe in my fortress in the forest. Far from the world. As good as dead. I laughed and roamed around the couch.

"I don't know what you're talking about," I said.

"I met you, but you wouldn't remember. It was at the book signing in Denver. You had your face in your hands. Of course, I had this carefully prepared speech." She chuckled. "And you . . . you didn't even look at me. You looked pretty pathetic, Sky."

Pathetic? What the hell? I opened my mouth to snap, then shut it.

"Are you recording this call?"

"No," she said, "but I doubt you believe me."

"Mm, you're right about that. And let me just say—if you are recording it, if you make a move with your crazy theory about who I am, I *will* come after you. I don't care who you are. I have the resources to find out, and I'll come after you with all my family's formidable power, so don't fuck with me. Understand? Don't fuck with me."

"And here I thought I wasn't in trouble." She chuckled again. I frowned.

Okay, the stranger had a point.

"You're not in trouble," I said. "Look, let's start again. Hello."

"Hello."

I perched on the arm of the couch. "Have you got a name?"

"Melanie."

"Anything to go with that?"

"Yeah. Like most humans, I have a last name. Should I give it to the strange man threatening me with his family's . . . formidable power?" She wanted to giggle again; I heard the humor simmering in her voice. She was laughing at me. She found me comical and pathetic.

"Fine," I snapped. "Do whatever the fuck you want."

"Fine. My last name is vanden Dries." She pronounced it *Dreese.* "It's Dutch. It means 'of the shore.' I'm telling you that as a good-faith gesture, Sky. Let's not—"

"Stop calling me Sky."

"Then what do I call you?"

"You don't call me anything." I smiled and ran a hand through my hair. *There.* I'd regained control. "Melanie vanden Dries. Melanie of the Shore. Sounds good."

"Yeah, I like it."

"Convenient. Okay, Melanie vanden Dries, let's get to the point. Why did you turn my forum post into an e-book?"

"I never said I did." Now Melanie was on the defensive. The humor faded from her voice. *Good girl,* I thought—*you ought to take this seriously.*

"Assuming you did. Why would you?"

"Fine. Assuming I turned your forum post into an e-book, which would make me insane, I might have done it because . . . the story deserved to be shared."

"Deserved to be shared?" I laughed. "You *are* insane. Have you heard of this thing called copyright infringement? You are selling *my* story, *my* words. How much have you made?"

Melanie went quiet.

Her answer could condemn her.

Meanwhile, I said nothing to condemn myself—but I was guilty. I wrote *Night Owl* and I posted it on an Internet forum. Worse, I told Hannah I had no idea how the story "leaked online." *Someone must have hacked my e-mail,* I said. *I e-mail all my writing to myself, for backup.*

Hannah believed me.

And why wouldn't she believe me? Who could imagine that I, so obsessed with privacy that I faked my own death, would write that intimate and honest novel and throw it on the Internet for the world to see?

But that is exactly what I did.

I yanked open the sliding door and strode barefoot onto the deck. Winter air swirled around me. The snow quickly numbed my feet.

I lifted the cell.

"You are insane," I repeated, this time in a softer voice. "So am I. You know I am. What I'm doing—it's insane. Icarus on fire? I get it, Melanie. You're flying too close to the sun, but I'm not

going to be the one who burns you. I'm right up there with you.
Now be honest with me, please. I just want to understand . . ."

I began to shiver. Gooseflesh rose along my arms, and my teeth
chattered.

After a long gap, Melanie said, "Ten thousand. I've made about
ten thousand dollars. I'm selling it cheap. Do you want the money?
It's yours. I don't care."

"Ten grand? I don't want your lunch money, Mel. Thanks,
though. Keep it."

"Then what do you want? Do you want me to take it down?
It's all over the Internet."

I hugged myself, pinching the TracFone between my jaw and
shoulder. The absolute silence rang in my ears.

What do you want? Do you want me to take it down?

I hesitated, as if I were considering.

"No," I said. "Quite the opposite."

"I don't understand."

"Keep selling the book. That's all."

"But why?"

I smirked. "Why should I explain myself to you?"

"I . . . I dunno."

"I'm sure you don't, Melanie. Maybe you published my story to
make some cash, or"—she butted in to disagree, but I talked right
over her—"maybe you published it on a whim, because you wanted
to share what doesn't belong to you. People like you act without
thinking, but don't for one moment imagine that I am so simple."

Melanie made a small, hurt sound.

"All you need to know," I continued, "is that I wanted *Night
Owl* to go viral, and you helped that happen. Don't try to understand, just keep selling the book. You're making decent money,
right? Good for you. Keep it all."

"It's not about the money," she mumbled.

"I don't care what it's about." I didn't. I had accomplished my
goal—contacted the stranger who published *Night Owl*, urged
her to continue selling the book—and now I wanted to go. "Look,
I'm running out of minutes."

"Prepaid cell?" Melanie giggled suddenly, and I narrowed my eyes. How old was she? The giggle was girlish, but she spoke with an adult's poise.

"Well . . . yeah," I said.

"You're like a spy, living on the run. Do you go out in sunglasses? Did you dye your hair? Get plastic surgery?"

"No, no." An involuntary smile quirked my lips. I ruffled my hair, which was dirty blond and in need of a cut. Melanie had given me an idea. "Actually, ah . . . my hair. I dyed it . . . black."

"Black?"

"Mm, black. Dark hair runs in the family. It looks good, of course." I cocked my head. Nate looked sharp with his raven hair. So would I.

"Of course." Melanie laughed. "Hey . . . how are you surviving without her?"

"Excuse me?" My smile dropped.

"Hannah. How are you surviving without her? *Night Owl* . . . paints a picture of obsession. And I saw her with you, at the book signing. It's all true, isn't it? I—"

I closed my TracFone and let myself back inside.

Enough.

I shivered in the warm cabin and turned my phone over and over in my hand. My day was shot for writing, but I didn't want to write.

I wanted to go into town.

Chapter 5

HANNAH

Seth Sky.

He had Matt's attractive, angular features—the high cheekbones and expressive mouth. He had Nate's dark hair, which he wore to his shoulders.

I took his measure in a moment: long hair, leather jacket, sullen smirk aimed at me—plus the "little bird" comment, designed, I felt sure, to let me know he'd read *Night Owl.* Designed to embarrass me.

Yup, Seth fit the wannabe-rocker profile perfectly. Also, the quarter-life-crisis profile. What a chump. If he was trying to make me uncomfortable, he could take a number.

"Seth," Nate said, "when did you get here?"

"Few minutes ago. You playing chauffeur?"

The brothers embraced. Seth stood a few inches taller than Nate. As he hugged Nate, he locked eyes with me. I raised a brow.

Fucking Sky men with their presumptuous stares.

"Oh, Hannah." Nate broke from his brother. I smiled sweetly at Nate and angled myself away from Seth. "This is Seth, my brother."

"Mm." My eyes slid over Seth. "Nice to meet you." I hoped my voice, posture, and expression conveyed my real meaning. *Go to hell.*

"Yeah, same," said Seth.

Something in Seth's voice made me want to look at him, but I didn't. I wouldn't gratify him. Still, and I hated to admit it, Seth reminded me of Matt more than Nate ever would. The sneering tone, the lanky frame, and the way I felt his stare glued to me . . . it was Matt through and through. Also, the asshole demeanor.

"Hannah, can I get your coat?" Nate moved behind me. I hugged myself. All of a sudden, I didn't want to be seen in my dress.

I wanted layers.

When I prepared for the memorial, I assumed every guest would know about *Night Owl.* Thus, my goal was to look as wholesome and nonslutty as possible. I wore a black dress with lace sleeves, midheel boots, and my hair clipped at the crown of my head.

"Hannah?" Nate touched my shoulder. I lurched away.

"I'm cold. I'll keep it on."

"All right. Would you like to have a seat in the study? I can send Shapiro your way."

"Uh, sure. The study."

"Off the living room. Thank you, Hannah. This means a lot to me. To us. I know the timing isn't ideal." He grimaced. Poor Nate; he was so sincere.

"Ciao, bird," Seth called as I moved away.

I glanced over my shoulder to see Nate gesturing at Seth, his face like thunder.

Great. I was already a source of contention.

The main hall of Nate's home bristled with flowers. White lilies, white roses, white orchids. All white. I flinched as a waxen petal brushed my hand.

Valerie, Nate's wife, greeted me in the kitchen. Her eyes filled with tears as soon as she saw me. "Oh, Hannah," she said. "Oh, God, darling."

We hugged, and she dug her long nails into my back.

When I left her, she dried her eyes efficiently and resumed lecturing the caterers.

I found the study and dropped into a leather armchair. One tall window stood behind the desk. Bookshelves covered two walls and Vermeer's *The Geographer* hung on another.

I got up and closed the study door, then retook my seat.

I slouched in the chair.

I sighed. A moment's peace.

As I waited for Shapiro, an antique mantel clock ticked off the seconds.

How was I going to handle the lawyer? I wanted to know who published *Night Owl* as much as the next person, but *Night Owl* couldn't afford a legal level of scrutiny. I couldn't afford it. Matt especially couldn't afford it.

Yours is the strongest case, Nate said. He expected me to spearhead the lawsuit. Maybe no one else had a case.

After ten minutes, I began to scroll through pictures on my phone.

I opened my Matt album.

There was Matt on Thanksgiving, seated between Chrissy and me. He looked gorgeous in a dark cashmere sweater. And he looked adorable, hunched over his plate, staring at me.

I had a shot of Matt setting up the fake Christmas tree in our condo. I caught the picture just as he smiled over his shoulder at me. One of his rare relaxed smiles. The image had energy—a little blur, the twist of his body in motion.

Oh, yes . . . he got up, I remembered, and pushed me onto the couch.

I curled my toes in my boots.

I looked at the study door, then the clock, and opened another album. The "My Eyes Only" album.

I swallowed as the thumbnails loaded. Damn . . . .

It hadn't been easy, convincing Matt to let me take those pictures. "What are you going to do with them?" he'd demanded. "Think about you," I replied. He was still reticent. Then I reminded him how many pictures and videos *he* had of *me,* and he relented.

First, I opened a tame photo: Matt sleeping, the sheets tangled around his waist and his strong back bare.

In the next photo, I had tugged down the sheets to get a shot of Matt's perfect ass. Then lower. His lean thighs.

The fourth photo made my heart quicken. Matt was sitting up halfway, his cock stiff. I recognized a telltale darkening of his eyes.

I squirmed on the armchair as the pictures got racier. My hand on Matt's thigh. My hand around his cock. His hand around my hand. Then: a clumsy shot of our bodies, my sex sliding over his head. I was on top, a rare thing indeed.

Matt's need for control showed in each successive image. Positioning himself. Spreading my lips. Tugging on my hips.

Holy hell.

My finger hovered over the next media, a video.

The study was exceptionally quiet. I heard no footfalls approaching. I thought I heard Valerie's voice drifting through the house.

I hit Play.

The video wavered crazily with the motion of our bodies.

We leaned apart to make room for my iPhone and to get a clean shot of Matt's cock drilling into me. In and out, slick with my desire.

I panted. Fuck . . . even watching was intense.

I risked a little volume. Tinny moans piped into the study. I heard Matt snarling my name, groaning it. *Hannah* . . . like I was killing him. *Hannah . . . God, fuck . . .*

The video didn't capture the words Matt whispered in my ear, but I remembered them.

"Is this what you want?" he said. "You want a video of me fucking you, Hannah? You want pictures of me hard? Do you like this? Watch . . . watch me fuck you . . . watch my dick . . ."

He went on and on like that.

On and on.

I touched my forehead. God, I needed to take off my coat.

"Miss Catalano?"

My eyes shot up. I jammed my phone into my purse.

A slight man stepped into the study, paused, and closed the door.

"Do you mind?" he gestured to the door.

"Not at all. Call me Hannah."

We shook hands—after I discreetly dried my palm.

"Very good. The boys call me Shapiro. You may do the same, if you like." Shapiro took a seat behind the desk.

Shapiro must have been in his sixties, but his smiles were boyish and his quick eyes missed nothing. He wore a navy suit with subtle plaid and silver circle-frame glasses. His hair was gray and neatly combed.

"I won't take much of your time," he said, "and let me express how sorry I am for your loss, Hannah. That dear boy . . ."

Shapiro gazed at his lap. I watched him, trying to get a read. *Dear boy.* This house was full of people who knew Matt better than I did.

I, who was guarding Matt's greatest secret, and who set the night on fire with him countless times, had known him for only nine months. And not nine solid months. Nine months of turmoil. Nine months of secrets and lies and now this—Matt's vanishing act.

When would things be normal for us? When would it be my turn to truly know him?

"Thank you," I said. "My condolences to you."

"Thank you, Hannah." Shapiro riffled through a leather folio. "So, let's get to it. I'm pursuing this case on Nate's behalf. The charge will be libel, defamation of character. Shall we review the facts?"

"Sure." I fiddled with a button on my coat. "Will I have to testify at a trial?"

"Most likely not. When we present our material, after we locate the defendant—ah, the original author—he or she will surely settle."

"But money isn't going to change anything."

Shapiro gave me a withering glance.

"Here we are." He withdrew a sheet from his folio. "If you would, Hannah, correct me where you hear inaccuracies, if any. I'll read the highlights." His eyes skipped over the page. "The text titled *Night Owl* first appeared online in a forum on January first of this year, 2014, approximately seventeen days after Matthew Sky went missing."

Shapiro paused and eyed me.

"Right," I said.

"Very good. About two weeks thereafter, the text was uploaded to several online vendors and sold in e-book format with the author cited as W. Pierce."

"Yeah, that's right."

"To the best of your knowledge, the author of the text titled *Night Owl* is unknown to you, and is not Matthew Sky."

"No. I mean, yes, to my knowledge. It's not Matt. He didn't write it."

Shapiro scribbled on his page.

"Hannah, have you been negatively impacted by the dispersion of the text titled *Night Owl*? Has your work or personal life been compromised in any way? The text is very ribald. I assume you read it, at least in part."

I twisted the button on my coat. Shapiro's legalese was driving me crazy. *The text. The defendant. Libel.*

"I read it, yes. A few people have made the connection . . . that I'm, you know, the Hannah in the book. Some people came to the agency wanting to meet me." I shrugged. "They were fans of the story. They weren't mean."

"Readers came to your workplace?" Shapiro peered at me over his glasses.

"Yeah, but they weren't rude or anything."

He took more notes.

"Have you been harassed subsequent to the text's appearance? Have you received any communications with violent or sexual implications?"

"God, no." I glared at the floor. Where was this going? "Hey, do you know who wrote it yet? Do you know who published it?"

"Not yet, Hannah. We can't compel the original Web site owner to divulge user information until our suit is under way. The same goes for the online vendors. We'll subpoena the records, but first we need to build a case."

"I see," I said, but I didn't see. I didn't want to see.

Nate assumed I would help with the case and Shapiro assumed I would *make* the case. It was time for me to let them down.

I cleared my throat.

"To be honest, Mr. Shapiro, I feel very . . . overwrought, I mean with Matt's death and all, and now the book." I wiped at the corner of my eye. "Of course I want to protect Matt's legacy and defend his name, but I have to protect my emotional well-being. I don't believe I can—"

"She probably wrote it, Doc."

I jumped at the voice. Matt!

No . . . *Seth.*

Seth Sky loped into the study. He leered at me.

"I did *not* write it," I said.

"But it makes you look like such a vixen." Seth draped his arms over the back of my chair and grinned down at me. Close, I saw that his hair was not black but a very dark brown, like mine. It moved fluidly with the tilt of his head.

"Seth, Miss Catalano and I are having a meeting."

"Actually, we're done." I clutched my purse and made for the door. Seth's intrusion was a perfect excuse to bail.

"Seth makes a fair point," Shapiro said. "We assume the author was someone close to Matthew and close to the events described in the text."

I paused in the doorway. My hands shook. Instinct told me to deny it again—I didn't write *Night Owl*—but if Shapiro suspected me, maybe he didn't suspect Matt.

"Whatever," I said. "I'm done talking about this."

"Then we'll be in touch."

"Maybe."

I hurried out of the study and through the house. I ducked around Valerie in the kitchen. She had placed framed pictures of

Matt all over the house—here on a coffee table, there on a shelf. Inescapable, beautiful Matt.

I stumbled into a long room dominated by couches and a baby grand. More pictures of Matt stood on the piano. I picked up a frame.

I was still shaking, and a kernel of dread was growing in my stomach. A young Matt beamed at me from the picture frame. He was crouched in a shed with three large dogs fussing for his attention. His eyes were alight.

When would it be my turn to truly know him? Fear answered: *Never. You'll never know him. You can't hold on to a man like that.*

"So, did you?"

I spun.

Seth grasped my arm and shook me. I met his eyes. Wild eyes . . . storm dark.

"Did you write it?" he said. I tried to yank my arm out of his grip. His fingers tightened until they hurt.

"Let me go. I'll scream."

"*Très dramatique.*" Seth drew closer to me.

"Let me *go.*"

"You are every bit as feisty as the book makes you out to be."

"I didn't write it. What the hell is wrong with you? Get away from me."

"You sure that's what you want? Rumor has it you like pushy men."

My eyes darted around. Where was Nate? With my back to the piano and Seth's death grip on my arm, I was trapped.

"What do you want?" I whispered.

"I don't know." Seth searched my expression. "You seem fun. A fun diversion from my . . . mourning." His voice dried with humor.

"You're sick."

"Runs in the family. You aren't being very sympathetic, Hannah. My brother is dead. I need someone to talk to."

"Not me." I wrenched my arm uselessly.

"No? Then how about a quick fuck before the service?"

My heart stuttered and began to thud. In that moment, I wanted to run back to Shapiro babbling about *Night Owl* and sexual harassment—and then I felt ill. This was Seth Sky. Shapiro was on his side, not mine.

Seth leaned in and brushed his lips to my cheek. I gathered a breath to scream. Seth shoved me, and the force of his push sent the air out of my lungs.

"Don't be so damn dull," he muttered, and he left me reeling against the piano.

Chapter 6

MATT

Radiant black. Midnight black. Jet black.

Soft black, blue black, silken black. Black with highlights. Black with lowlights. Black with three tones for more natural color.

I shuffled up and down in front of Smart Mart's hair dye section, glaring at the boxes.

Gorgeous models with glossy hair smiled back at me. One resembled Hannah—pale skin, smoky eyes, and curling black-brown locks—and I lingered over that box.

How are you surviving without her?

Melanie had no right to ask me that. So what if she read *Night Owl*? That didn't mean she understood me—or me and Hannah.

Finally, I chose a L'Oréal blue-black hair dye kit because it cost more than the others.

I loitered in Smart Mart, enjoying the warmth.

I'd spent the better part of an hour hiking from the cabin into town. I wore sunglasses, a North Face jacket with a high collar and hood, a wool hat, gloves, scarf—the whole nine yards.

Concealing my face was priority number one.

Staying warm came in at a close second.

I carried a day pack with some cash, water, two granola bars, a compass, and my phone. No one looked at me twice. In Colorado, things like me materialize out of the woods every day.

I wandered to the SUPER SALE section at the back of the store. A woman was studying the discount pastries, which were ninety-nine cents because they sat out for days. I watched her.

Damn, did it ever feel good to be out in public and not M. Pierce. When people know you're an author, they turn into weirdos. I swear. A woman who would normally spit in your coffee is suddenly quoting Whitman and reminiscing about AP English, or a guy who would try to cut you in line instead harangues you with the story of his third divorce.

You can't see the real world anymore. Everyone becomes a caricature.

"Anything good?" I asked the woman perusing the pastries.

She gave me a wary look. "They've got doughnuts," she mumbled. "And the bear claws."

I smelled alcohol on her breath.

"Huh, yeah." I picked up a container of cinnamon buns, pretended to inspect them, and smiled at the woman. I felt such pity for her, and such gratitude, too—because she let me be nobody. She let me be a stranger, and not M. Pierce. "These look decent. Thanks."

I browsed the books and magazines. I sneered at the bestsellers. There were a few young adult series, a legal thriller, a thick fantasy. The usual suspects.

The Surrogate, my last novel, would be "posthumously published" next month, in March. It would be a bestseller. It would sit on the list for months. It would do so not because it's good, though it is, but because my name is on the cover—and because I just died from a rare puma attack while attempting a solo ascent of Longs Peak.

Brilliant. I'd have a cult following.

I couldn't find any John le Carré, so I grabbed the latest Jack Reacher novel.

I paid for the hair dye, pastries, book, and a pack of beef jerky with cash. I carried no ID and no cards of any kind. Driving was out of the question.

I hiked out of town by the shortest route. I avoided the roads and popular trails, instead retracing my path through the woods. It was four in the afternoon.

The air chilled as evening approached and shadows fell long through the forest.

"Stupid," I muttered, hiking faster. It was stupid to go out so late. Soon it would be dark; night comes early in the mountains.

But if I survived my own fake death, I could survive anything.

I guzzled half a bottle of water as I hiked. I checked my watch: 4:30, 6:30 on the East Coast. The memorial would be over by now. Even if Hannah stayed for the collation, which I hoped she didn't, she should be back at her motel. Why didn't she call?

I paused to check my phone. Nothing.

"Whatever." My breath steamed in the air. No big deal. Hannah could hold her own on the East Coast, and I would see her soon. I would see her in just a few days.

It was February 8, 2014, and I hadn't seen Hannah since the day I staged my death, December 14 of last year.

I'd spent exactly fifty-six days without Hannah. Fifty-six days without her smile. Fifty-six days without her body. But who was counting?

My breath grew ragged as I trekked up a snowy incline.

Whenever I missed Hannah like that, I remembered the last time. The last time we lost our minds together.

It was Friday night—Friday the 13th—the night before the day we drove out to Longs Peak. Hannah would see me off at Glacier Gorge Trailhead. Then she would drive to Kevin's cabin, turn on the cellar freezer, and drop off my food and supplies. We already had a key to the cabin courtesy of Kevin, for an innocent "weekend getaway."

My Jeep would remain at the trailhead lot.

Hannah would return to Denver and stay away until the search cooled.

We went over and over the plan until there were no holes, no questions.

We were mentally exhausted, but neither of us could sleep.

"We should turn in early," I said. "Big day tomorrow."

"Are you having second thoughts?" Hannah came to sit on the edge of the bed with me. I pressed a hand to her thigh and she smiled feebly.

"No," I said. "Are you?"

"No. I'll miss you, but . . ." She watched my hand. Her eyes glistened in the dark and her milky skin was lambent. "This is about your writing, and I know I come second to that."

"Hannah—"

"No, listen. I'm okay with that, Matt. I don't . . ." She traced her fingers over my knuckles and pursed her lips as she thought.

Reflexively, my fingers stirred against her thigh. *We should turn in early.* Yeah . . . right. Hannah was wearing a tiny turquoise nightie and I was in nothing but lounge pants. And after almost two months of living with Hannah, I still felt crazy when I looked at her.

"I don't want to be the sun in your sky," she continued. "Do you get what I mean? I'm happy being the moon. I'm happy coming second to your writing. I don't *want* to be your whole life. And if this—" She kissed my shoulder. The imprint of her lips burned on my skin. "If this crazy thing we're going to do is what it takes to protect your first love, then I'm game. We're in this together, Matt. You can count on me."

"Hannah." I spoke her name slowly. I dragged my fingers up her inner thigh. "You're stronger than I am. Do you know that?"

She shivered. "We're different . . ."

"Night and day," I murmured. The air between us was charged. A few touches, a kiss—that was all it took.

My fingers reached the top of her thighs and brushed bare skin. No panties.

"Hannah," I growled.

I wanted that pleasure to go on forever. Never to say good-bye to it. That heat, her nails digging into my ass, the frantic union of our bodies.

She drove me mad. She knew how to do it. One look from those dark eyes, her soft face framed by a spill of curls. I was powerless.

When we were spent, I sank against her.

I curled her hair around my hand and kissed her ear. "Think . . . of me," I said, gulping in air between words, "when you do it . . . alone. Me. My body. This."

"I will. I will. I love you, Matt."

I lifted myself enough to gaze down at her. I stripped off her nightie so that we could be naked together, and I pulled the covers over us. In a moment like that, it would have been easy to say Hannah was my sun—my whole life. But that was a feeling, and I know a feeling from a truth. The truth was that I loved Hannah, but I loved my writing more, and what I would do the following morning was the surest testament to that fact.

Faking my death. Separating us for months. Reclaiming my anonymity while Hannah played out our lie and bore the guilt alone.

That night, I had walked through our condo and brooded over the memories it held.

Our Christmas tree stood in the living room. We would spend Christmas apart. There was the deep-button sofa where we cuddled and watched movies, and our small kitchen crowded by an island and breakfast nook. I often sat there, staring at Hannah's backside while she cooked.

Hannah filled that place. Hannah laughing, Hannah in my arms . . . every room, Hannah.

I had ached for her suddenly—a hot stab of sorrow that nearly doubled me over. *What the fuck?* I missed her, and she was only one room away.

God . . . I *was* having second thoughts.

I returned to bed and found Hannah still awake. She wiped her eyes on the sheets. I climbed over her, entangling our limbs and kissing her longingly.

"Brave bird," I whispered as our lips parted. "Come with me. Please."

I had made this case before, and a familiar look of fatigue came over Hannah's face. It was my first idea—my best idea. Why die, after all, when I could escape the public with Hannah? We could drop off the grid together. The hope of it rose inside me again.

"Please," I repeated. "Let's go somewhere no one knows me. We can disappear; there's no law against that. I'll take care of you. I have enough money—we'd never need to work—and we wouldn't have to leave *this*." I emphasized my point by pressing my long, firm body against hers. She responded with a sigh. "This is my life. You're my life, Hannah . . ."

"No, Matt." Her fingers slid through my hair. "You know I'm not. You've got cold feet. We'll get through this, but don't—" She turned her head away, resting her cheek on our pillow. "Don't ask me to leave *my* life. My job, my family . . ."

I tried to turn Hannah's face toward me, but her neck stiffened.

She sniffled, and a bright tear rolled from her eye.

It broke my fucking heart.

Freezing wind whipped through the woods. Flecks of ice stung my cheek. I rose from that memory like a ghost.

Through the dark, I saw a light glowing in the cabin. I imagined Hannah was there, though I knew I'd left the light on for myself, and I hurried toward it.

Chapter 7

HANNAH

I stood shivering on the front steps of Nate's house, waiting for the driving arrangements to be settled.

Valerie was inside giving last-minute instructions to the caterers.

Madison and Owen huddled close to me and I held their small hands. Madison was quiet, buried in a book, and Owen seemed cowed by the somber atmosphere.

"Are you warm enough?" I said. I squeezed his hand. He was adorable, a miniature Nate.

"It's cold." Owen kicked a clump of snow with his little boot. Then he lowered his voice and fixed me with his serious dark eyes. "I don't like Uncle Seth," he whispered.

I glanced toward the brothers. They were conferring at the end of the driveway. Nate gestured to the road. Seth shrugged. His posture said they were having an argument.

A pearly white Bentley was parked in front of the house. Seth's car? Rich asshole . . .

"Why not?" I said, smiling down at Owen.

I was shaken by my exchange with Seth and I almost told Owen that I didn't like Uncle Seth either, but nine-year-olds have a habit of broadcasting secrets.

"He's mean," Owen said. *No kidding,* I thought. I trembled as I remembered the force of Seth's grip and the crazed look in his eyes.

"She can come with me." Seth's voice cut through the air. "Let's go, Hannah."

I blinked at Nate and Seth. They were both staring at me.

"Excuse me?"

"I said let's go. You're riding with me." Seth strolled toward the Bentley.

I shot a pleading look at Nate. Fuck, what could I say? *I don't want to ride with your sociopathic brother who assaulted me in your house?*

Nate was oblivious to my discomfort. He breezed up the driveway and took Owen's hand.

"How did it go with Shapiro?"

"Fine, it . . . went fine." I forced a smile. It went *terribly.* I needed to call Matt ASAP and tell him about the lawsuit. But right now, I had more pressing problems, like psycho Seth.

Valerie swept out of the house and took Madison's hand. She smiled at me. I smiled back, but I felt queasy. I was trapped—again.

"Well, we'll see you there," Nate said.

"Yeah . . . see you."

Seth stood by the passenger-side door of his car and gazed at me. I stalked over and climbed in without looking at him.

"My lady," he quipped.

Seth smiled as he got in.

"It'll warm up in here soon," he said. His leather gloves creaked on the wheel.

I stayed quiet as he spoke, and after he spoke. I planned to stay quiet the whole way. *Don't engage him. Don't look at him. Get a ride back with Nate.*

We wound through Nate's neighborhood and I tried to focus on the mansions instead of the oppressive silence in the car.

"I hope you're not waiting for an apology," Seth said.

I closed my eyes and clutched my purse.

"You know, it's forty minutes to the cemetery. At least."

I sneered. Did this asshole think I couldn't freeze him out for forty minutes? I could freeze him out for a lifetime.

"Presbyterian cemetery," he went on. I opened my eyes and watched him on the edge of my vision. He didn't *look* psychotic. He looked tired and irritable and bored. He watched the road as he rambled. "Oak Grove Presbyterian Cemetery. Our parents have headstones there. Just markers. I've got a plot, too."

Seth grinned at me suddenly. I flinched and pressed against the door. Panic flooded me. I gripped the door handle.

"Please." Seth shook his head. "Don't jump from my moving vehicle, okay? I don't need that shit. I'll happily let you out at the next stoplight."

I swallowed.

"No," I said. "Just drive."

"She speaks." He chuckled. "Happy to 'just drive.' Call me Chauffeur Seth. Oh—Shapiro wanted me to give you this." He dug in his jacket pocket. "He's leaving right after the service, otherwise I'm sure the good doc would give it to you himself."

Seth produced a folded paper and tossed it onto my lap.

"The doc?" I unfolded the page. The car had warmed and my heart rate slowed. Maybe I was freaking out about nothing. Sure, Seth had acted crazy back at the house, but he was probably trying to scare the truth out of me. He probably really believed I wrote *Night Owl* and that I was turning a profit at his dead brother's expense.

I would be just as harsh if someone used Jay or Chrissy like that.

"Yeah, the doc. Doctor Shapiro. He makes our problems go away."

"Lucky you." I scanned the printout. It listed details of the case—the time line of events, dates, and Web sites. "It must be nice to have a lawyer on call whenever you get into trouble."

"Hey, whatever you say, Hannah. Maybe we have a lot of trouble."

I rolled my eyes. I was about to reply—*maybe you wouldn't have so much trouble if you didn't go around assaulting strangers*—when my eyes stopped dead on the page.

What the hell?

Shapiro had listed the Web sites where *Night Owl* appeared—mostly blogs and forums.

The first line of the list read: ORIGINAL FORUM POST OF "NIGHT OWL"—themystictavern.com.

Seth was saying something, but I didn't hear him. The landscape of the highway swirled into a blur. I pressed a hand to my head.

The Mystic Tavern was the Web site where Matt and I first met. We connected on the forums. We were strangers then, anonymous writing partners.

The Mystic Tavern was the beginning of everything.

And no one knew that except us.

What was happening? What did this mean?

"Hey, you all right, kid?"

With shaking hands, I pushed the paper into my coat pocket. Seth's eyes flickered between the road and my face.

"Fine, I'm . . . I get dizzy reading in the car."

"Yeah? Anything on that paper ring a bell? Shapiro is damn sure the author is someone close to you two, maybe someone who—"

"No. Nothing rings a bell, and I don't want to think about it now." I closed my eyes and leaned my head against the car door. Seth took the hint. He flicked on the radio and we drove the rest of the way to the cemetery with a meandering jazz melody filling the car.

"I remember our first winter ascent of Longs Peak." Matt's uncle leaned back as he spoke, rocking on his heels. He was a powerfully built man with salt-and-pepper hair and dark Sky eyes. "That boy loved to climb, and he was a great climber."

He actually laughed, the sound ringing in the cemetery.

Oak Grove Presbyterian Cemetery in winter was the quietest place I had ever been. Snow muffled everything. Bare oaks surrounded our small group and drifts gathered on the graves.

Under any other circumstances, I would have loved that place. But not now.

Matt's uncle stood beside a picture of Matt.

Floral arrangements clustered around the stand.

Matt was giving the assembled mourners one of his million-dollar smiles—a little wry, a little secretive. The photo must have been candid. His dirty blond hair was wild and he looked entirely at ease, which was rare.

"Solo ascents," his uncle boomed. "They test a man. They demand all a climber's skill, all his focus. Matt soloed the Diamond twice and summited both times."

I tried not to scowl as I listened to Matt's uncle. I was getting an annoying manly-man vibe. No grief. No real memories. Just this blather about dangerous, testosterone-fueled climbs.

If Matt were really dead, I thought, *I'd deck this guy.*

Seth touched my shoulder and I looked at him sharply.

"Do you want to speak?" he whispered.

Matt's uncle retook his place next to his wife, a petite woman with black hair. Was it my turn? I scanned the faces around me. Shapiro was there, a few cousins and other family members, my boss Pamela Wing, Nate and his family, and Seth. A pathetically tiny group. And almost everyone had said a word, except for me.

I shrugged off Seth's hand.

The group parted for me and I moved to stand by Matt's picture.

Again, I took stock of the faces before me—all eyes on me. How many of these people read *Night Owl*? How many thought I wrote it? And how many hated me for it?

I caught a small smile from Pam. God, at least I had one friend here.

"I lived with Matt," I began, "for . . . for almost . . . two months."

A patch of clouds closed over the sun. The graveyard dimmed.

"Two months. Two . . . of the happiest months . . . the two happiest months of my life."

A day ago, I could recite this speech in my sleep. Now the words scattered.

"I . . . we met, um . . ."

A flash of movement caught my eye.

I looked toward the motion, which came from a figure standing apart from our group. It was a man. He seemed to be visiting a nearby grave, but as I focused I realized that he was watching our service. With a camera. What the hell?

He was taking a picture . . . of me.

"You motherfucker," Seth growled.

"Seth!" Nate grasped his brother's arm. Seth broke free and ran at the man with the camera. Owen began to cry.

The peace of the cemetery dissolved.

The other guests and I watched in a trance as Seth caught the man by the collar of his coat. "I'll kill you!" Seth bellowed. "I'll fucking kill you!"

The man's arms flailed. The camera flew from his hand.

"Hannah Catalano!" he called to me. "Hannah! Aaron Snow! Please, we need to—"

His words cut away with a groan. Seth's fist hit the man's jaw with a dull thump. The reporter went down clutching his face. He curled on his side in the snow.

From where I stood, I could see the blood seeping from his cupped hands.

Chapter 8

MATT

I dyed my hair that night for the first time in my life. As I watched the charcoal swirls spin down the drain, I thought of Hannah.

Would Hannah like my hair black? It would be a surprise.

I slicked my fingers through my hair and shut off the shower.

I should prepare other surprises. I should have bought something special at Smart Mart—food for a nice meal or candles, maybe something sexy. Warming lube? A ribbed condom?

Ha, a condom. If Hannah and I didn't use a condom the first time, we weren't about to start now. And fuck if she wasn't crazy to let me have her without a condom that night, IUD or no IUD. I knew I was clean, but Hannah couldn't have known.

Sometimes, she was as reckless as I was.

I wiped fog from the mirror and inspected myself.

"Fuck," I muttered. Black is . . . black. My skin looked pale against the wet spikes of hair. I needed a haircut. Long pieces matted against the back of my neck and across my brow.

But I looked less like Matt Sky, and that was the goal. Another way to hide. I dried my skin and padded out of the bathroom.

Most days, I didn't give one fuck about how I looked. I looked damn good on my worst days. Hannah, though, made me want to look my best. I liked to make her stare. I liked the way she touched my body, with obvious appreciation.

The cabin had no treadmill, no pull-up bar, nothing—but I improvised. I had a one-hour routine of sit-ups, push-ups, crunches, and squats, plus the occasional jog through the woods and chopping firewood.

I pulled on jeans and built a new fire.

I wondered, not for the first time, if I would ever feel forgotten enough to stroll into a gym or barbershop. And if not, how would I live? What if I needed to go to the doctor? What if I needed a hospital? *What if, what if?*

I studied my phone as I lay on the couch. Those moments were the worst, when I missed Hannah and the future felt impossible.

But the future feels impossible for everyone. That's life, I told myself—a series of impossibilities ending in the greatest impossibility, death.

I waited for a call I had no reason to expect. Night thickened around the cabin. I turned out the lights and let the fire illuminate the main floor. Always, a fire. It was cheery and warm and it reminded me of—"Christmas," I said aloud.

A broad smile spread on my face. *Christmas.* The perfect surprise for Hannah. We'd missed Christmas in December, so I would give her Christmas in February. Our own Christmas.

But how much time did I have?

I slid my finger along the kitchen calendar.

Hannah flew back to Denver tomorrow. I knew she wouldn't take a week off work, meaning she would drive up to see me . . . on Friday, the 14th. Valentine's Day.

How strange.

How perfect.

I jumped when my phone rang.

"Matt." It was Hannah. I could barely hear her above what sounded like music and a crowd. "Are you there?"

"Bird, hey. God . . . I'm glad you called. I was just—"

"Matt, listen. We have a problem."

Chapter 9

HANNAH

Noises from the main floor filtered to the basement. Classical music, muted steps, a hum of chatter. And the tone: cautious.

Funeral talk.

Now and then, laughter flared and died fast. Probably someone was reminiscing about Matt. A funny anecdote, I imagined.

I wanted to hear those stories, but I couldn't be up there. I couldn't stand another condolence for my loss; I couldn't hug another tearful cousin who believed the lie of Matt's death. More—I couldn't handle another look of contempt.

During the memorial, I caught Matt's aunt eyeing me with a gaze that said: *slut*.

But I had bigger problems than that.

What did it mean, that *Night Owl* first appeared on the Web site where Matt and I met? Who else knew about that? How were we going to handle Shapiro's lawsuit? And what the fuck did that reporter want? *Aaron Snow.* His name rang a bell.

I shrugged off my coat and draped it over the bed in the guest room. I smiled as I touched the comforter. Once, Matt and I slept in this bed.

After a moment, I drew back the sheets and slipped under them. I closed my eyes and reached out. Soon I would be with him. Soon my hand would find his skin, the body I loved. And the voice, the mind, the soul.

A light came on in the basement. I scrambled off the bed.

"You're in the dark," said someone who sounded just like Matt, but this time I wasn't fooled. Psycho Seth.

Another light came on in the main room. I stepped out of the bedroom.

"I was lying down," I said.

"Hell of a time for a nap." Seth glanced at his watch. He still wore his leather jacket. I saw a strip of medical tape around his knuckles. "Who drove you home?"

"I have a headache. And one of your cousins drove me. What do you want?"

"I brought you some food." He held out a plate. "Peace offering."

I took the plate and retreated to a couch.

"No peace offering needed. We're not at war. Earlier, the way you"—*the way you assaulted me?*—"the way you approached me about the book, that was . . . unacceptable. But I get it. Matt's your brother and you think I wrote that book, but I didn't. And if Shapiro has his way, we'll all know who wrote it soon enough."

I picked at a glorified piece of toast.

"Olive tapenade," said Seth. "And egg. On the toast. It's good. That's a . . . cupcake." He pointed, keeping his distance.

"Thanks, I see that." I stuffed the tiramisu cupcake in my mouth.

I chewed and swallowed, and Seth stared at me.

"I like your dress," he said.

"Uh . . . thank you. Yeah." I jammed the toast in my mouth. I wanted my coat. I also wanted more food to stick in my mouth to avoid speaking.

I knew Seth's eyes were strafing along my lace-covered arms. Something about skin peeking through lace is always sensual. I tucked the hem of the dress over my knees.

"I get what Matt saw in you," he said.

I frowned and brushed crumbs from my lap.

"What is your deal?" I stood and moved away from Seth. "Have you been drinking? Because I haven't, okay? I don't really know anything about you, but it seems like you're trying to make me uncomfortable . . . again. So please stop. Please leave me alone."

"What did you see in Matt?" Seth took a step back. A laughable amount of space stood between us, plus a couch.

"I love him."

"Loved."

"I *love* him," I said. "That doesn't change because he's gone."

Seth smiled wolfishly. He sauntered over to a bookshelf and touched a spine. His posture was relaxed, his tone far cooler than mine. "I get it, Hannah. 'Love is as strong as death,' right?" After a space, he added, "Song of Solomon."

"I know," I snapped, but I didn't. The reference was lost on me.

"You're like a cornered animal. So defensive. I guess I deserve that. I'm not attacking you, though. I brought you some food, and I'll go away soon, if that's what you want."

"Why did you hit the reporter?"

"He was taking pictures at my brother's funeral." Seth's lips curled. Fire glimmered in his eyes. "I split his lip. And you ought to know he's upstairs right now, receiving care from the good Doctor Nate. In return for not making trouble for me, the reporter gets to talk to you, just as soon as Nate finishes stitching him up."

"What?"

"Yeah. Nate struck that deal. Obliging, huh? I knew you wouldn't be happy about it. You weren't happy about talking to Shapiro, either. Pretty fucking tense in that study. You going to thank me for giving you an excuse to bolt?"

Seth drifted into the guest bedroom and emerged with my purse and coat.

"Thanks," I muttered.

"You're welcome. And I'm sorry."

"What for?"

"You know what." Seth glared at the wall, struggling with his apology as Matt always did. "For earlier. For what I said. What I did . . ." He flexed his long fingers, and I remembered the force of his grip on my arm. Then I remembered him plowing across the cemetery to punch the reporter who dared to take pictures at Matt's memorial, and my anger faltered.

"Apology accepted, Seth."

"Nate and Snow will be looking for you in about . . . five minutes, Hannah." He offered my coat and purse, and he gazed at me earnestly. "You want to get lost?"

Seth drove too fast and I didn't care.

We made our escape by the patio door. I actually laughed as we rushed across the snowy lawn. Seth almost fell. So did I.

"What's so funny?" he said when we were on the road.

"I feel like we're bad children."

"Oh, I *am* a bad child." He grinned.

I hadn't thought about where we would go, and though I was alone with Seth, I wasn't frightened. I just wanted to get away from Nate and the reporter.

I needed to talk to Matt before I answered any more questions about *Night Owl*.

Besides, Matt and Nate were fundamentally good guys, and I assumed Seth was, too.

As if reading my mind, Seth said, "You're not scared of me, are you?"

"No."

"Good. I was rude earlier, I know. I wanted to see what kind of person you are. I thought you wrote that book, but you say you didn't, and I believe you now."

"Good." I gave him a small smile. He looked ahead into the frozen night. He was part Nate, part Matt, part something of his own. The white tape on his knuckles shone in the dark.

"Where to, Miss Catalano?" Seth withdrew a flask from an inner coat pocket.

I laughed. "Wow, really?"

"Not for me. Not yet." He offered the flask without taking his eyes off the highway.

"I have a plane to catch tomorrow. And my motel is . . . in the exact opposite direction, just FYI." I took the flask and twisted off the cap. I sniffed the mouth. Vodka.

"You want me to take you back to your motel?" Seth glanced at me. His face was a mask of shadows. *Yes. No. I want you to be Matt asking me that question, Matt driving me back to a roadside motel to do bad things to me.*

"Whatever," I said. I took a pull off the flask. The vodka was surprisingly smooth and pooled warm in my belly.

"You can come with me if you want. I'll get you back to the motel later."

I checked the time: 6:15 P.M., too early to be alone in my motel, aching for Matt.

"Okay, where are we going?"

"Surprise," said Seth.

I tried to return the flask. He shook his head, so I took another slug. I felt like I was in college again, going wherever the hell with people I barely knew, a little buzzed, happy and trusting. I remembered my cigarettes.

"Mind if I smoke?"

"You're endlessly surprising, Hannah. Go on. Light one for me."

"Only when I'm buzzed," I explained. I lit two cigarettes and passed one to Seth. We smoked with the windows down and threads of icy air cutting through the car. I didn't care. The cold, the buzz, the way Seth pushed his Bentley to eighty—none of it bothered me. I needed a release after the memorial.

Matt was right. That had to be the toughest part of our whole charade. And it was over.

"DJ, will ya?" Seth tossed a white jack onto my lap. I plugged the cord into my phone and searched for a good song. Was it wrong to listen to something happy?

I chose "Nara," the theme to *Cold Case*. No vocals, just a haunting melody that spiraled upward and almost out of control.

That was how I wanted to feel: almost out of control.

"Too cold?" said Seth.

"I like it."

"Good, me too."

We smoked second and third cigarettes. I finished off Seth's flask. He laughed when I returned it empty.

I was in the zone, playing all my favorite songs by Radiohead and Elliott Smith, and I barely noticed when we pulled into a crowded parking lot.

"Let's go, little bird."

"Don't call me that." I unplugged my phone. "Where are we?"

"Outskirts of Trenton. Come on." Seth bummed another smoke off me and we climbed out of the car. The cold felt amazing. The night's momentum, greased with alcohol, pulled me along at just the right pace.

Seth caught my hand and guided me toward a large building with dark windows. People stood outside smoking and laughing. This was a bar, I realized, or a club. Cool. My postcollege life had been pretty straitlaced, and I missed this scene.

"You all right?" Seth led me past a bouncer.

"I'm fine, no worries."

Jeez, we got inside so easily. One moment I was standing in the cold, the next I was in a chic low-lit club with hardwood floors and a semi-industrial look—brick walls, exposed pipework. A crowd filled the floor. Toward the front of the room was a stage studded with speakers and washed in blue light.

A DJ called out from a booth I couldn't see. "My man Seth is finally in the house!" The crowd cheered. I blinked up at Seth. "Here's one more song and then I'm off, thank God."

The volume amped up. I recognized a remix of . . . "Come & Get It" by Selena Gomez? I must have been drunk; it actually sounded good.

The crowd swirled around us and colored lights strobed overhead. A petite brunette with a buzz cut appeared out of the throng. She and Seth hugged.

"Steffy, hey!" Seth shouted to be heard.

"Hey, baby, who's this?" The girl smiled at me.

"Oh, this is Hannah! Take care of her, yeah? I'm doing *three* songs and leaving—" Seth held up three fingers emphatically. "We didn't get to practice! I had the thing for Matt!"

"Oh, yeah, the thing! Oh, my God!" Steffy hugged Seth again. Her arms lingered around his back. "Okay, get going! Wiley is going to kill you!"

Seth smiled at me. I smiled back at him, though I was confused as fuck. Maybe Seth was a DJ, but who the hell schedules a gig after his brother's memorial?

"Cool?" Seth shouted.

"Yeah," I mouthed.

Seth vanished into the crowd, leaving me with Steffy. I turned my uneasy smile to her.

"Cool! I'm Steffy! Okay, drinks!" Steffy hooked her arm through mine and dragged me to the bar. Her pupils were dilated, a thin rim of iris visible. She was rolling, I guessed.

Two screwdrivers later, I found myself at the foot of the stage with Steffy. Shaggy-haired band guys were messing with mike stands and cables. They did a sound check and the crowd went crazy, pressing against us and screaming.

"Oh, my God, finally!" Steffy squealed.

I laughed and let the crowd jostle me.

The stage darkened, then blared with orange light. A man jogged to the mike. "Okay, without further fucking ado"—the crowd laughed—"give it the fuck up for *Goldengrove*!"

I blinked against the bright light. Goldengrove? I tugged Steffy's arm.

"Goldengrove?" I shouted. "Like . . . *Goldengrove*?" I knew this band, an indie rock group notorious for turning down record deals. I liked their stuff.

"Yeah! *Wooo!*" Steffy waved her hands and pointed. I followed her finger to the stage and my jaw dropped. Seth stood at a mike about five feet away. He was shirtless and laughing. He wore an ironic little smile, as if the whole scene embarrassed him.

"Good to be home," he said into the mike. He shook out his

hair. The crowed exploded and surged forward, shoving me against the stage. I stared up at Seth helplessly. Of course, he had Matt's lean, sculpted torso, flat abs, and a teasing treasure trail.

Fitted jeans clung to his hipbones.

Two large tattoos covered Seth's flanks, curling ink scrawled from his waist to his ribs. One read GOLDENGROVE. I caught a look at the other as he twisted. THE PENNY WORLD.

"What's up with the tattoos?" I yelled to Steffy.

"Oh! The thing, like, about childhood! You know, like—"

Sound erupted from the speakers—drums and muted cymbals, then the howl of an electric guitar. I found myself laughing and cheering. Live music is intoxicating.

"This is a cover," Seth shouted. "'In One Ear'!"

The band played for a while and then Seth started to sing. His voice, smooth at first, turned gravelly at the chorus. He swayed as he sang, pulling the mike stand with him. He was good. He was actually good. And he was a beauty on stage, though I felt guilty looking at him.

What would Matt think of all this? What *did* Matt think of it?

He never told me Seth was a singer.

The band played an original song, one I knew from the radio, and Seth transitioned to the piano and played and sang through the third song. He rocked on the bench, his thighs tense as he shifted his foot on the pedals. Under the blue and orange lights, I saw sweat on his neck and toned muscles on his arms. His tattoos seemed to writhe.

He played like he wanted to break the piano.

If his hand hurt, he gave no indication.

I danced halfheartedly with Steffy, who danced wholeheartedly with me, grinding on my leg and rolling her hips.

A writer. A doctor. A musician. The Sky brothers. They were fascinating, or I was drunk. I wanted to be in their world.

"Encore!" the crowd wailed.

Seth loped back to the mike. His silky hair looked perfectly disheveled. Part of me thought *cool,* and part of me resisted his crude appeal.

Seth made a big show of debating the encore, tossing his hair and sighing.

"*Wellll,*" he said. For the first time since he stepped on the stage, he looked at me. Directly at me. My eyes widened.

Seth smiled. *Trust me,* his smile said.

He reached down and caught my hand, or maybe I gave him my hand. He hoisted me onto the stage. I wobbled on my heels and he snaked an arm around my waist.

His body was electric, vibrating with energy. I clung to him. I missed Matt with sudden, crippling intensity, and I pressed my face into Seth's bare shoulder.

"One more song," Seth said into the mike, "if my new friend Hannah kisses me."

I jumped.

"Only if she kisses me! I want a kiss from this beautiful girl."

Seth hugged me tight. Shock lanced through me, and the fog of my buzz lifted abruptly.

"I will *not!*" I rasped right into his ear.

"Kiss him!" the crowed screeched. "Kiss! Kiss!" It became a chant.

I made the mistake of glancing down at Steffy. Her eyes were hard and black.

"It's a show," Seth murmured in my ear. I felt the full slow trail of his finger up the nape of my neck. "Kiss me on the cheek or something."

I grabbed Seth's jaw and jerked it aside. The crowd cackled. Seth winced. I planted a kiss on his cheek and climbed off the stage.

"Damn!" I heard him saying. "Better than nothing, right? Okay, one more song!"

I forced a smile as I pushed my way to the back of the club. Strangers whistled at me and girls glared. My lips burned hotter than my cheeks. What the hell was that about?

I found a pay phone in the lobby and jabbed in Matt's new number.

Chapter 10

MATT

That night, I couldn't sleep.

I kept replaying my conversation with Hannah.

"We have a problem," she said. She hiccupped in my ear. "I—I just—today—"

"Slow down, bird. I can hardly hear you. Where are you?"

"At a bar. Er, a club . . . thingy."

"A bar?" I frowned. Maybe Hannah needed a drink after the memorial. Understandable, but . . . "Did something happen? Are you okay?"

"It's about the book. *Night Owl.*"

I stilled, and then I smiled slowly. *This is it,* I thought. Hannah went to my memorial . . . and everyone knew about *Night Owl.* I could easily imagine her embarrassment. I felt the same embarrassment when *Fit to Print* exposed my identity last year, and the media ran with it, and suddenly the whole world knew the most private details of my life.

Night Owl had become a phenomenon, just as I was a phenomenon. And Hannah was the star of *Night Owl.*

Soon, I knew, she wouldn't be able to stand it. The gossip. The speculation. The way my family must have treated her. She would understand how cruel the media can be. She would fear the public, with its vulgar curiosity and sickening sense of entitlement.

And then she would come to me. Then, finally, we could leave the country together. Disappear . . . start over . . . be free . . . just as I'd hoped and planned.

Hannah's voice broke into my thoughts.

"Matt, it was posted on the Mystic Tavern. Like, first. What the hell?"

My heart stammered. *What?* No, this wasn't in my plan. How did she find out?

"The Mystic Tavern," I repeated.

"Yes! You know, the site where we—"

"I know." I rubbed my mouth. "That . . . that's . . ." *That's something you weren't supposed to figure out.*

"That's fucking insane, is what it is," she said. She sounded breathless. "Who else knows about that site? I mean, who—"

"A couple people, actually." I got up from the couch. *Get a grip, Matt. Get control of this situation.* "Yeah. Mike, my psychiatrist . . . he knew. I think I told Kevin, too. And Hannah, let's be logical here. Whoever put the story online must have hacked my e-mail, like I said. We're talking about a . . ." I closed my eyes. My lies sounded truly ridiculous. "A really tech-savvy person," I mumbled. "Someone who could trace me to that Web site . . . no problem."

"Yeah . . . I guess." Hannah sniffled.

"Babe, are you crying?"

"No. I'm in the lobby. It's cold. I just . . . stopped for a drink before heading to the motel."

"Hannah, how do you know it was posted on the Mystic Tavern *first*? I mean, it's all over the fucking Internet. Maybe it got posted there randomly . . . a coincidence."

Hannah told me about the lawsuit then. She told me about her meeting with Shapiro and Nate's minor obsession with *Night Owl*. I gave her hollow reassurances. *They have nothing. The book doesn't prove I'm alive. Refuse to cooperate and Nate will drop the lawsuit.*

Now I was lying for both of us.

I checked the bedside clock: 2:49 A.M. The gears in my mind wouldn't quit turning. *Night Owl* . . . Shapiro . . . the Mystic Tavern . . . Melanie.

I told Melanie she wasn't in trouble—but she was, apparently, and so was I. *Night Owl* pointed to Melanie. Melanie pointed to me.

I took my phone to the deck and sat on a snow-coated chair. The cold and damp quickly crept through my lounge pants. I lit a cigarette.

When the day's first light hit the treetops, I flipped open my cell and called Melanie.

"Hello?" Her voice was muzzy.

"Hey. It's me."

Melanie coughed and went quiet for a moment. I heard water running. "Jesus. It's like . . . six in the morning."

"I know. It's also Sunday. I assume you don't have work."

"I'm between jobs. But if I were working, I think I'd want to sleep—"

I barked out a laugh. "Between jobs. That kills me, that phrase." I waved my hand. "Like the next job is right around the corner."

"You really *are* an asshole."

"Yeah, the legends are true." I wanted to laugh—really laugh. "Listen, Mel, sorry I woke you. We've got a little problem."

I paused and Melanie waited.

I was about to speak when she said, "How did you do it? The mountain lion. All that."

I squinted against the sunlight. I was still thinking about Hannah and my failing plan to drive her to me, and wondering why I was such a dick most of the time, and why I couldn't seem to change. And then I was thinking about the mountain lion. Her muzzle was pure white, like she dipped it in paint. Beautiful—and so terrible.

"The cat wasn't part of the plan," I said.

"Jesus . . ."

"Mm. I cut my wrist and my forearm. I took codeine . . . not enough. I had a tourniquet around my arm. The idea was to bleed enough to . . ."

"Enough to make it look like you bled out."

"Right. Like I fell on my ice axe or something. Sounds stupid now." I lit another cigarette with trembling hands. It felt good to tell someone what happened—someone besides Hannah. I'd spared Hannah the details because she'd go crazy with worry.

Melanie waited for me to continue.

"I fell," I said simply. "I lost consciousness. The pain meds, the blood loss . . . the cold or the altitude, I don't know, all of it. I blacked out. My plan was to hike out and wait for a fresh snow to cover my tracks. The cat . . ."—a cylinder of ash broke from my cigarette—"found me. Dragged me, I guess. Mel, I was out cold. I don't know for how long. When I came to, she was shaking my leg, she was just shaking it and shaking it, and the skin, she was . . . it was tearing, she was shredding it without even trying. I was stuck on a rock. I saw, you know, I saw how she was trying to pull me over a rock and my pack was stuck."

"Oh, my God," Mel whispered.

I stared into the memory.

I wouldn't tell Melanie how I thought I was dying—how I thought, *This is it.* How I wasn't ready. How desperately I wanted to live, and how scared I felt.

"Anyway." I laughed. "Long story short, I woke the fuck up and I screamed my fucking head off, and I waved my arms and all that, and I scared the shit out of the cat. She took one look at me and she was like, *You really are an asshole,* and she beat it."

I forced another chuckle. I slid my bare feet through the snow on the deck. Cold. Cold that hurt, because I was alive.

"That's insane," Melanie said.

"Yeah, for sure." I struggled to sound blasé. "Couldn't have bribed the cat for a better performance. Blood, animal hair, the trail into the woods—mountain lion attack, case closed. I threw on my snowshoes and hiked out of there, and that was that."

"Your leg—"

"Was fine, shallow wounds. I had a first aid kit. I'm fine." I winced. *Fine* could never describe my hike off Longs Peak with a torn calf and bleeding arm in subzero conditions. Every few steps I stopped to make sure I wasn't trailing blood. Every few steps I thought, *I'm too weak to get to the cabin, if I sleep I'll die, I'm going to die, I'm really going to die out here.*

"Was it worth it?" Mel said.

"Was what worth what?"

"All that. Everything you went through to disappear. Was it worth it?"

"Hey, you don't know me." I stubbed out my cigarette in the snow. "You don't know what matters to me. You don't know how fucking bad it was, with half of Denver breathing down my neck every fucking time I went out for a cup of coffee—"

"Okay, okay!"

"Yeah. Okay. Story time's over. You need to pull *Night Owl* off the Internet. Now."

"What? Yesterday you told me to—"

"I know what I told you." I sneered and dug my fingers into my palm. I wasn't mad at Melanie. Not at all. I was mad that my plan was failing. Hannah didn't seem to care how many people read *Night Owl,* or how much they might guess about her life. She was, as far as I could tell, no closer to leaving Denver and disappearing with me. And now she knew *Night Owl* was posted on the Mystic Tavern forum. How long before she suspected me?

I relaxed my grip and sighed slowly; I felt so fucking powerless.

"Just pull the e-book," I said. "Everywhere you're selling it, pull the title. My brother has a lawyer looking into it. We're both fucked if they figure it all out."

"Oh . . . shit. Shit."

"Yeah, shit." I rolled my eyes. "Hence my six A.M. wake-up call, okay? Do it now."

"I will. I promise. I'm so sorry . . . if this . . . shit, if this comes back to you . . ."

I smirked and pushed myself out of the chair. I brushed snow off my pants.

"Hey, don't worry about me, Mel. I could lie my way out of existence." *I practically did.*

Melanie was still talking when I shut my cell.

She would call again, I knew she would, when *Night Owl* was gone from the Net.

Chapter 11

HANNAH

My phone and watch alarms went off simultaneously, chiming and beeping in the dark. I groaned. It was five in the morning. I had a flight to catch at seven.

And I missed Matt.

I missed waking beside his warm body, our limbs tangled together. I missed the things he muttered in his sleep.

I told you, he insisted once. *I told you!*

And another night: *Peaches. No, a picnic. A picnic . . .*

We laughed like crazy when he woke up and I told him. Now it was our little joke, signifying nothing. "Peaches. No, a picnic!"

I checked the packing job I did last night. Not bad, I only missed my boots and nylons.

I popped two Tylenol and showered quickly. As hangovers go, I was feeling all right.

My plan was to call a cab and be gone before Nate showed. I would text him from the cab, saying I decided to head out early.

I frowned as I rinsed shampoo from my hair. It was too bad about Nate and his *Night Owl* fixation. I actually liked Nate.

Seth, on the other hand . . .

I shivered and plucked a towel off the rack. *Seth* . . . I felt a swirl of emotion when I thought of him. Anger, interest, confusion.

I pulled on a gray V-neck sweater, skinny jeans, boots, and my Burberry coat—a gift from Matt. He spoiled me terribly. I dried my curls and tied them back. My hair was getting long again, hanging around my shoulders. I think Matt liked it that way. I know he loved when I dragged it over his body . . .

My cell rang.

It was Nate, of course. I let the call go to voice mail.

He called again. *Really, Nate?*

I rubbed my neck and sighed. But of course he was calling . . . and calling and calling. He'd committed to giving me a ride to the airport, and like the gentleman he was, he wanted to remind me. We hadn't exactly touched base after the memorial. I rode back to Nate's house with two of Matt's cousins, hid in the basement, and then made my escape with Seth. (And then made my escape *from* Seth by calling a cab.)

When my phone began to ring for a third round, I peeked through the curtains. *Fuck.* Nate stood in the motel parking lot, phone to his ear, eyes aimed in my direction.

I grabbed my cell.

"Hey!" I said. "Sorry, I was drying my hair."

"There you are. I was worried, Hannah. We should get going soon. Are you ready?"

"Yup . . . all ready."

"I'll meet you in the lobby."

I watched Nate through the window as we talked. His posture relaxed the moment I answered. He nodded and raked a hand through his hair.

God, now I really felt like a scumbag.

Nate beamed at me in the lobby. I caught a touch of guilt in his smile.

"Hannah. Good morning." He took my suitcase. "Did I scare you off with Shapiro yesterday? Did you get one of these?" He handed me Matt's memorial card.

Matthew Robert Sky Jr. November 9, 1984–December 2013.
"The Lord is my shepherd, I shall not want. He makes me lie
down in green pastures, He leads me beside quiet waters, He
restores my soul . . ."

There was a picture of Matt on the back.

I skimmed the Twenty-third Psalm until I got to the "valley of
the shadow of death" bit. I shoved the card in my pocket.

"Val helped me choose that. Matt liked the Psalms. Beautiful
language, right?"

"Yeah, thanks." I turned up my collar as we headed to the car.
I decided not to mention Shapiro. Instead I said, "Matt liked the
Bible? That's news to me."

Nate put my suitcase in the trunk and started the car. We
swung smoothly into morning traffic and my eyes drifted shut.

"Oh, yes, of course. Matt always believed in God. His books
are full of biblical allusions. Surely you've noticed."

"Sort of . . ." Sort of not. My biblical background was woefully
weak.

" 'The silver cord,' that's from Ecclesiastes 12. Matt's with God
now, of that I have no doubt. He had faith. He had principles. I'm
sorry you didn't get to know that side of him."

Matt's faith . . . Matt's principles . . . more of Matt I didn't
know.

"Me too," I said.

I dozed.

The speed bumps in the airport parking garage woke me,
though Nate eased over them as gingerly as possible. He winced
when he saw me waking. "Sorry."

"No, I'm sorry. Jeez, I passed out."

"You had a long day yesterday. I'm sorry about Seth, you
know. He's bad with introductions. He thinks . . ." Nate waved a
hand.

He thinks I wrote Night Owl.

"I know," I said. I was suddenly wide awake, and I did and
didn't want to talk about *Night Owl*. Now that I knew it first ap-

peared on the Mystic Tavern, I was more confused than ever. I felt like someone was out to get me—or Matt. Or *us*. But why?

Who stood to gain by sabotaging us like that?

"I want to give you a heads-up, Hannah. Shapiro might be in touch. Also, that reporter at the service?" Nate pulled a face. "I knew his name sounded familiar. Aaron Snow. Turns out he ran that online magazine, *Fit to Print*. I'm sure you remember."

"I remember." I wished I could forget. Last year, *Fit to Print* exposed Matt as M. Pierce and had a field day with his personal life.

"Seems he's part of a new online outfit, *No Stone Unturned*. I swear, some people don't know when to give up. He thinks he's a great investigative journalist, I'm sure. He was fixated on Matt, and now on *Night Owl*. He wanted to speak to you last night. I meant to humor him, only because he wasn't pressing charges over Seth's idiocy, but—"

"I snuck out."

"Right." Nate chuckled. "Just as well, Hannah. Snow doesn't know about the lawsuit, and we'll keep it that way. We don't need his help. We surely don't need the media's attention, online or off. The book has done quite enough damage as is."

I felt Nate gearing up for another *Night-Owl*-is-filth-protect-the-family-name speech and I stammered, "I'm starved. Wow, I better grab something to eat before my flight."

"Please do. They have a lot of eating places in here." Nate carried my suitcase into the airport. I struggled to keep up with his long-legged stride.

He stood at my side as I checked my bag and received my boarding pass.

"They have those dots. The ice cream dots. Owen loves them." Nate was peeling bills out of his wallet. "But it's early for that, isn't it?" He tried to press the money into my hand.

"Nate, I—I have traveling money."

"Hannah, please." He stared off as he pushed the bills against my palm. He closed my fingers around them. "There. Don't be a stranger. Aren't you almost part of the family now? It feels that way. I know how much Matt loved you. What a mess we dragged you into."

I blinked rapidly and took the money. Oh. Oh . . .

Nate was trying to say good-bye.

"It's not a mess," I whispered.

"You'll come see us again? What do you think, in the spring? Or we'll come see you. The kids love that zoo in Denver. I know Matt hated the zoo, animals in cages and all that, but the kids . . ." Nate frowned. He was rambling and seemed to realize it.

I clutched my purse and Nate's cash and stared up at him, afraid I would cry if I spoke. Here was the most decent guy I knew—truly—and I was lying to him in the worst possible way.

"The kids." He pulled me into a hug. "They love it."

"Yeah." My voice was barely audible.

Nate kept me in his arms, and I felt fine there. Nate wasn't sleazy like Seth. He wasn't impulsive like Matt. He was responsible. He was good. I trusted him.

Just before I got in line to go through security, Nate drew an envelope from his inner coat pocket. He handed it to me and nodded. I narrowed my eyes.

"What—"

"Read it on the plane," he said. He walked away before I could return the envelope. I watched his dark head disappear around a corner. *Typical.*

Chapter 12

MATT

Melanie didn't call. One hour turned to two, turned to six, and when my phone finally rang, I recognized the number of Hannah's prepaid cell. I smiled and closed my notebook.

"Hannah. Hey."

"Hi. I just got home." Something thumped, a door closing or a suitcase hitting the floor. Hannah exhaled. "You won't believe your brother."

"Which one?"

"Nate. He drove me to the airport, and—"

"Of course he did." I scowled.

"Matt, relax. This is Nate we're talking about. You know, married Nate with a medical practice and kids, who probably goes to church every week."

"He does. You underestimate your charms."

"My charms?" Hannah giggled. She only giggled for me.

"Yes, your charms. You know, the charms I threw over my whole life for."

Hannah got quiet.

"Hey, I'm kidding," I said. "But I wouldn't put it past anyone to fall for you, all right? Even Saint Nate. So what happened?"

"He . . . he gave me this letter. Before I got on my plane. It's all technical and . . . well, listen." She began to read. "'It will be some time before the court orders a death certificate for Matt, months possibly, though I have Shapiro working on it. In a case of imminent peril such as this, presumption of death is typical. I apologize if this is'—"

She skipped something.

I already knew what was coming.

"Here. Okay. 'As I was last aware, Matt willed his estate to myself and Seth, and secondarily to any living nephews and nieces. I know, however, that if Matt had reason to anticipate his death, he would have willed his estate to you. I know how he felt about you, Hannah. We spoke about you more than once. I want to give you my portion of Matt's estate and I won't hear no about this.' So, he goes on like that . . ."

"Mm." I lowered my head and rubbed my temple. "He's right," I said after a while. "I would have given it to you. What's the problem?"

"I don't know, Matt. You mean besides lying to your brother about your death and taking your money, *his* money? I don't think I can do it."

"Hannah, he won't take no for an answer. Trust me. Anyway, this is what I want and you'll do it. Think of it as me giving my money to you. I would have, and you know that, but I couldn't rewrite my will and then disappear the way I did. This is perfect. This is better than I could have hoped." I forced some enthusiasm into my voice.

All told, I left Hannah with fifty thousand dollars in cash. I kept fifty thousand at the cabin with me. It was my rainy day fund, which I held first at my Denver apartment and then in the wall safe I had installed in Hannah's condo.

"Always have some cash on hand," my uncle used to say, "because you never know."

Maybe my uncle didn't mean one hundred grand, but I'm an overachiever.

"I have to think about it," Hannah said.

"Fine, think about it." I flipped open my notebook and began to doodle. I drew a fat little bird on a branch. "We'll talk about it. You're coming out, aren't you?"

"Yeah. I was thinking . . . Friday night." Hannah's voice lightened and I smiled.

Yes, here was a good thought: Hannah at the cabin with me all weekend. *Finally.*

"Great," I said. "Perfect. I can't wait . . ."

"Me either," she murmured.

"I *can't* wait, Hannah." I pressed the point of my pen against the page. Black ink bled out. "You're home. I'm glad."

"Me too. I don't . . . want to wait." Whenever Hannah got embarrassed, which happened often and easily, her voice softened. I grinned and tilted my head. Mm, Hannah's shy side delighted me. It made me feel like a devil.

"Let's not wait. A week is a long time. Do you need to get settled?"

"Yeah . . . let me go get Laurence. I might grab a shower, if you don't mind waiting."

"Shave."

Hannah took a moment to process my imperative.

"Oh . . . yeah, okay. Yeah."

I could barely hear her, she spoke so softly.

"Take your time, Hannah. I'll wait for your call. I love you."

"I love you, too. I won't be long."

We said our good-byes—my good-bye involving anything but the word "good-bye"—and I left the desk and headed toward the bedroom.

Chapter 13

HANNAH

The charms I threw over my whole life for.

I threw over my whole life.

Hey, I'm kidding.

I shuffled down the hallway with Laurence's cage digging at my belly.

"You'll be out of here soon," I said to the rabbit. He slid along the newspaper and scrabbled to stay steady. His eyes were big as quarters.

I had tried to pay Jamie for watching him—Jamie lived in the condo above mine—but she refused my money. Maybe I could slip a gift card under her door.

I stroked Laurence's ears, kissed the top of his head, and set him in his hutch in the living room. He began a full fur clean, the way he always did after I touched him.

"Hey, I'm not so bad," I said.

I changed Laurence's food and water and dragged my suitcase to the bedroom. God, I didn't feel like unpacking. I felt tired and greasy after a four-hour flight, and I couldn't turn off my brain. Seth, Nate, Matt . . . Seth with his confusing kiss, Nate with his

excessive generosity, Matt with his tongue-in-cheek comment . . .
I threw over my whole life.

I'm kidding, he said. But it was true.

Matt *did* throw over his whole life for me.

His anonymity, his relationship with Bethany, his safe and
stable routine—I broke it all apart when I bumbled into his world.
My picture and my clumsy mistake started Matt on the path that
ended with him risking his life on Longs Peak. And that, I realized with a shudder, was why I agreed to help him fake his death.

Not just because I loved him.

Not just because I wanted him to be free.

Because I felt responsible for his unhappiness.

And that unhappiness had surrounded Matt, no matter how
he tried to hide it. "It's one thing," he told me, "to share your
life in fiction, on your own terms, and another thing entirely to
see your personal history all over the Internet."

Sometimes I caught Matt looking very pale as he surfed the
Net, and I knew he'd seen another article about his life—about his
botched suicide, his dead parents, his old partying habits, and petty
crimes. I would hug him then and find his heart beating rapidly
under my hand.

And even after his birthday, when I finally coaxed Matt out of
his funk, he lived like a hermit. The condo was his cell. From its
windows he watched the city he loved, where he used to move
freely, an unknown observer. But that city had turned on Matt
with its insatiable twenty-first-century curiosity, and the more Matt
hid, the hungrier people got. He was "Denver's author," and they
were proud and proprietary. His good looks, his wealth, his damaged past, and wild youth became the stuff of tabloids, literally.

M. Pierce sightings were tweeted.

Young writers haunted the agency's steps.

Pam received a never-ending deluge of mail for Matt. Cloth-
ing, food, books, love letters.

"Wait it out," I used to tell him. "You're a fad. This craziness
won't last."

But he couldn't wait.

"My life will never be the same," he said. "I'll never be free."

I ran the shower too hot and hissed when the water hit my skin. Unwelcome thoughts kept cropping up—Shapiro, Snow—but I tried to focus on Matt. *Shave,* he said. I lathered pear-scented gel over my legs and began to work a razor around my ankles.

I shaved before the memorial and my legs were smooth, but Matt liked me velvety. He liked one particular area bare.

My thoughts clouded as I shaved over my knees and up my thighs to my sex. Lord, Matt even made shaving sexy.

Shave. It was an order. I loved taking orders from Matt.

I imagined him lying along the couch by the fire, nothing but a throw draped across his hips . . . and I dragged my razor over my pubic bone, shearing away the short, stiff hair.

I felt light-headed by the time I stepped out of the shower. I patted my skin dry and rubbed in my DollyMoo lilac body oil. Another thing Matt liked: rubbing oil into my skin.

I pulled on Matt's bathrobe, which reached my feet and smelled of his body wash, and a black lace thong. I fetched my box of toys from the closet.

The box held two LELOs, toy cleaner, three kinds of lube, the collar with clamps that we first used at Matt's apartment, a blindfold, silk ties, a gag, and a roll of black tape. Matt sometimes joked about adding a leash or riding crop to the box.

Or maybe he wasn't joking . . .

I lit the candles on the bedside table and sprawled across our comforter. I dialed Matt's number. He answered immediately.

"You," he said.

"Me." I smiled. "And you."

"Did you have a nice shower?"

"Very." I caught the first whiff of my candles—sandalwood and jasmine. Their light pulsed on the ceiling. "It was only missing you. I think this place misses you."

"Soon we'll be together. And before long, we can live together again. When things die down . . . we'll get a place. Now you'll have my money, or some of it. That's one less worry."

"Yeah . . ." I shoved away the thought of the money. Truth be told, Matt and I had no idea what our future held. We didn't plan that far ahead. Sometimes he talked like this, idly and optimistically, and I agreed because the alternative was painful.

"What are you wearing?" he said.

"Your bathrobe and a black lace thong."

Matt chuckled. My smile expanded at the sound.

"Very nice. Let the robe hang open. Déjà vu, little bird. Do you remember—"

"Of course." I reclined against a stack of decorative pillows. Matt's robe slipped open, exposing my breasts. My nipples stiffened instantly and my skin prickled with anticipation. "The first time, online? You must have thought I was crazy."

"No crazier than I was. Granted, I thought I was pretty fucking crazy."

"What if I had been someone else?" I slid my fingers over the slope of my breast.

"You weren't. This is our reality, Hannah. I don't have time for what-ifs. You shaved?"

"Yes." I smiled again. I loved the way Matt dismissed things out of hand—always with ice in his voice. *I don't have time for what-ifs.*

"Where? What did you shave?"

"My legs."

"What else?"

"My—" My cheeks warmed. "My pussy."

"Mm." Matt sighed roughly. "Touch it for me. I miss it."

I slipped my hand into my thong, over the soft bare hill of skin. Matt missed this. I remembered his mouth between my legs and circled my fingers around the wet folds.

"Tell me what you're doing," I whispered, "and where you are. I want to know."

He laughed and I felt the color rising in my face.

"Okay, bird. I'm lying on the bed. You know, in the bedroom—the one whose windows face east. I keep it warm in here. I'm not wearing anything." Matt paused for a beat and I envisioned his firm, naked body. My sex throbbed under my fingers. "That's how I want to be with you, Hannah. Nothing between us . . . your body and mine."

I moaned softly and spread my legs. "Matt, I miss you. I miss you so much."

"I miss you, too. I miss your cunt. I'm already hard. You make it easy."

I groaned and shoved down my thong, dragging it off with a foot. Matt hard. Now, that was a beautiful thought.

"Play with your clit. How does that feel?"

I rolled my fingers over that bundle of nerves. My calves tensed.

"G-good," I mumbled. Matt stayed quiet, but I could *feel* his deadpan smirk. "Um . . . it feels . . . strange, I can't—"

I missed Matt's body like hell and maybe I resented our relapse to long distance, but phone sex has its virtues. Just this—putting words to my pleasure—turned me way, way on.

"I can't quite explain. It's like I'm chasing something, a sensation, an itch. It's hard to stop." My hips twitched as I skimmed my fingers over my clit. "And it makes me so wet."

"God, Hannah."

"Tell me . . ." I bit my lip.

"Tell you how my dick feels?"

"Yes. Please."

"Sensitive. Warm. So fucking sensitive, Hannah. It's not always this way—" Matt hesitated, breathing softly on the line. My eyes slipped closed. I could see him in my mind's eye, his muscled forearm working, his hand gliding up and down his shaft.

"But fuck, when I get hard," he said, "it gets so sensitive. I can't ignore it. I can't think about anything else. All I want is you. All I want is to come. My mind, it's . . . good for nothing . . . a pornographic reel of you. You on your hands and knees. Your ass. Your pussy. Your tits. I want to fuck you. I want to fuck you Hannah, *fuck.*"

My eyes flared opened. Matt could still shock me. His anger. His raw honesty. And *whew,* the way he laid it all out there . . . like he was possessed.

"I miss your body, your tight pussy around me." He panted in my ear. "My cock inside you. Deep. God, *fuck*. Fuck yourself. Do it."

I groped at my box of toys and pulled out the plum-colored LELO. It was long and thick and smooth. And powerful. I didn't need any lube; I was soaked.

"Hannah . . . fuck yourself. Tell me. I'm hard for you. Touching my head . . . my balls . . . thinking of your sweet mouth . . ."

"I'm . . . p-putting it in," I whispered. Matt moaned his appreciation. I pressed the tip of the vibrator to my slit and inched it in and out.

"God, baby. Think about me fucking you. I can't wait . . . I can't wait a week. I can't wait five fucking minutes."

I turned on the vibrator and whimpered as I slid it deeper. *Think about me fucking you.* I did. I thought about the way Matt looked at me when he entered me, and the way I felt when he took me. The way he held me down as he moved. His relentless pace. His arousal filling me.

"Matt," I breathed. My legs trembled. I dropped my phone on the pillow and rubbed my clit. I brought myself closer and closer to the edge.

"Hannah . . . move it in and out. Fast, the way I'll fuck you this weekend. I think about it all the time. I dream about your tight ass. I wake up hard and—" He gasped. "I get off thinking about your cunt."

"More," I panted.

"I wish you could see me." Matt's sexy voice was fraying. "My cock. How hard I am. How I'm oozing. God, *fuck*. Are you going to squirt for me? You are. You *are*."

"I will . . . I p-promise."

"You want to see it, don't you? You miss my cock. Say it."

"I miss it." I did. I groaned as I plunged the toy in and out of my body. I got crazy when I got close, willing to say and do anything, the maddest thoughts in my head.

"I'm close—close—want to come inside you . . ." Matt's breaths grew sharp and erratic. My spine arched. I held back because it felt so damn good, and I wanted to come with Matt.

Maybe Matt was holding back, too. He kept swearing and moaning—sounds I loved—and telling me to fuck myself. "You only fuck yourself for me," he rasped. Then, "God, I'm coming— *fuck*—I'm coming."

I let myself go. My pleasure was right there waiting. A little shift in pressure, a subtle change of pace, and that incendiary ribbon of feeling unraveled in my body. How is it that this feeling never grows old? Ecstasy is strange fire.

I came down slow and smiling. Little aftershocks of pleasure tickled my limbs.

"My bird," Matt murmured. "Baby. Did you come?"

"I did. With you."

A gray day and drawn curtains lent a deceptive darkness to the room, but it was only one in the afternoon. I rubbed my eyes and sat up.

"Let's talk awhile?" Matt said. The hope in his voice hurt my heart.

"Hey, of course. I've got nowhere to go." I folded Matt's bathrobe back around my body. It smelled like a freshly showered Matt hug.

"Me either." He laughed.

"You holding up all right out there? How's the food? How's your leg?"

"Leg's fine. Really, it was minor. Totally healed . . . you'll see. Food's fine, too. Stop worrying about me. I'm good. I'm writing. How was the thing?"

The thing. He meant the memorial.

"Oh, you know. Formal. I met Seth."

"Mm."

"You didn't tell me he was in a band."

"I didn't think it was important." In an instant, Matt's voice went from warm and open to cold and closed. "I don't know what *your* brother does."

"Matt, my brother's in high school."

"Fine, he's in high school."

Laughter burbled out of me. I clapped a hand over my mouth, but the giggles slipped through my fingers. Oh, Matt . . .

"What's so funny?"

"You. You're adorable."

He snorted. "Excuse me?"

"Nothing. Hey, I can't wait to see you. Want me to bring anything special?"

"Mm . . . your cute little ass and a few thongs. That'll do."

"You're turning into a sex-starved recluse out there, huh? Subsisting on ink and fantasies. And ramen noodles."

"I was always a sex-starved recluse. And I'll have you know I made SpaghettiOs today."

I pinched the bridge of my nose. God, this was killing me. Matt couldn't cook to save his soul, and now he couldn't eat out. Left to his own devices, he was living on Pringles, Pop-Tarts, and SpaghettiOs—I just knew it.

"I'm going to cook for you this weekend, I swear. Every meal."

"In an apron?" he said.

"Uh, sure. In an apron."

"Mm . . . my little bird in just an apron."

Just an apron? I laughed again, shaking my head.

We talked about my job. I asked about the weather. We avoided the lawsuit, Matt's money, and *Night Owl*. I also decided not to mention Aaron Snow and his online magazine, *No Stone Unturned*. Maybe Matt already knew about that. The cabin had dial-up, though we never used the Internet to communicate. Too easy to trace, Matt said.

Finally, around two, I pushed myself off the bed and blew out my candles.

"Plans for the evening?" Matt tried to sound upbeat.

"Nah, I've got nothing. I might go to yoga. There's a class at seven."

"Don't forget your little bird mat."

I grinned and rubbed my neck.

"Yeah, can't forget the mat. I dunno if I'll really go."

"Make yourself go. You'll feel better."

I paused by the window, my hand on the curtain.

"How do you know I'm not feeling good?"

"I know, Hannah. I know you like I know my own self."

"How come I don't know you like that?" I remembered the memorial guests relating stories about Matt. I remembered Nate discussing Matt's faith. I even remembered the laughter I heard as I hid in Nate's basement, which seemed to mock me for being an outsider. Outside of the mystery of the man I loved.

"You do, Hannah. You know me. Let's not say good-bye. Say you'll see me soon."

"I'll see you soon," I said.

"So soon. I love you, Hannah."

Matt hung up first. I tossed the phone onto the bed, but I picked it up immediately and returned it to the wall safe in the closet. *Don't leave this lying around,* Matt told me the day he came home with two prepaid cells. *Keep the minute cards in the safe too. No one can see these things. And we can't use them all the time; we can't talk every day. It's too risky.*

How did he know all that stuff?

Sometimes, I got a feeling that Matt had contemplated vanishing before.

I changed into my yoga pants and workout top.

I set my yoga mat and water bottle by the door.

Music. I needed music, or TV or maybe a movie. I needed noise and distraction—which reminded me.

I unpacked my laptop and booted it up. I sat cross-legged on the bed as I waited for iTunes to load.

Then, with a smile on my lips, I deleted every Goldengrove song in my library. *Good-bye, Seth Sky,* I thought.

I never expected to see him again, and I resented the swirl of confusion I felt when I thought about him. It was Matt I loved. Matt I wanted. I didn't need anything from his dark-haired, cynical brother.

Chapter 14

MATT

Hannah sat on our bed, angled away from me. Her shoulders moved with quiet sobs. The room was dark, and I could just make out the silvery satin of her nightie.

"Hannah?" I reached for her. "Baby, why are you crying?"

"I miss you," she whispered.

"Bird, I'm right here."

"You're not. You don't want to be."

Something tightened inside me. *I* didn't want to be with Hannah?

"You're the one who won't run away with me," I said. "You won't leave Denver . . . won't leave your life. *You* don't want to be with *me*."

"Matt . . . I miss you. Where are you?"

With that, Hannah slipped off the bed and rushed out of the room. I watched, mesmerized, as her little nightie shifted around her body, as her curls fanned across her back, and she disappeared out the bedroom door.

"Hannah!" I darted after her.

I reached the hallway in time to see her rounding the corner into the kitchen.

I heard the condo door opening.

When I got there, I found the door hanging open and no Hannah.

"Hannah!" I called. "Where the hell are you going?"

Barefoot, I dashed down the complex stairs and out into the Denver night. A wall of cold air crashed into me. Improbably, a crowd filled the street—masses of strangers milling and laughing. I glimpsed Hannah's body vanishing into the mob.

Silver satin. Pale skin. Dark, thick, heavy hair.

Mine. Mine. Mine.

"Hannah!" I lunged after her. A commanding anger filled my voice. "Hannah, get back here!" The crowd on the street closed around me. Hannah slipped away effortlessly; I slammed into an immovable jam of bodies.

"M. Pierce!" someone shouted.

"Matt! Matthew Sky!" said another.

Strange hands touched me. Eyes staring. Voices rising.

"Hannah!" I roared. "Hannah!"

My eyes flared open.

I lay alone in the cabin bedroom, my arm outstretched and hand grasping air. *Fuck.* My heart pounded in my ears.

Was I screaming Hannah's name? My throat was raw.

I sat up and checked the time. Seven at night. My cell and Jack Reacher novel lay at my side. I must have dozed after getting off with Hannah.

When I collected my breath, I forced myself out of bed and pulled on jeans. The wind had picked up. It gusted against the cabin—a lonely, howling sound—and I felt hollow.

I hardly needed to analyze my dream. I knew what it meant.

It meant that Hannah wasn't mine, not truly, and that my best efforts to bring her to me were failing. It also meant that I couldn't live without her, no matter what I'd thought. Wanting Hannah plagued me all day. Now it invaded my dreams.

And it wasn't enough, getting off miles apart. It wouldn't be enough, seeing her this weekend. I needed her with me—always.

That evening, I tried to get back into my writing, but the scene was closed to me. I flipped to a clean page and sketched Hannah.

I checked my phone periodically.

"Melanie, Melanie." I sighed. "Where the fuck are you?"

She'd better be busy erasing *Night Owl* from the Internet—at least insofar as she could. I doubted Shapiro and Nate would go after torrents and forum posts. No e-book, no case.

I messed with my sketch a little more, and then, hurriedly, as if I could convince myself that I wasn't doing it, I keyed in a Google search: *Night Owl by W. Pierce.*

I hit Enter.

The search results loaded with agonizing slowness. Agonizing because I had plenty of time to realize I was making a mistake. Sure, I read news and reviews of my other books, but *Night Owl* wasn't like my other books.

Night Owl was about Hannah and me. It was precious.

Google found four hundred thousand results. I smirked and scrolled down, my eyes jumping from one link to the next. I saw Facebook pages, fan pages, forum posts, blog reviews, and URLs from Goodreads, Amazon, the iBookstore, Barnes & Noble. Damn . . .

And there was a link to the e-book, which wasn't supposed to exist. I clicked it. Still available, still ninety-nine cents. I balked. *Night Owl* was number thirty-five on the digital bestseller list. It had six hundred reviews and a 4.6-star average rating.

My cursor hovered over the one-star reviews. I clicked.

The first was a refund request with "pornographic quotes."

TERRIBLE, said another reviewer. *Pure porn, no story!*

The negative reviews went on like that, attacking my plot, my writing, my person. I was *mentally disturbed.* I was single-handedly *sending women back to the Dark Ages.*

By the time I got to the last one-star review, my hands were shaking.

"Hannah," I said aloud. Her name was a talisman.

I forced myself to read the last review. I always twist the knife.

Don't waste your money, it said. *Matt is a psycho and Hannah is nothing but a slut.*

My eyes widened.

Oh, it was one thing for me to call Hannah a slut. She was *my* slut. She was a slut *for me.* When we went mad together, when she got on her knees . . . only I called Hannah "slut."

But this? This was a backhanded slap—a stranger calling my lover a whore.

I slammed my laptop shut. I nearly snapped my phone in two as I opened it.

When I rose, my chair tipped over with a crash. I found Mel's number in my recent calls. "Answer," I snarled as soon as I hit Send. "Answer!"

"Hello?"

At the sound of Mel's voice, my anger erupted.

"Take it down, you bitch!" I snarled. "I told you to take it down. Take it down. Take that fucking book off the Internet *now.* Now!" Flecks of saliva wet my lips.

"I did!" Melanie's voice was tiny.

"You. Did. *Not.*" I spat the words into the phone. The heat of my rage scalded my throat.

"Calm down," Mel bleated. "It takes—it can take up to t-two days for the—"

"No!" I shouted over the small voice on the phone. "Don't you try to fucking handle me! You have twelve hours—twelve fuck-ing hours—"

My threat broke into silence. Twelve hours, or else what?

I ended the call.

My phone began to ring. It was Mel. I ended the call. It rang again. I hit End. Again, then again. *Ring* . . . end call, *ring* . . . end call.

I set the volume to mute.

The screen lit up. I ended the call. It lit again. She called again. Again and again, and I couldn't walk away. Leave me alone!

I threw down the phone, which bounced off the floor with an unsatisfying pop. I drove my heel into it. The plastic plates snapped.

Implausibly, the mangled phone lit up. The cracked screen glowed with a new call.

I smashed my foot into it. I did it again.

Again, the frame cracking, fragments skittering across the floor. Shards of metal stabbed at my sole, but it didn't hurt enough to make me stop. A mountain lion dragged my body off Longs Peak. That didn't hurt enough to make me stop. I was living apart from the only woman I wanted. That didn't hurt enough to make me stop.

When the phone was a shapeless mosaic of debris, I turned to the chair. I lifted it easily and swung it against the wall. I did it because I could, because I was as strong as any animal. *A psycho,* they called me. They were right. They were wrong. They couldn't come close to my fire. They couldn't touch my heart.

Chapter 15

HANNAH

When I strolled into work on Monday morning, I found my boss, Pam, dressed in a winter white skirt suit. I was wearing a too-bright blue turtleneck and dress slacks. Our outfits shouted: *Not in mourning!* I suppressed a grin.

Really, I was getting tired of being treated like a porcelain doll. The sad eyes, the lingering hugs, the artless dodges of Matt-related topics drove me crazy.

Maybe Pam knew the feeling.

"Come in here," she called from her office to mine. "No, wait, stay there. One moment." She typed and swore at her mouse. "There. Check your e-mail."

Pam grinned and peered at me over her glasses.

I opened my work e-mail. A hideous number of queries loaded—my new duties included reading queries—and at the top was an e-mail from Pam: SURROGATE JACKET.

My heart skipped.

I opened the e-mail and then the attachment.

Pam moved to lurk in the doorway.

"Knopf sent it over this morning," she said.

I took my first look at the book jacket for *The Surrogate,* Matt's last novel. The title, in unadorned white type, hung on a backdrop of stars. Tall towers or tree trunks lined the sky like bars. Behind the bars, a dark figure. Visible and invisible. The surrogate. Matthew Sky.

Matt's pen name was a splash of red, front and center. M. PIERCE. No blurbs busied the cover, no needless accolades announcing that Pierce was a bestseller everywhere.

I let out the breath I was holding.

"Beautiful," I said.

"Yes." Pam came to stand behind me and we admired the jacket in silence. After a time, she said, "This is the book jacket everyone will remember this year."

I knew she was right.

I blinked rapidly to keep back tears.

Sometimes, I almost believed my own act.

"Well, it looks like you have your work cut out for you, Hannah." Pam nodded at my in-box, then went clicking out of my office and closed the door.

The workday flew by. I had a sandwich delivered for lunch so that I could stay in my warm office. Besides, I was having fun. I worked at the center of a world I loved—the world of publishing—and I believed in the old romance of book writing, bookmaking, and bookselling.

I bundled up and left the office at six. I brought two manuscripts home with me.

My thoughts turned to the empty condo, and instead of driving home, I headed to Cherry Creek for a little retail therapy.

The mall was surprisingly busy. I smiled as I wandered through Macy's and into the open shopping center. This almost made me feel less lonely. Almost . . .

I paused in front of Fragrance Hut and glanced at the rows of perfume and cologne. Hm. I should buy something for Matt. Something for . . . us.

I hesitated outside Victoria's Secret. The windows displayed super-lean, leggy mannequins in getups that probably required instruction manuals. I swallowed and looked closer. Well, Matt *did* like me in lingerie . . .

I headed into the store, a light blush warming my face. The simple act of choosing lingerie to wear for Matt was a turn-on.

I drifted around the tables, trailing my fingers over satin and lace, bustiers and corsets. The more risqué lingerie hung in the back. I picked out a delicate black baby doll and held it up for inspection. It was tiny, and it was all sheer lace. I draped it over my arm. Perfect. What else?

As I shopped, I began to feel more daring. Matt would flip when he saw me in this stuff. I chose a form-fitting garter slip with polka dots, ruffles, and matching thigh-highs. I bought mesh panties with a bow on the back and a slip with a bustle that would barely cover my ass.

I left the store with a smile on my face.

I made a shopping trip each evening after work, ticking off items on a list I titled "Weekend Getaway." Matt's list-making habit had rubbed off on me.

I stocked up on canned foods and frozen meals for Matt. I bought a big cooler, a new first aid kit, two flashlights and a wholesale-sized pack of batteries, a can of bear spray, camping rations, antibiotic ointment, even long underwear.

And that was when I made myself stop. I was standing in Cabela's with the underwear removed from its package because I wanted to check the length. I unfurled the scrunched, withered white legs, and I began to giggle. My giggles turned to laughter, which turned to louder laughter. Louder laughter turned to fitful howls.

I couldn't stop, even when other customers began glancing at me. Oh . . . my God . . . what was I doing? My worry for Matt was somehow manifesting as thermal underwear.

I bought the long underwear because I knew Matt would get a kick out of it.

It was Thursday. *Enough is enough,* I told myself. My pile of Matt supplies looked like Y2K prep plus lingerie. Everything was laid out on the living room floor. Laurence eyed me as I added the thermal underwear to the pile.

"I know," I said, holding up my hands. "I'm done. Seriously."

On a whim, I flicked on the Christmas tree lights. They winked merrily and lit the condo white and blue. I sighed.

Yeah, it was definitely time to take down this tree . . . so why couldn't I?

In our haste to plan and execute Matt's disappearance, Matt and I forgot all about the holiday. Two presents sat under the tree, one from Matt to me, one from me to Matt.

He'd wrapped mine in gold paper with black ribbon. I shook the small box. *Hm.*

"What do you think?" I said to Laurence. He flicked an ear. I grinned and moved both gifts into my suitcase.

Chapter 16

MATT

The chair listed left a little. I tilted my head. Good *enough*.

It was broken at three joints, where two legs met the seat and again where a spindle fit into the top rail. Really, I could have done worse.

Duct tape formed a lumpy seal around the joints. I set the chair in a corner.

"It was like that when I got here," I said. I frowned. No, no. I should sound more offhanded. I tried a little laugh and eyed the chair as though seeing it for the first time. "Oh, that? No idea. Kevin is weird."

I even rehearsed the truth.

"The chair? No big deal. I lost it after I read some bad reviews. Oh, and I crushed my phone with my bare foot because I'm manly like that. Ha . . ."

On second thought, I carried the chair to the cellar. Out of sight, out of mind.

I swept the fragments of my TracFone into a dustpan.

I would buy another phone in town and give Hannah the

number when she arrived. I doubted she would call between now and then. We kept communication to a minimum.

I replaced the desk chair with a kitchen chair and scooted closer to my computer.

"Okay, Mel," I said, opening my laptop, "let's see the damage."

A new e-mail announced three private messages on the forum. This poor fucking girl. I skimmed the messages, all from Melanie, all apologies.

I sent a reply.

SUBJECT: "Matt is a tool"
by nightowl on Sunday, February 9, 2014
Hi, Mel,
Thanks for your messages.
I'm the one who needs to apologize. I was an out-of-control ass-hole on the phone. I am a "tool" and a "psycho" according to cus-tomers who should know. And they want their money back. (I'm laughing.)
Can you guess what happened here? Yes, I decided to read the Night Owl reviews. Just the one-star reviews. Fuck me. I wigged out and called you. You know the rest.
Of course you forgive me because I'm charismatic and winning.
—M
P.S. You should still remove the book before my brother sues your ass.
P.P.S. I broke my phone. I'll send you my new number soon.

Mel's reply was waiting in my forum in-box the following morning.

She forgave me, of course, and iterated that I was "an out-of-control asshole on the phone (and probably off it, too)." I laughed as I read.

"The book is off Amazon, B&N, and Smashwords," she wrote. "I like my ass and don't want it sued." She said she understood my anger. She said she was "waiting for it, actually."

My grin faded as I read the last line of Mel's message:

So, Night Owl is no more. What now?

I pondered the question: What now?

I had to admit, I liked this Melanie chick. She had guts and wit. And she was straight-up insane, so we had something in common.

Plus, it was nice to have someone to chat with occasionally. No man is a fucking island.

I typed, "I told you, I'll give you my new phone number soon. I pulverized my phone after you called fifty times and activated man mode."

I sent the reply and logged out of the forum.

I couldn't write worth a damn that morning, couldn't focus on anything but Hannah and her upcoming visit. So I made a list.

SEX ALL WEEKEND
Hannah, in the flesh (and nothing else)
Candles/atmosphere/flowers?
Nice meal (how?)
Lube . . . or something
Nonsexual gifts (books?)
Clean the cabin
Do your fucking laundry
Xmas tree/lights etc.

I prowled through the cabin collecting laundry and rereading my list. Hannah, Hannah, Hannah. *Finally*. Friday would be Valentine's Day. It would be our Christmas. I would make it romantic and special—unforgettable—and maybe, just maybe, she would stay with me.

I checked the food situation in the cellar. I had a lot of food—canned food, frozen food, untouched bags of pasta and rice—but nothing that would cohere into a "nice meal."

My thoughts strayed helplessly back to Hannah.

God, I wanted her sprawled by the fire on a pile of shearling blankets. Naked. The firelight playing on her curves . . .

Ten minutes later, I was sitting on the couch with a heap of laundry at my feet and the hard-on of the century. I had to laugh.

If this wasn't the epitome of my life without Hannah, then nothing was.

"Do you want me to wrap these, hon?" said the cashier. She lifted one of the twenty votive candleholders on the belt. "I don't have paper, but I can wrap bags around them."

Twenty scented candles followed the holders.

Also: a new TracFone, two boxes of chocolates, two fresh flower arrangements, three books, warming lube, massage oil, wrapping paper and ribbon, two cards, a plush rabbit holding a heart, a bottle of white wine, and two bags of frozen shrimp and penne dinner. "Ready in 10 minutes," the bag claimed. "Just heat and serve!"

Hell, I could heat and serve.

"Yeah, please," I said, "if it's not too much trouble. I have a long way to go with them."

I slid off my hat and ruffled my black hair. I watched the cashier from behind my shades. I expected her to do a double take, to hesitate and then say I looked familiar, but she only nodded and began swathing the glass with plastic bags.

"Is it too much?" I gestured to my purchases. "I have a date. For Valentine's."

"Oh, it's never too much." The cashier smiled so hard that the apples of her cheeks reddened. "Some lucky girl."

"Mm."

I plucked the plush rabbit off the belt and studied it. Lucky girl. Yeah, right. Merry super-belated Christmas and ghetto Valentine's, Hannah. Here's a thirty-dollar bottle of wine and a bunch of wax that doubles as chocolate. Run away with me?

With a sigh, I handed the stuffed animal to the cashier.

"Cute!" She passed it over the scanner.

I pulled out my cash and started counting off twenties. "Yeah, I think she'll like it," I said, and I did. Hannah would like any gesture from me.

I pocketed my change and carried my bags out to a bench. There, I arranged the candleholders and other items in my pack. The wrapping paper and bouquets poked out the top.

It was Thursday morning. The flowers would easily survive until tomorrow. I couldn't find Christmas lights in the store, but fuck it. This was good enough. More than good enough.

As I hiked back to the cabin, I laughed and remembered little things about Hannah. I pictured her every which way. My chronic anger and harsh moods stood far off when Hannah filled my thoughts, and no drug could do that for me, and no other human. Just Hannah.

Chapter 17

HANNAH

The garter slip fit me like a sleeve. It hugged everything and covered nothing. My nipples showed plainly through
the sheer cups. The ruffled hem flared around my hips.

I spun before the standing mirror.

I thought of Matt's gaze and curled my toes.

I don't know when I decided to drive up to the cabin in nothing but lingerie and a coat, but the idea excited me. Maybe I saw
it in a movie: a sexy woman shrugging off her coat, nothing beneath but skin and lace.

Besides, knowing Matt, I'd be lucky if he didn't fuck me
against the car. So why not give him a treat on our way to bliss?
I rolled up my black thigh-highs and clipped on the garter straps.
I grinned as I slid my feet into pumps. *There.*

I pulled on my coat, collected my purse, and hoisted Laurence's
portable cage.

He thumped his displeasure.

"Yeah, yeah," I said. "Tell it to someone else. I *could* be leaving
you with Jamie again."

I locked the condo and headed out to my car.

Cold air whooshed under my coat. Oof, what a draft . . .

I giggled as I arranged Laurence's cage on the backseat and got behind the wheel. I was being quite bad. Matt would love it.

Though I'd left work early, I hit Friday night traffic on I-25. I sighed as the string of cars slowed, smiled when it picked up, and groaned when it came to a standstill.

What should have been a one-and-a-half-hour drive stretched into two.

The sky darkened as I cruised west toward the mountains. Shivers raced through me.

I sipped a Red Bull and plugged in my iPhone to play music.

With a jolt, I remembered Seth.

DJ, will ya?

Matt's memorial felt a lifetime away, but the memory of Seth was so fresh that he might have been in the car with me.

I get it, Hannah. "Love is as strong as death," right?

I highly doubted Seth would "get it" if he knew the truth. Death wasn't in the picture here, just deception.

My mind trailed over the Goldengrove gig, and I frowned when I remembered I'd deleted all their songs. Yeesh, overreact much? I started a song by Broken Bells.

It was, I realized, very possible that I overreacted to all of it—Shapiro's interrogation, the looks the other memorial guests gave me, even Seth's request for a kiss.

I was hypersensitive, crazy with guilt. Maybe there was no harm in any of it . . .

I turned onto the narrow road leading out to the cabin. My palms began to sweat. God, why was I nervous? I wiped my hands on the seat.

The road steepened and my Civic labored over the snow. My wheels spun. The car pitched forward and slid back.

I found the driveway and veered onto it. Matt had shoveled the dirt drive as well as he could. I slowed the car as I neared the cabin. My headlights swung across the snow.

Matt.

He jogged through a drift. Jesus, he was barefoot! And his hair was . . . black? But it was Matt. My Matt. My night owl.

As the last light of day peeled off the snow, he closed the distance between us. I lunged out of the car. He caught me in a hug and crushed my body to his.

"Hannah. Goddamn." He lifted me off my feet. His hands were in my hair, against my neck, on my back and arms. He touched me all over as if to make sure I was real. And maybe I wasn't. This felt like the best dream.

"Matt. Baby. Hi. Hey . . ." I stroked his face. I scrubbed away the beginnings of tears from my eyes. "Your hair." I ruffled it.

"Black," he said, his voice muffled as he kissed my neck.

I couldn't stop laughing. "Yes, black."

Matt came up for air long enough to look me in the eye. "You like it?"

"I love it. You look great. Beautiful. My beautiful night owl." I fit my hand to the contour of his cheek. His eyes shone with happiness . . . and something a little darker.

He resumed kissing my neck, sucking hungrily on my bare throat. I moaned into the night. *I was so right,* I thought—I was going to get fucked against my car. But Matt was barefoot. And Laurence was in the car. And there was food, and—

"Your skin tastes so fucking good," Matt whispered. He dragged his teeth over my jaw. The way his tongue touched my neck . . . the way he pulled my body against his, forcing me to straddle his thigh . . . I groaned.

Through my coat, through Matt's thin lounge pants, I felt his erection trapped between us. Oh, Lord.

"B-bunny . . . in the car," I panted.

"Hm? You want it in the car?" Matt wedged me against the door. It felt like a sheet of ice. "How about against the car? Right here."

"No, Laurence. Laurence. He's in the car."

Laughter overtook me, fueled by happiness and relief. Matt

started to laugh, too. We were helpless with it, sagging against one another and the car.

And God, if it wasn't heaven to see Matt laugh like that.

"Well, I'm not horny or anything." He rubbed his face. "Goddamn, Hannah. I missed you so much." He kissed my mouth. He slowed it down, rocking against me and teasing my tongue with his. I moaned and clung to him.

"Mm, birders . . . if you start moaning like that. Shhh." He silenced me with a finger and peered into the car. "You really brought him. Crazy girl."

"He missed you." I grinned. I couldn't take my eyes off Matt. With his black hair, he looked like a rascally Nate. Maybe he'd lost a pound or two, but I'd expected worse—an emaciated Matt with a limp and a chunk missing from his leg.

My relief swerved toward disappointment. Matt looked just fine. Gorgeous, strong, passionate—the same old Matt. He wasn't wasting away without me. I guess I wasn't wasting away without him, either. At least, not on the outside.

"What is it?" Matt caught me staring. He smiled uncertainly.

"Nothing." I smiled back at him. He had the back door open and was working Laurence's cage off the seat.

"Nothing, huh?" He returned to me. He slid a hand under my coat and got a handful of my bare ass. I squeaked. His eyes widened. "What . . . are you wearing?" Matt tried to get a look.

I tugged down my coat. "Inside!"

With a laugh, I broke away and headed toward the cabin. The food would keep in the car. The night was like an icebox.

Matt followed with the rabbit cage.

"Ah . . . wait!" he called.

I giggled and flew into the cabin. Hot air enveloped me. It smelled of cinnamon and pine and . . . something burnt. I wrinkled my nose. My eyes adjusted to the firelight. Votive candles glowed in a misshapen heart formation on the dinner table.

On the far side of the room, a huge spruce slumped against the corner. From it emanated the powerful scent of pine. A bit of ribbon drooped around the tree's middle.

Either I felt hysterical or this was seriously funny, because I found myself hugging my belly and fighting new waves of laughter.

Matt backed into the cabin. He hefted Laurence's cage and kicked snow from his pants. "Let me explain." He slid the cage onto the coffee table. He was half laughing, half crooning to the terrified rabbit. "Hey, little guy. It's okay. Too hot for you? You're too fat, is what it is."

Matt adjusted the thermostat, then pulled me back into the circle of his arms.

I smiled up at him. Dear God, I'd missed this handsome face, this strong grip.

"Merry Christmas, baby," he said, the edges of laughter in his voice, "and happy Valentine's Day. I made a snack." He hooked a thumb toward the table. I glanced over his shoulder. It *was* Valentine's Day, wasn't it? I had forgotten.

In the candlelight, I saw two paper plates, a bag of Wonder Bread, a jar of peanut butter, and one spoon. I pressed my lips into a line to keep from laughing.

"Oh, sweetie. Wow. And . . . a tree." My mouth twitched. "Did something burn?"

I was still acutely aware of Matt's arousal pressed against me. His fingers gathered up my coat as we spoke. I trembled against him.

"I was making pasta. I threw it out. It came out all . . . weird. Hannah, what—" Matt's fingertips trailed over the tops of my thigh-highs. Again, confusion flashed through his eyes. He began to undo my coat, freeing one button after another and finally throwing it open. I swayed on my heels. Fuck . . .

Matt's expression grew serious, and my own giggly mood floated into oblivion. Already, my chest rose and fell with heavy breaths. My nipples stood stiff against the mesh cups of my slip. I lowered my eyes.

"Do you . . . like it?" I whispered.

How did this work? Matt's desire seemed to suck the sound out of the room, and the breath out of my body. And he was only staring. I peeked at him through my lashes.

The look I found on his face is with me forever. It was need mingled with satisfaction. A hunger in his eyes, a thin smile on his lips.

Matt wanted me, and Matt already had me. I was his.

He pushed the coat from my shoulders and it flopped to the floor. I dropped my purse. Matt shucked off his T-shirt and I stared at his torso.

I came alive then, flattening my palms to his chest. His heart knocked under my hand.

"Yeah," Matt said. He nudged me toward the wall. I let him move me; I yielded easily and started to pant. Heat gathered between my legs. "Yeah . . . I like it, Hannah. I like this . . ."

He pinched my nipple through the polka-dot fabric. I moaned. My hands flew to the drawstrings on his pants. He grinned down at me as I fumbled with the knot.

"I like this," he whispered, shifting out of my reach and slipping a hand between my legs. My thong was soaked. Matt pulled it down. He unclipped my garters and let my panties slide down my thighs.

"This." He squeezed my ass with both hands. I squirmed.

"Please." I reached for his pants again. It was humiliating, being the only one exposed, and I wanted . . . I wanted to see Matt's need. I wanted him naked.

Again, Matt moved his hips out of reach. He chuckled and pressed my back into the wall. I stamped my foot.

"So precious, Hannah. So fucking sexy. Touch your breasts . . . your nipples." Matt trained his green eyes on my chest. "Do it, and I'll take off my pants."

I clenched my teeth and closed my eyes, lifting my hands to my breasts. Matt *always* embarrassed me during sex. And some part of me . . . loved it.

"Eyes open, look at me." His voice tickled my ear.

I forced myself to meet Matt's gaze as I squeezed my breasts. He tilted his head. The tent in his lounge pants said he was enjoying the show, but fuck, I wanted to see his body. When I rolled my nipples between my fingers, I gasped and Matt's mouth dropped open.

"God, Hannah." He pushed off his pants. He braced a hand against the wall and gripped his shaft. My eyes broke from his. I drank in the sight of his sculpted body, his stiff cock, his strong thighs. "This . . . is how it was, wasn't it? You touching yourself . . . me touching myself."

My eyelids fluttered.

"It was," I said. "Not anymore."

"Not anymore." Matt touched my face. He turned me gently to face the wall and rested his shaft along the cleft of my backside. "Can you tell, Hannah?" Matt gathered my hair with one hand. He kissed my ear. "Can you tell I like it, your tight little lingerie?"

"Yes," I breathed.

"How? How can you tell?" Matt slid his sex up my crack. I pushed out my bottom and clenched my cheeks to grip him. Matt hissed. I grinned. Two could play at this game.

"The way you stare," I said.

"Mm, what else?" He kissed the corner of my mouth. Lightly, he teased a fingertip over my sex. My desire oozed down his finger.

"Your cock," I said quietly. I knew that was the answer he wanted.

"Yes. What about it?" Matt rewarded me by lazily circling my entrance with his finger. He pushed his chest against my back, and my heaving breasts met the wall.

"Hard," I mumbled.

A whisper of laughter crossed the nape of my neck. I reached back and gripped Matt's hips, trying to draw him closer to my body. His cock throbbed against my bottom.

"That's right, Hannah. You make my dick so fucking hard."

I moaned and tried to drive my body onto Matt's finger, but I couldn't move.

Matt released me suddenly. My heavy hair fell around my shoulders; the pressure of his body eased and air rushed into my lungs. And then he dragged me down.

Chapter 18

MATT

Fuck . . . the lingerie. Fuck.

My brain went haywire when I looked at Hannah.

"On the floor," I said, pulling her down with me. Not for a moment did I let my cock lose contact with her skin. Hannah's pert ass gripped me—that little devil—as I pressed her onto her hands and knees. I climbed over her.

It was easy, that position, and so intimate. My limbs were longer than Hannah's. I was stronger, firmer, taller; she fit under me perfectly.

Hannah tried to part her knees on the floor, but her thong constrained her. I tugged on her hair. She moaned and lifted her head.

"I'm going to fuck you on the floor," I told her.

She stilled beneath me. "Yes, please," she said in her softest voice.

"I'm not going to come. Not here. But I have to remember . . ." I reached between my legs. I positioned my head against Hannah's sex. That touch—her wet cunt brushing the most sensitive part of my body—sent a violent shiver through me.

"Get on my dick," I growled.

"Matt . . ." She began to rock back, the tiny motions sliding her onto my cock.

I have to remember how this feels.

"Good, that's good," I whispered. "Come on. That's it . . ." I didn't move. I let Hannah take her time, and she took her time. She pushed backward, then slid off me, then back, again and again. Our harsh moans mingled.

At last, Hannah sank onto me fully. Her satin thighs pressed at mine. Her ass fit snugly against my abs. And her tight pussy held my cock. She quivered below me.

"I love you," she murmured.

"Hannah, I fucking love you so much." I bit her shoulder.

We didn't move—not much. I reached under Hannah and lifted her tits. She circled her hips subtly, moving my dick inside her.

I pinned Hannah's hand to the floor. I thrust into her once, slowly, and we moaned. Goddamn . . . I should have rubbed one out earlier in the day. I was never going to last.

Hannah met my second stroke with a backward push. I snarled. "Fuck. Hannah . . . fuck. I changed my mind. We're going to come. You're going to make a mess for me. *Right here.*"

I began to move in earnest. I got up on my knees and held Hannah's hip; I snaked a hand beneath her to tease her clit.

Her sex clamped around mine. Already? I gazed down.

One look at Hannah's body in that tight getup and I needed to come. I thrust frantically, watching my cock and her ass, the curve of her spine, her swollen pussy. Excitement rushed through me. I couldn't stop. I couldn't stop moving. Hannah was here—under me. For one weekend. Not long enough.

My pace grew punishing, my thrusts brutal. I poured my anger and frustration into that fuck, and Hannah bucked and moaned in response.

How could she live without this? I couldn't.

"I need . . . to come," I managed. "Come for me, Hannah . . . come."

"Don't stop," she panted. "I am—I am—" And she did. With

a cry, she convulsed and tightened, the pressure of her body practically painful on my dick.

I swore and released. My pleasure spilled into Hannah; her pleasure dripped over my hand and ran down her inner thigh.

She always made a mess for me.

We collapsed across the floor. I rolled Hannah's body onto mine and lay there gasping. She curled on top of me and held me.

"I was . . ." I laughed. Some of my anger evaporated in our afterglow. "I was . . . planning to draw that out a bit more."

Hannah giggled. "Me, too."

"Oh, yeah?" I tugged on a garter strap. "Is that why you wore this? I just about spontaneously combusted, Hannah."

"I think that's exactly what you did . . ."

"Hey, now." I slapped her bottom. "I wouldn't put too fine a point on it." I stood and lifted Hannah easily. She wrapped her arms around my neck.

"We have plenty of time," she murmured.

I carried her around the room. My sweet little bird.

"Mm . . . plenty of time." *One weekend.*

Laurence watched us in a mild state of alarm, and when we noticed him watching, we laughed all over again. The things that rabbit has seen . . .

I set Hannah on the couch, dressed, and retrieved her things from the car. It took three trips. She had a suitcase, a cooler, and about seven loaded grocery bags.

She smiled each time I returned.

"Hannah." I frowned at the pile of stuff. "You know I have food, right?"

"Hm?" She shrugged and hopped off the couch to inspect my tree. The fucking tree. After I cut it down and hauled it into the cabin, I realized I had no base for the massive thing. Hence standing the tree in the corner. It looked like a joke.

But Hannah didn't seem to care. She buzzed about, bending over and examining the gifts. "Presents!" she said.

"Mm . . ." I stared at her pussy. She was trotting around in the slip and thigh-highs and no panties. I walked into the coffee table and nearly ate it. "And—*fuck!*" I rubbed my shin. "And flowers. Here. For you." I tapped the vase of roses on the dinner table.

Hannah flew over and hugged me tight. "So sweet, Matt. Thank you."

I brushed my hands against her ass while she clung to me.

"Oh, hey, before I forget. I've got a new number. Did you try to call?"

"No." Hannah's brow knit.

"Yeah. Here." I'd written my new TracFone number in my notebook. I tore out the page and brought it to Hannah. "I dropped my phone."

She blinked and accepted the paper. "You dropped your phone? And it broke?"

"Yes. In . . . water." I nodded. "Rushing water. Icy cold. Outside. A stream." I made a streamlike gesture with my hands. Hannah was not buying this shit.

"In a stream," she deadpanned.

"Mm." I did the hand gesture again. A smile tugged at her lips.

"Okay, Mr. Mysterious. I'm guessing you dropped it in a stream called the toilet and you're too embarrassed to tell me." She fetched her phone and began changing my contact info, then paused. "Hey, how did you get a new phone?" She surveyed the room. "Actually, how did you get all this stuff?"

"I've been hiking into town."

Hannah's eyes widened. "You have?"

"Yeah. I mean, I dyed my hair."

"Matt . . . you still look exactly like yourself with black hair."

"Okay, okay, wait." I disappeared into the bedroom, emerging some minutes later in my incognito ensemble: hat, jacket, sunglasses, scarf. "How about now?"

Hannah fought her amusement. Her dark eyebrows drew together. She wanted to be pissed, I could see that.

"It's just . . . Matt, if you get found out"—she laid a hand on her chest—"I get found out. Your family will hate me. Your fans will hate me. Everyone. Have you thought about that?"

"Hannah, I'm not going to get found out. I promise. Believe me, I want that less than you. I have to go out sometimes, you know?" I returned to the bedroom and pulled off my winter clothes. Hannah followed me to the door.

"As long as you're careful," she said.

"I'm a paragon of caution." I balled up a shirt and tossed it to her. "Bird, if you don't put your cute little butt away . . ."

Hannah snickered and pulled on my shirt. The sleeves flopped over her hands and the hem reached her thighs.

"Maybe I was hoping for an encore." She lifted a brow.

"An encore, huh?"

Hannah leaned against the doorway. Even in my oversized shirt, she was a bombshell. Her sumptuous curves, her heavy hair, her plump lips . . .

"Mm, you." I padded across the room. Hannah was here, finally, with me—and we were alone. The knowledge went straight to my head.

I took her hand and drew her toward the bed.

"Let me see," I said, "what I can do about an encore . . ."

Chapter 19

HANNAH

It was eleven at night by the time Matt and I finished in bed. Or maybe we were just taking a break.

My hair was a nest and the sheets smelled of sweat and sex.

I curled against his side.

"*Mm,*" I hummed. "I'm spent."

"I don't want to sleep," Matt said. "I don't want to waste my time with you."

"Then let's stay up as late as we can." I kissed his temple.

Sadness overlaid everything and I couldn't ignore it. *Whatever else life contains,* Matt once said to me, *it's sad because it has to end.* At the time, I thought he was strange and morose. Now I understood. No happiness that weekend would go untainted because on Sunday I had to leave. And maybe I could see Matt the following weekend, but I was still looking at another week without him—and another, and another. How long?

I sat up and stretched. A paperback lay on the bedside table.

"Lee Child?" I grinned down at Matt.

Even after hours of fucking, my breath hitched at the sight of Matt naked. He sprawled on his back, hair wild and lids at half-mast. His lean, muscled limbs lay gracefully over the sheets. One arm bent above his head. And my eyes kept straying to his beautiful cock, which lay against his thigh. Good Lord . . . I felt like I was getting a full frontal from a male model.

He smiled lazily at me and I wanted to jump his bones. Again.

"Yeah," he said. "Jack Reacher. He's a badass."

I finger combed a knot from my hair. "I wouldn't know. I'm just surprised to see genre fiction on your bedside table."

"Are you?" Matt sat up and moved behind me. He lowered my hands and began to carefully untangle my curls. "Well, for one thing . . ." He kissed my shoulder. "I write genre fiction, remember? *The Surrogate* is sci-fi. And then there's *Night Owl* . . . which is romance."

My shoulders stiffened and I dug my fingers into the bed.

"You okay, little bird?"

I bit my lip. How could I explain to Matt that my defenses flew up at the mention of *Night Owl*? He would feel guilty, and it wasn't his fault.

"It's nothing," I said.

Matt's hands stilled.

"Is it horrible for you, Hannah? The book being out there. Are people bothering you?"

"No. It's fine, really."

"Are you sure? Babe, I know how it is . . . when your private life becomes public knowledge. I know how terrible that feels."

"Matt, it's no big deal." I reached back and rubbed his thigh. What was he getting at? "People don't know *Night Owl* is true, and no one is really harassing me about it. I'm not famous like you, remember? Nobody cares." I smiled.

Okay, so I was lying. I *did* feel uncomfortable with *Night Owl* out in the public. The book was so raunchy . . . so detailed. And even my boss had read it. Mortifying.

I cleared my throat. "Nate's obsession is a little worrying, but other than that . . ."

"He'll drop it." Matt sounded vaguely disappointed. "Trust me. He has no case."

"Yeah, I hope so . . ."

Matt loosened another tangle from my hair. "Anyway . . . I like genre fiction, Hannah. Literary fiction teaches you how to write. Genre fiction teaches you how to plot."

"You and your surprises."

"You and your bird ways. You want some hot chocolate?"

"That sounds good. And I want to open my presents."

I dressed in Matt's shirt and he pulled on flannel pants. The cabin was delightfully warm.

Matt watched me as he filled the kettle. I loved it; he couldn't take his eyes off me.

"You sure you don't want me to boil the water?" I grinned.

"Ha. Stand back and watch a pro."

I touched my lips as Matt struggled to get the burner lit. *Do not laugh, do not laugh . . .*

He narrowed his eyes at me.

"This one burner requires some finessing," he murmured.

"Fortunately you're good with your hands."

"Don't you know it . . ." The flame burst out and Matt flinched. So did I. My poor adorable lover. How was he surviving?

He lit a fire and we sat on the couch with our cocoa. He brought my presents to the coffee table, piling them around Laurence's cage.

"Sorry, Laurence, nothing for you. I didn't know you were coming." When Matt leaned toward the cage, Laurence pressed himself to the bars and sniffled at Matt's nose.

Okay, that was the cutest fucking thing . . .

"Oh! Wait." I dragged over my suitcase and retrieved the presents I packed, one for me and one for Matt. "From the condo, remember?"

Matt tilted his head. "Huh, you're right. How the hell did we forget to open those?"

"It wasn't Christmas. And we had a lot on our minds." I smiled and leaned against Matt. His hand strayed up and down my bare thigh. "But this . . ." I moved my gift for Matt away from the pile. "Let's open this one tomorrow."

Matt was smiling roguishly. "No problem," he murmured. "You sure that's a gift for me, or is it a gift for you?"

"Both of us?" I grabbed one of my presents. My cheeks burned.

Matt had wrapped my gifts with plain red paper. He kept up a running commentary as I opened them. "I only go to one little grocery store," he said. I hugged the stuffed rabbit and kissed Matt's frown. "They only had Valentine's stuffed animals." Lube. "Not sure if you like that type." Massage oil. "That was the best one I could find." Chocolate. "You don't have to eat it." Three books—a new biography of Elliott Smith, Patti Smith's memoir, and a romance novel.

"This is brilliant." Matt tapped the memoir. "And this, I don't know, it's new and acclaimed. I know you like Elliott Smith."

"And this?" I giggled, displaying the romance.

"Ah, that . . . I thought it would be funny."

I read aloud from the back cover. " 'Destiny's powerful new employer' "—I whipped my hair dramatically—" 'becomes a dark horse in the race for her heart.' "

We laughed.

I thanked Matt for my gifts and he went on apologizing. I gave him a long, languid kiss—and that silenced him.

"Matt, really," I whispered against his mouth, "I'm so touched. I didn't expect any of this." I sat on his lap while I opened the present from the condo. "Did you wrap this?" The gold paper was creased like origami; the black ribbon wound around the box just so.

"Nah, I had it wrapped. I wrapped those—" He nodded toward my other gifts. "Which is why they looked like lumpy pillows."

I laughed and kissed his chin. Lumpy pillows was putting it nicely.

"What can I say? I'm domestically challenged." Matt lifted my shirt and stroked my bottom while I opened the box. I shivered. Absence doesn't make the heart go yonder *or* grow fonder. Absence makes people horny as fuck.

Nestled in the box on a little satin cushion were a pair of silver earrings and a matching bracelet and ring. Delicate owl-shaped charms accented the jewelry. Rhinestones winked in the silver. I traced a finger over them. My night owl . . .

I kissed Matt's chest. "They're beautiful."

"So you don't forget about me."

"Oh, please. I'll never forget about you. Never."

We kissed again and got tangled up. Matt's hands drifted under my shirt. He caressed my back and sides, gently at first and then with growing urgency.

I didn't know if I could go another round, but Matt wasn't pushing it. In fact, he only seemed to want to touch me.

I savored our kiss and moaned as he touched my stomach, my breasts, my thighs.

"So beautiful," he sighed against my neck. "Sometimes, I can't believe you're mine."

I pushed my fingers through his thick black hair. "I feel the same way. I want to know you, Matt. I want to know you better."

He sat back and his hands settled on my thighs. He gazed at me evenly.

"I hope you mean that in the biblical sense."

I thwapped his shoulder. "You know what I mean."

"What is this lately? You . . . feeling like you don't know me."

I tucked my head under his chin, avoiding his eyes. "Your memorial. Everyone at your memorial knew you better than I do."

"Everyone at my memorial thought I was dead. I think you know more than they do."

"Come on, I'm serious. You never talk about your parents, your brothers, your faith."

Matt tensed beneath me. He slid me off his lap and stood. He began to pace beside the coffee table, watching the fire.

"What faith?" he said. "And what exactly do you want to know about my family?"

"Nate said you're religious." I fidgeted with my new earrings.

"Oh, you know me, a regular churchgoer." Matt scowled. "Nate has a lot to say lately."

"He said you believe in God."

"So what if I do?"

"Matt, I'm not attacking you."

Matt ranged over to the fire and I watched his back. *Hmmm,* I loved the way his spine disappeared into his low-slung pants.

"What do you want to know about Nate? Nate is Nate. Beautiful home, beautiful wife, beautiful kids. And he's the only doctor. Our parents would be proud."

"He seems happy. With the kids and all . . ."

Matt glanced over his shoulder at me. I dropped my gaze.

"Kids, huh? Is that what you're driving at?"

"I'm not *driving* at anything. Chill. God." I held up my hands and Matt frowned. "You're being way feistier than this conversation warrants, do you realize that?"

He glared at the fire.

"I don't remember my parents," he said.

I knew that was a lie—or I had a hunch it was—but I let Matt keep rambling.

"Seth, there's no love lost between us." He waved a hand. "When I went through all my bullshit, you know, drinking and partying and . . . rehabbing . . . Seth wanted nothing to do with me. He saw the toll my behavior took on our aunt and uncle. He thought I'd be the death of them. Hell, I was almost the death of myself, but he didn't seem to give a fuck."

I began to crumple wrapping paper. I scanned the cabin for a trash can. Wow, had I ever dispatched the happy mood. Here I was, wanting to "talk" and get to know Matt, and now I couldn't think of a thing to say. Matt was brusque. The conversation was morbid.

"Your inheritance," I hedged. "How—"

"Not billions." Matt collected the wrapping paper from my hands. He carried it to the trash can in the kitchen. "Millions. And since I know you'll ask, my grandfather and his brother made their money opening factories in South America. All kinds of factories—tiles, bottles, energy plants. When a company was doing well, they sold it and moved on to something new. They were brilliant businessmen, worked all their lives, stayed ahead of the trends."

Matt sounded bored. I cringed as I listened.

"The money's been passed down. Mine is tied up in IRAs and investments, a little property in Montana, an offshore account. And of course there will be royalties."

I closed the jewelry box and went to Matt. I hugged him from behind. His skin felt hot, firm and yet smooth. I laid my cheek against his shoulder blade.

"Is it so terrible, that I want to know this stuff about you?"

"No, Hannah." He turned and tucked my body against his chest. "It's not. But like this, it feels forced. I don't want my phony memorial and a bunch of people who don't even get me to be the reason you want to know me better, you know?" Matt cupped my face and lifted it. He watched me intently. "I want things to be natural between us. Let's not live like other people. Let's not be like other couples."

Matt brushed a fingertip over my lips and I kissed it.

"I'm pretty sure we're not like other couples," I said.

He chuckled and a weight slid off my shoulders. *Whew.* Matt's bad moods were steep and unpredictable, but they passed quickly.

We went back to bed and chatted about nothing serious. We fought sleep as long as we could, but around two we drifted off, Matt still mumbling as he slipped into dreams.

Chapter 20

MATT

I woke to the smell of coffee.

It's Saturday. The realization hit me in the gut. My only whole day with Hannah.

I splashed water on my face and brushed my teeth, and then I went to find her.

She sat on the kitchen counter with her iPad on her thigh. She wore a black lace baby doll and nothing else. When she saw me, she smiled and slid off the counter.

"Coffee?"

"Hm, maybe." I nuzzled my nose into her hair. "Maybe you, then coffee."

Hannah hugged me tight. I pinned her body against mine and ran my fingers over her ass, which her attire did nothing to hide.

"What time is it?" I murmured.

"Nine. I didn't want to wake you."

"Fuck, I'm sorry. I'm usually up earlier." I gazed down the back of Hannah's body, trying to get a look at her legs.

"I think I wore you out last night. Do you want to write? I can entertain myself."

"You seriously think I'd do that—with you here?" I drew back.

"I don't know. I don't want to mess with your . . . writing routine."

I glanced in the direction of my desk. Before Hannah arrived, I'd stowed my notebook in the drawer and unplugged my laptop. I wanted no distractions. I also didn't want to discuss my new story, because my new story was still our story. A continuation. A continued fixation with Hannah, or a new chapter in my obsession.

"What did you think of *Night Owl,* anyway?" I set her down on the counter and nudged my hips between her knees. She hooked her legs around my waist. "I mean, apart from the crazy online leak. What do you think of the book itself?"

Hannah frowned.

"Come on," I said. I stroked her neck. "Let's see those literary knives. I hope Pam's rubbing off on you a little."

"All right." Hannah licked her lips. "I'll be Hannah the almost literary agent and not Hannah your lover, is that what you want?"

"Yes, that's what I want. You know I think of you as an equal."

A shock of surprise passed over Hannah's face. I frowned at that.

"Well. Okay. *Night Owl.*" She drew circles on my chest as she thought. "It's different, of course, from your other stuff. So different. Even the language, the style."

"Yes." I nodded.

"It's much simpler. Not . . . dumbed down, but faster. No philosophy, no cultural commentary. And the characters . . ." She laughed shakily.

"Go on," I said.

"You—Matt, whoever—he feels very authentic. My character . . ." Hannah's nose wrinkled. I kissed it. "Okay, my character feels a little 2-D at points. Sort of cliché."

I laughed and backed out of Hannah's legs.

"Thank you. Mm, I know. I know you don't always ring true in that book. It's hard to get in your head, Hannah." I flashed a smile at her. I wanted to reassure her, to let her know that I wasn't upset. Criticism from Hannah I could handle. And, from what I'd seen of her work at the agency, her editorial instincts were spot-on. "You see, I want us to be able to talk like this."

"Me, too." She smiled. "I loved it, by the way. For what it was, it worked. It succeeded."

"Do you want to know how I feel about my books?"

"Of course." Hannah took my hand. We walked through the cabin hand in hand as if strolling through a park, me in flannel pajama bottoms and Hannah in a bit of lingerie.

"They bore me, Hannah. They bore me before they're even done. I outgrow them. I become better, and they embarrass me. By the time the world is reading them, by the time the critical acclaim starts rolling in, I'm sick with it. The books in my mind are better. I have something more, something greater in me. Do you understand?"

Hannah nodded and squeezed my hand. When I talked like this, I tried to detect if I was boring her, but I only ever found interest in her expression.

"They never sing," I went on. I grimaced and tugged at my hair. "The books never really sing. You have to make sense for people. People are scared of anything that doesn't make sense. But we need a new alphabet, a purer language. I want to get it right. Will I? Will I ever?"

"Oh, Matt." Hannah sighed over my neck. Her fingers wandered over my bare back and awoke my desire. I pushed against her. "I don't know what to tell you. Even when a book captures an emotion and I feel it, it's only for a moment."

"Exactly," I said. "*Exactly*. A moment. I want to hold on to them. Hannah . . ." I lost the sense of my talk. She understood, and that meant more to me than anything she could have said. I filled my hands with her breasts and nudged my cock against her.

"Come with me, Matt."

Hannah led me toward the bedroom, then through to the master bathroom.

The corner tub there was far larger than our claw-foot at the condo, where we nevertheless tried to bathe together. The results were comical: Hannah on one side of the tub, me on the other, my long limbs cramped, and finally a lot of splashing and swearing when we got mixed up. I chuckled at the memory.

Hannah plugged the drain and ran a bath.

"What's up?"

"Oh, thinking about the condo."

She lifted her baby doll. She drew the lace off over her head, and just like that, Hannah stood naked before me. I gaped.

She still stunned me. Still. Hard nipples peaked her round, heavy breasts. Her pussy was bare, the way I liked it.

"God," I whispered.

I grasped her wrist and yanked her to me, pressing her naked chest against mine. My hunger, always simmering, boiled up. I pulled at her sweet body—harder and harder, closer and closer. *Sweet,* yes. Soft and sweet. Hannah's curves provoked me; they were the stuff of my wildest fantasies. "I love your body, Hannah . . ."

She shifted against me, her luxurious thighs rubbing along mine.

"When I fuck you . . . I love to watch your breasts tremble." I bit her neck. She shuddered. "When I hit your ass . . . I love to watch it quiver. I love your name. I love to moan it. You know I moan your name when I jerk off alone. *Hannah . . . Hannah . . .*"

I slapped her backside—hard. She yelped and I groaned. God, her little sounds of surprise drove me crazy. I hit her ass again with the flat of my hand, and the slap resounded above the rushing bathwater. Hannah moaned.

"Is that right?" I whispered in her ear. "You like that?"

She nodded and clung to me. She sucked at my neck while I spanked her, each meeting of my hand with her bottom making her jump against me. Making her lush body rub along my dick. Exciting me.

I kicked off my pants and we climbed into the tub.

Hannah's cheeks were apple red, and so was her bottom. I crawled across the tub to her. Her delight was contagious. She pressed herself against the side of the tub and sank until her chin touched the water. Her long curls floated on the surface like fronds.

"My Hannah," I whispered.

Beneath the water, I parted her legs and touched her sex. I watched her face. She held my stare as I slid one digit into her, then another, and fingered her at a leisurely pace.

"Watch me do it," I said, nodding at the water.

The color of Hannah's cheeks deepened. She lowered her eyes and, through the water, watched my fingers slide in and out of her body.

I watched, too, my gaze playing between her face and her cunt.

Soon, I felt the moisture of her body coating my fingers. I smiled.

"You're getting wet. Even here, underwater. Isn't that right, lover?"

She swallowed and nodded.

"Say it."

"Yes," she said.

"Yes what?"

"Yes, I'm . . . getting wet."

"Mm, turn over. I want to finger your ass."

I saw what my words did to Hannah—the way they took her by surprise. I felt what they did to her, too. Her body tightened on my finger and she got wetter still.

Obediently, Hannah turned over and around, kneeling in the tub. She looked over her shoulder as she presented her backside.

"You look good like this, little bird. Stay put."

I stepped out of the tub and dried my feet. I was at the door when Hannah said, "Bring my present for you."

Chapter 21

HANNAH

Waiting for Matt in any position turned me on, but waiting for Matt with my ass in the air did a number on me. He was right; I was soaked, bath or no bath. And the longer he took, the wetter I got.

Some minutes passed before Matt reappeared. He smiled wickedly and looked me over, his gaze lingering on my rear.

"Looks good, baby," he said. "You have a gorgeous ass."

Matt set his present on the edge of the tub, along with two votive candles and the warming lube he bought me. He lit the candles and flicked off the bathroom light. He closed the door and drew the curtain over the window so that only candlelight lit the room.

"So, I get to open my present this morning?" He settled back in the water.

"Yes." I was glad for the darkness, which hid my blushing cheeks.

"I'm excited. Very excited, actually." Matt neared me, touching his hardened cock to the back of my thigh. I shivered in the hot water. "Still wet, Hannah?" He brushed a finger along my slit. "Oh, even more wet."

He opened the bottle of lube and squirted it along my crack. Matt was always overgenerous with lubricant. I think he liked to make a mess, to watch it run down my body as it did then, trickling from my ass to my sex in a slippery trail. My skin began to tingle.

"Perfect." He sighed and rubbed the lube against my entrance, the tight muscle twitching in response. "Always so tight, no matter where I put my finger. Move back onto my finger, Hannah, the way you did with my dick last night."

Some incoherent word escaped me. I inched back and moaned at the strange, pleasurable sensation of my ass parting for Matt's finger. No matter how often we played like this, it felt . . . forbidden, almost shameful to enjoy, and therefore exquisite.

"There you go, Hannah. Nice and slow." Matt held my hip, guiding my motion until his finger was deep inside me. In our steaming hot bath, I couldn't tell whether the warming lube was warming at all, but it tickled like a good itch.

"Should I try to guess what my present is?" Matt moved his finger inside me and I groaned. "Maybe a cute little plug for your ass? I'd love that, you know."

My nails scraped along the bottom of the tub. Matt fingered my backside slowly and I moved to meet the motions. The sweet cinnamon scent of the candles and their wavering light put me under a spell. God . . . this felt good . . . and it made me long for more.

"L-let me show you," I panted. How did Matt manage so much dirty talk during sex? I could barely form a word.

He withdrew his finger and I sank against the edge of the tub. When I got turned around, I found him smiling indulgently at me.

"You . . ." I grinned. "You look like the cat that caught the canary."

"Do I? Well, I sort of am." He dried his hands and untied the ribbon from the present. My heart fluttered. Would he like this, or was I in for the embarrassment of a lifetime?

Beneath the paper, which Matt peeled off quickly, was a black LELO box. I stared at my foot, the wall, anything but Matt.

"LELO? Nice choice, Hannah."

He lifted the lid and I closed my eyes. Dear Lord, where did I get the balls to give Matt a vibrating waterproof cock ring? I wanted to disappear beneath the water. Urgh . . . the silence was killing me. I drew up my knees and cracked open one eye.

Matt's stare burned into me. He'd removed the ring from its holder and set aside the packaging. I couldn't read his expression. Candlelight glimmered on his damp skin, limned his profile, and flickered in his eyes.

"It's, uh, waterproof. I ch-charged it . . . so . . ." I sank behind my knees.

Matt extended the ring to me. Mute, I accepted it. My fingers drifted over the butter-soft silicone. Wow. This felt like a brilliant idea when I was ordering the toy, but now—

"Put it on me," Matt said.

He stood smoothly. Water streamed down his naked body and his rigid length jutted from his pelvis. I dropped the ring in the water, swore, and snatched it.

Okay, he wanted it on . . . *I got this, I got this.*

"Tell me . . . tell me if it hurts. I'll just . . ." I scooted forward along the tub bottom and wrapped my fingers around Matt's cock. His lips twitched. My heart was doing acrobatics in my chest. I was excited, nervous, pleased, terrified, turned on—everything.

I leaned forward and kissed the tip of Matt's cock.

"God . . . Hannah . . ."

There wasn't a note of protest in his voice, just slow-burning desire. He gripped my wet curls. I wrapped my lips around his head, suckling and swirling my tongue. I laid a hand against his thigh to feel the muscles tensing. He *loved* this.

And sure, every guy I'd dated loved it, but not like Matt. When I looked at Matt while I sucked his dick, I saw the most powerful longing overtaking him, accompanied by a furious, stubborn resistance. He never wanted to show his need. He fought the pleasure as it overcame him, and he surrendered to it with low, long moans. Only in those moments did I have the upper hand, and I relished it as much as I relished submission.

I licked my way down Matt's shaft before sliding the elastic ring over it. It stretched around his girth as I worked it down to the base. I looked up at him.

"Does it hurt?"

I caught a ghost of a smile on his lips. "No," he said. "It feels good, Hannah."

I massaged Matt's balls lightly and turned on the ring.

He moaned—the sound so sharp that I jumped.

"Fuck," he snarled. He gripped his shaft.

"Uh, sorry—sorry, let me—"

"N-no, no . . . it's fine." Matt stroked himself a few times and closed his eyes. "Fine . . ."

"Does it feel good? Bad?" I peered up at him.

"Good," he breathed.

I pried Matt's fingers off his dick and tried not to giggle. He was always taking matters into his own hands. "Let me." I pumped his shaft and licked his head back into my mouth. I relaxed my throat and moved him deeper, moaning as I did.

Matt's pleading began when I dialed up the ring. Powerful vibrations trembled down his cock to my tongue, turning my moans into purrs.

"Don't—don't," he hissed, tugging at my hair. "Don't make me come. I want to come with you—fuck, Hannah, fuck . . . suck me . . ."

I savored his desperation, along with his indecision. One moment he was trying to guide my mouth off his sex, the next he was trying to push it deeper. Swearing. Snarling my name. His head thrown back or pitched forward, eyes glued to me.

"Come on," he rasped. "No, *no.* Hannah . . ."

And I won't lie; it drove me just as wild. The way Matt felt in my mouth and the way he begged for me—it was pure need, raw honesty.

I drew back, licked my lips, and leaned against the slope of the tub. I spread my legs and Matt sank over me, lowering his gorgeous body into the water. Into me. His eyes were stormy.

I felt every inch of his invasion.

The bullet at the top of the ring hit my clit and I gasped, digging my nails into Matt's back. "Fuck!" I cried.

"Yeah?" Matt's voice curled with delight. "I know, I know."

He didn't move; he simply pinned me against the tub with his cock buried in me and the ring vibrating against my clit. Before long, I was writhing under him.

"Come on," he coaxed. "I know you can come like this. Come for me."

My coiled pleasure released in a rush and I groaned. My back bowed. My sex squeezed and milked Matt's length, and only then did he begin to move.

The bathwater seesawed in the tub. Matt fucked me single-mindedly, oblivious even when a splash extinguished a candle. My pussy, he kept telling me, was tight, so fucking tight, and he loved to fuck it, he wanted to come in it, and how did I like to feel his cum?

He groaned and pressed his face into my neck as he came. Whatever crossed his features in the throes of bliss, he hid.

Afterward, we bathed one another. Matt was sedate. He lathered shampoo into my hair, smoothed body wash over my skin, and rinsed me clean. We kissed and didn't speak. We'd created a sanctuary—in the bathtub, in the cabin—and I felt such peace.

Matt blew out the rest of the candles and turned on the light. We dried one another, smiling faintly whenever our eyes met. Then—for the first time, though I don't know how I missed it last night—I caught sight of the white-pink scar on his calf. I knelt and brushed the towel over it.

"Baby," I whispered.

I could see where the cat's teeth punctured his flesh, four large spots with smaller splotches around them. I covered my mouth.

"Let me see your wrist," I said. "Let me see it."

"Hannah, stop. It's nothing."

"No." I caught his hand. I scanned his arm until I found a pink bar on the inside of his forearm and another over his wrist. I stared at the scars.

"They don't hurt. Stop this. We're happy. Everything is working out." Matt lifted my chin. The confidence in his voice was absent from his expression. His eyes were haunted. And no wonder . . .

Matt opened his mouth to say more—and then, from the kitchen, his cell began to ring.

Chapter 22

MATT

Hannah and I hovered over the phone. She looked afraid to touch it, her dark eyes so round. The silence between each ring was dead air. And then it stopped.

Mel, I prayed, *don't leave a message, don't leave a message . . . please.*

How could I have forgotten to tell Mel not to call this weekend? I bought the new phone on Thursday and sent her the number as soon as I got back to the cabin. Then, in my rush to prepare for Hannah's visit, I completely forgot about Mel.

And here she was—Melanie, the stranger responsible for *Night Owl*'s publication—calling me while Hannah listened in horror.

My cell began to ring again. *Fuck.*

"What the hell?" Hannah whispered. She looked between me and the ringing cell. "Who has this number besides me?"

"No one," I stammered. "No one, I swear. It's got to be a wrong number."

"What if . . . someone figured this out? I'm answering it."

"No!" I grabbed the phone.

Hannah's eyes narrowed. *There.* For the first time since she arrived, I saw suspicion flash across her face.

I eased the TracFone back onto the counter.

Its loud, persistent ring was the sound of panic.

"Why answer it?" I said. "I mean, there's no point."

"Matt, we have to know who it is. And *you* can't answer it. I'm answering it."

Before I could stop her, Hannah flipped open my cell and brought it to her ear.

"Hello?" she said.

My heart thudded into a thin, fast rhythm. I could do nothing but stare and strain to hear. No voice came from the phone. Or maybe it did and I missed it. My ears were ringing.

"Hello?" Hannah demanded. "Who is this? Hello?"

Her face fell. She glared at the phone, then snapped it shut. Her hand was shaking.

"They hung up," she said. "They didn't say anything."

Another muffled ringtone sounded.

This time, it was Hannah's phone.

She frowned and opened her purse, digging out her phone and peering at it.

"Shit, it's Nate."

"Oh, of course." I threw up a hand.

"I have to answer this."

"Do you, now?" I folded my arms and regarded Hannah carefully. Why did she *have* to answer a call from Nate?

"It looks weird if I don't, okay? Let me handle this." She took the call and walked off a few feet. I followed her like a vulture, looming at her shoulder.

"Nate? Hey. No, it's fine." She paused. "No, out at Kevin's cabin. Yeah. Yeah, I needed to get away. He said I could stay here." Another pause. "He really is, yeah."

I leaned in, but I couldn't catch Nate's voice.

Hannah glared and twisted away from me. Then something changed in her expression. Her hesitant smile fell and her dark brows drew together.

"What?" She walked toward the deck. She was silent for a minute. "I see. I see. I don't know anything about that." Her shoulders hunched as she listened. "No," she said. "I realize that. It's really weird, but I—yes, believe me."

Hannah's one-sided conversation continued to make no sense. While her back was to me, I shut off my new cell.

"All right. I will, Nate. I'm sorry. I'll be in touch. Bye."

She ended the call and lowered her phone. She took her time turning to face me. She tightened the towel around her bust and returned the phone to her purse.

"Nate," she said.

"Mm."

Hannah's guarded expression worried me, along with her slow and careful motions.

"It seems like . . ." She looked through her purse. "It seems like *Night Owl* has been removed from the Internet. All the places selling the e-book have discontinued it."

I looked down at the countertop. Too late . . . the slow-dawning realization of how suspicious this looked. Hannah told me about the lawsuit last weekend. Within days, *Night Owl* disappeared from the Internet.

I wasn't clever at all. Not at all. I was the world's biggest fucking idiot.

"Wow," I managed.

"Yeah, wow." She continued to go through her purse, and when I looked at her hands, I saw that she wasn't really searching for anything. She mechanically raised and replaced items. Lip gloss. Her keys. A coin purse. A pill holder.

I grasped her wrist. Her hands jerked to a stop.

"Did you?" she said. Her meaning was clear. *Did you publish it?*

I shook my head.

"Matt, you could have told me if you did. You can tell me. I won't be upset, just—"

"I didn't turn *Night Owl* into an e-book," I snapped. That, at least, was true.

I turned away from Hannah and dragged a hand through my wet hair.

"I'm sorry, but I had to ask," she said. "Do you get how weird this is? It makes no sense. I told you about the lawsuit, and the only other people who know are Seth and Nate . . . and Shapiro, obviously. And me. That's it." Her voice faltered as she worked through the logic.

"I know."

"Like . . . what are the odds, I mean . . . it's as if the person who published it *knew*. About the lawsuit. To suddenly pull the title off the Internet—"

"Coincidence," I said. "It has to be a coincidence."

"I guess. I know *you* didn't tell anyone. I didn't tell anyone but you."

I moved away from Hannah, heading toward the couch and the broad western windows. A run through the woods would clear my head. That, or a swim in some half-frozen lake. Something painful and rigorous.

"Nate is seriously pissed," Hannah persisted. She gnawed at a nail as she spoke. "At first, he was basically accusing me. You know, they all think *I* wrote it, and now—"

"You?" I laughed. "Please."

"Excuse me? What is that supposed to mean?"

"You don't write. I don't get why they'd think you wrote it."

"Uh, okay. I actually *do* write, just FYI. You remember how we met on a *writing* forum? But anyway . . . yeah, this is looking pretty bad for me." Hannah laughed, the sound as bitter as mine. "Doesn't matter, I guess. It's not like they can prove I wrote it, since I didn't."

"Mm."

Soft snow began to fall, slanting across the sky. It was hard to believe that a moment ago Hannah and I stood in the bathroom together, feeling so content.

No trace of that harmony remained.

"And Nate still plans to pursue the lawsuit," Hannah said.

"Mm."

"I'm glad you're so concerned."

"Hannah . . ." I rubbed my face. In the wake of strong emotion, I always feel void.

"Look, if it comes down to it, why don't I just tell them you wrote it?"

"What?" I turned.

"Yeah. The truth, Matt. I'll say that you wrote it, and that I have no idea how it got online. I'll tell them you always e-mailed your stuff to yourself, and that maybe someone hacked your e-mail. You know, it would feel good to tell the truth for once."

No kidding.

"No," I said flatly. "No, I—"

"Matt, please. Let me say that. Nate will probably drop the lawsuit, and if he doesn't, who cares? Let him sue the asshole who hacked your e-mail and put the book online. I know the book is embarrassing, trust me, but you don't have to save face. You're dead, remember? You're never going to—"

"Stop it!" My voice echoed off the cabin walls. Hannah jumped about an inch in the air. "Please, just . . . stop it. I can't—" I unclenched my hands. *I can't let Nate sue the person who put the book up for sale. I can't let a stranger take a fall for me.* Besides, would Melanie even take that fall? No, she'd roll over on me in a heartbeat. "I can't think about this right now."

Hannah's shoulders fell and she wiped her eyes quickly.

"Fine," she said. "Later, then. We'll . . . handle it later. It's just, I don't live in a cabin in the woods, Matt." She gestured around the cabin. "I can't not think about this, okay? I have . . . Nate calling me, and I'll have Shapiro hounding me. I live in the real world."

I crossed the cabin and returned to Hannah. I folded her into a hug. If she doubted me, or if she suspected something was up with *Night Owl* and Mel's call, I would have felt it. She didn't. She melted against me with a sigh.

"Let's not live in the real world." I swayed with Hannah in my arms.

She gave a defeated laugh.

"Disappear with me," I persisted. "It can be done. I don't live in the real world."

"I know you don't." She kissed my collarbone. "I've always known that. But I do, and I like it. I love my family, my job . . ."

"Mm, I know. It's a nice thought, though, isn't it? The two of us on the run. Sort of daring and romantic . . ." I smiled and sighed and let it go. I knew better than to push Hannah now. On the inside, though, I was exultant. The book *was* complicating her life. She called it *embarrassing,* said Shapiro was *hounding her.* To me, that meant she was one step farther from Denver and one step closer to us. I tapped her nose. "So you write, do you?"

"You know I do."

"And what do you write, little bird?"

"Well." She fidgeted. "There was . . . that story with you."

"What, Lana and Cal? Oh, yes, the stuff of Pulitzers."

Hannah grinned. "Uh-huh, super highbrow. But, no, I mean . . . I write."

I tilted my head and waited for her to say more, but she only smiled at me. Mm . . . beautiful Hannah with her little secrets. Fair enough.

"It's better that I don't know," I said after a while. "As long as it's not a tell-all memoir about me, hm? Suddenly you'll be auctioning off my e-mails."

We returned to the bedroom with our arms around one another. A small part of me refused to relax, and it pricked at me as we dressed and chatted.

Really, how could I be so stupid? I thought removing *Night Owl* from the Net would solve all our problems, but it only made more.

That morning, Hannah and I went for a walk in the woods. I showed her where I jogged and told her about the owls I sometimes heard at night. I displayed my giant pile of firewood. "Impressive." She giggled. She was all levity again, and I found myself smiling as I watched her.

We attempted to build a snowman in front of the cabin, but the powder wouldn't hold. Hannah flung snow at me and I tackled her soundly.

When we got back inside, Hannah showed me a pair of long underwear and told the story of her anxiety-fueled packing. We cackled.

"'I'll wear it sometime," I said, "and take a few hot pics for you."

She made tomato soup and grilled cheese sandwiches for lunch, and I gave her a glass of white wine. We settled down to watch Luhrmann's new version of *The Great Gatsby*.

I watched Hannah more than I watched the screen. It was pure pleasure, to see the nuances of emotion playing over her face.

I refilled her glass and she frowned at me.

"Matt, are you trying to get me drunk?"

"Mm." I wedged the cork in. "Drunk on cheap wine so I can have my way with you."

"It's not that bad." She sipped her wine and squinted. "But I . . . don't want to be all tipsy and silly while you're sober. I feel bad."

I leaned in to kiss Hannah's neck. I felt her pulse against my tongue. "I think you've seen enough of me drunk in a cabin for one lifetime, Hannah. Besides . . ." I set the bottle on the coffee table, "my tastes are way too refined for this shit."

Hannah huffed and smacked my arm.

I loved Hannah "all tipsy and silly," with her ready blushes and laughter. I knew that only I saw that side of her. When it came to work, she was professional and brisk. In social settings, she was friendly and polite, but finally reserved. She bloomed for me.

And I did have my way with Hannah that afternoon. When the movie ended, I took her out onto the deck and made her hold the rail while I slid a hand into her pants. I exposed her to the cold bit by bit, lifting her sweater and unclasping her bra, peeling down her pants and thong. I spanked her until her moans rang through the forest.

When I was ready, I made her tell me how she wanted it— hard and fast or sweet and slow. Hard and fast, she said. A good answer.

Chapter 23

HANNAH

Sunday arrived with the unsettling feeling of departure. I woke alone and shuffled into the main room, where I found Matt seated at his desk. The set of his shoulders—just that—told me we were going to have an argument.

He didn't turn.

As I was fixing my coffee, he said, "I'm not happy about this."

I frowned over at him. God, I couldn't get used to seeing that silky black hair where I expected dirty blond. I wondered how long he'd been awake. He wore a pale long-sleeved shirt and black fleece pants, and even those casual clothes fit him so elegantly. He must have looked like that when he was alone, relaxing at his desk, writing. Without me.

Matt turned and caught me staring.

"What? About what?" I said.

"You leaving. I'm not happy about it."

He rose and began to prowl through the cabin, stopping at windows to study the landscape. I watched him again, and I smiled. He couldn't be happy with a weekend. He was angry all the time—in his passion, in his contentment—as if he needed anger to survive.

"Matt, I'm not happy about it either."

"Then call Pam and take a sick day."

"No." I blew steam off my coffee. "I'm sorry, but I won't do that."

"Why? Why not?"

"Don't be childish, Matt. It's my job, it's my dream job, and you of all people should know that Pam can smell a lie for miles."

Matt glared a challenge at me from across the room. I met his gaze and shook my head. In bed, he could boss me around all night—and all day, for that matter—but not outside of it.

"Besides"—I swirled the spoon in my mug—"I'll drive up next weekend."

"Don't you want to spend another day with me?" Having failed with anger, Matt shifted into a far more persuasive mode: Mopey Matt. He flopped onto the couch and snatched a pillow, which he began to pick at and examine. When I said nothing, he set aside the pillow and went for Laurence, opening the rabbit's cage and leaning in to talk quietly to him.

Oh, Lord. He was like an outsized nine-year-old but with a man's guile. I grinned down at my coffee. To laugh at him now would be a mistake.

"Baby, of course I want to spend another day with you. I want to spend every day with you, but we can't, and you know that. You wanted this . . ."

My last words hung between us. Matt's hand stilled on Laurence's head, then resumed down the rabbit's back. He closed the cage and stood.

"I wanted my life back," he said.

"Your life minus me."

"I didn't want *this.*"

Matt stormed out of the room. The bedroom door slammed.

"Oh, for fuck's sake," I huffed.

I let Matt cool his heels in the bedroom. Whatever. If he wanted to fight, I had plenty of ammo. After all, I was the one taking heat over *Night Owl.* I was the one acting out our charade.

I gained nothing from his absence except his absence, which seriously sucked.

I never got to go to dinner with my boyfriend anymore . . . never got to walk down the street holding his hand . . . all week I slept alone in our king-size bed. The hell with him. *I* was the one sacrificing. He got his happy anonymous little life, and he just wanted more, more, more.

I sneered and dropped onto the couch.

I finished my coffee and had another cup. I played Candy Crush on my phone. I even stood on the deck awhile, enjoying the crystalline silence. I wanted to wait Matt out. He owed me an apology. But he didn't appear, and I heard no sound from the bedroom.

After an hour and a half, I knocked lightly on the door.

Nothing.

"Matt?"

Silence.

"Okay, I'm coming in, you big baby," I said.

I slipped into the room.

My suitcase lay open on the bed, and it was empty. Matt lounged against the windowsill smoking. Gradually, I noticed my clothes and toiletries in various places around the room.

There was my nightgown, still neatly folded, sitting on the bedside table. And there were my boots poking out from under the bed.

"Yes," Matt said. "I put all your things around here." He gestured to the room without looking at me. "And in the bathroom, too. And I won't help you find them, so good luck."

I fought to keep a straight face.

Finally, he glanced at me. "I'm glad you find this amusing."

"Matt . . ." I crept over to him and nuzzled his shoulder. "You're crazy."

"Mm." He blew smoke out the open window.

"And you're adorable."

"Handsome," he mumbled. His stubborn expression faltered.

"Okay, handsome." I laughed. I plucked the cigarette from his fingers and took a drag. Matt blinked at me.

"Are you smoking now?"

"Nope." I smiled and crushed out the cigarette. "And neither are you."

I left the cabin around the same time I'd arrived on Friday, when the day's last light stained the snow orange. Matt loved that time of day. He loved the sadness of it.

I knew he wouldn't want to say good-bye, so after we got my stuff and Laurence's cage into the car, we sat up front and talked about nothing. I wore my new owl earrings. Matt smiled and batted one with a finger.

"Let's go," he said. "I'll ride to the end of the road with you."

"You sure?"

"Yeah. I'll walk back. It's not far."

I pulled out of the driveway and onto the darkening road. Flurries swirled through the air.

Matt was silent, staring ahead and running a hand over my thigh. Through the denim of my jeans, his fingertips set my leg on fire.

I stopped at the bottom of the hill. To our right and left, the country lane was barren.

I turned off my high beams and the car idled in the cold.

A lump of emotion formed in my throat.

"Hey, come here." Matt pulled me over the console and kissed me. I sighed against his mouth. God, I already missed him so much.

I stroked his handsome face as we kissed and I kneaded the back of his neck. Our kiss grew hungry, and Matt tugged at my ribs to bring my body closer to his. The scent of his cologne filled my nostrils. His strong back shifted under my palms.

"Hannah . . ." He squeezed my breast through my coat.

I gasped and dug my fingers into his shoulders.

He stilled, breathing raggedly against my cheek.

"It's okay," I whispered. "It's okay." I touched his wrist and then his fingers. I fitted his hand around my breast and he groaned.

"Let me—" Matt's hand slid down my body. He rubbed the denim seam covering my sex. "Let me just . . . touch it, Hannah . . . let me put my mouth on it. *Please* . . ."

He didn't have to ask me twice. Together we fumbled with my zipper. I jerked my jeans and thong down my legs, worming around on the seat. I kicked off my boots. I spread my bare legs and gazed over at Matt, my chest heaving.

Damn . . . he looked so fucking good, serious as hell and hungry. And even if the roads were vacant for miles, sitting bottomless in my car felt deliciously illicit.

Matt pushed my legs open wider and leaned down to my sex, his beautiful body stretched over my lap. I curled my fingers in his hair. Oh, I loved this, and Matt loved it, too. He trembled like a starved animal every time he went down on me.

"I just . . . want to taste it," he said, his breath washing over my skin.

Matt didn't tease me like usual. He simply kissed my pussy, hard. His fingers gripped my thighs and his tongue slid into my sex. We moaned together, me into the silence of the car and Matt against my hot, wet skin.

"Matt, God . . . oh, God . . ."

His kiss was long and deep. His lips and tongue worked against my pussy; his smooth jaw caressed my thighs. Sometimes he bit down, pulling on my clit or the folds of my sex. "Good," he whispered, licking me as I got wetter.

I tugged his hair.

With Matt, I never faked it. Matt knew what he was doing. He began to work on my clit, pushing up its soft hood and sucking at the pearl of nerves. He licked it rhythmically and my insides tightened. I pressed his mouth closer to my cunt. He moaned. *Hmmm,* he liked that . . .

But of course he liked it. He loved my pleasure, and my need turned him on.

I arched against the seat and raked a hand down his back. I bunched up his coat and shirt and rubbed the skin beneath. Now that it came to good-bye, I wanted him more than ever. This skin, this back, these slim hips and strong flanks . . . I clasped them hungrily, panting as my pleasure spiraled higher.

"L-let's fuck," I gasped. "Fuck me . . ."

But I knew damn well there wasn't room in my little car.

As I neared climax, I began to buck against Matt's mouth, grinding my clit on his tongue. He slid several fingers into me. Over and over he stroked my G-spot. My legs trembled. I panted and writhed. I held back as long as I could, wanting Matt and my pleasure forever, and I screamed his name when he made me come.

He didn't linger.

He cleaned me with his tongue and watched the road while I pulled on my pants. I knew he wanted to ask me to come back to the cabin. I knew if I touched his groin that I would find him half hard in his jeans. I even knew that if I tried to return the favor, he would leave sooner and in anger. *That's not how it works,* he snapped at me once. *It's not a favor, when I make you come. It doesn't mean you owe me. How can you think about it like that?*

When Matt saw that I had my boots back on, he stepped out of the car.

"Next weekend, then," he said, and he strolled into the swirling snow.

Chapter 24

MATT

I lived for the weekends, driving myself through the week by writing relentlessly. I wrote as much as five thousand words a day. I hated the writing as I always hate the writing, and I was locked together with it and without Hannah.

How are you surviving without her? Melanie's question dogged me. *Night Owl . . . paints a picture of obsession.*

A picture of obsession.

She was right. I was addicted to Hannah.

I didn't return Melanie's call. I sent her a short message via the forum.

Pulling Night Owl off the net was rash—my bad. My brother is suspicious. Lay low about it and I'll be in touch. Don't worry. Don't call. Hannah is here on and off. I'll call you when I can. —M

Except I didn't call when I could.

I began to think I should never have contacted Mel. She was another blind spot, another chink in my armor. I didn't know her, I couldn't predict her, and I couldn't control her. If she decided to speak out about my existence, I wouldn't be able to silence her.

Friday came again and Hannah came again, and my worries faded.

She pulled onto the drive at that finest time of day, when the light is melancholy. She brought me little things, writing supplies and food, and she dressed up for me. She wore makeup and perfume and painted her nails. She wore new lingerie—once a strappy La Perla slip that barely covered her nipples. She drove me mad.

We fucked all over the cabin. I had her on the deck, against the bathroom counter, in the kitchen, on the floor, and on one very memorable occasion in the cellar. I trussed her to an empty wine rack and fucked her until she begged to come.

And then it was Sunday again.

I rode with Hannah to the end of the road. I told myself I wouldn't get desperate and lunge between her legs like last time.

I got desperate and lunged between her legs.

Afterward, I escaped quickly—no good-bye, just the taste of Hannah on my lips—and I climbed the road back to the cabin. Back to my self-enforced solitude.

By the second week in March, winter's edge was gone from the air. The days lengthened and the morning sun melted the snow, though the mountains froze overnight.

We set our watches forward together.

Hannah called on Tuesday. The phone's shrill ringtone startled me; I hadn't heard it in weeks. I smiled and pushed away from my desk.

"Baby bird."

"Hey." She laughed. "How's it going?"

"Oh, you know, crazy social calendar, dance card full, et cetera, et cetera. What's up?"

"Well, I talked to Kevin."

"Bad news?"

"Good news, actually. He said I can use the cabin all spring. He's going straight from Miami to Brazil, spending the season with his in-laws. And we got the utilities settled."

"Perfect." I smiled and tilted my head. Good news didn't

explain Hannah's careful tone. "One more season. Gives us time to think."

"Yeah. Maybe we should think now. I'm sure Kevin will want his cabin this summer."

"I'm not worried about it. Worst-case scenario, I stay at the condo for a while. Hiding in plain sight. That, or I could move to a hotel for a few months. When you get my inheritance—" A frown pulled at my mouth. It felt weird as fuck to talk about my inheritance. It was a lot of money, and it was *my* money. To think of that small fortune slipping out of my control . . .

"Matt?"

"Ah, the money." I ruffled my hair. "We can do whatever we want then. You could buy a cabin out here, something like that. Hey, I can't wait to see you, Hannah."

Hannah was quiet.

"This weekend," I prompted. "I'm missing you."

"Yeah. I miss you, too. This weekend, I can't come out this weekend."

Only then did I realize how much hope I pinned on Hannah's visits, because my heart dropped and my mood froze. Clouds seemed to gather over my week. Suddenly, I hated the cabin. I hated the cold and the snow. I especially hated my writing, which ruined my life—ruined any chance of happiness and normalcy for me.

"Why not?"

"Pam's throwing a party at the agency." Hannah paused. "For *The Surrogate*'s release. It's in stores on Tuesday."

"Tuesday. I'd forgotten."

"Yeah. I have to go to the party. And I want to. I'm excited about the book."

"Excited about the book." I smirked. "That's rich. I'm glad I'm not around for any of that shit. Did Mara totally savage the manuscript?" Mara was my editor.

"No. Almost no changes were made. Just some punctuation stuff . . ."

"Great. They fucked with my punctuation?"

"Pam says you're overly fond of semicolons."

My smirk softened. Pamela Wing, my stone-cold agent. I couldn't picture her shedding one tear over my loss, and the thought pleased me.

"God, I miss that bitch." I chuckled. Hannah laughed, too, relief flooding her voice.

"Anyway, I'll drive out next weekend," she said. "It's not so bad."

"Mm . . . not so bad."

We chatted for an hour and then Hannah had to leave for yoga. *Yoga . . .* I loved what yoga did for her body. She was all curvy and elastic and capable of assuming the most pretzelesque positions when I f—

"Matt?"

"Huh? I love you."

"You're daydreamy tonight. I love you, too."

I flipped my phone shut, and then I flipped it back open. I dialed Mel's number.

She answered immediately.

"Hey!" she said. "I thought you'd cut me off."

"I was thinking about it. You've become a problem for me, Mel."

She laughed nervously.

"Well, you have," I said, "but that's not why I called. Are you still between jobs?"

"Yeah. Are you going to make fun of me again?"

"Nope. I'm going to offer you a job."

Chapter 25

HANNAH

On Wednesday morning, I had to park two blocks from the agency. The joys of city living. I smiled as I hurried along the sidewalk. I thought about the cabin.

Yes, I would happily use Matt's money to buy us a cabin of our own.

I loved Denver, I loved the buzz and easy access to everything, but city life necessitates escape. I recharged in the mountains with Matt. When we lay in bed listening to the owls calling to one another, I felt satisfied at the deepest level.

They sound beautiful, I once said. Matt said they sounded lonesome.

I sighed and laughed.

I just couldn't understand that boy's fascination with sorrow.

Too late, I saw a figure standing on the agency steps. My vision of cabin life dissipated. It was Seth Sky. I veered away from the steps, but he'd already spotted me.

"Hannah!"

Seth looked no different than he had in New Jersey—long hair, leather jacket, stormy eyes—except that he wore dark jeans and boots instead of dress slacks and oxfords. I didn't let my gaze linger over how well Seth's clothes fit.

"What are you doing here?" I snapped.

That stopped him cold.

"Seriously?" he said. "You're still pissed?"

"I am not pissed." I enunciated each word. "I haven't thought about you since last month. But this is where I work." I gestured to the agency. "Which I think you know. So I believe this qualifies as stalking."

Seth cocked his head and smiled. He approached warily, hands in the air.

"I'm in town for a gig."

"Great. I'm in town for my job." I turned to go and Seth reached to stop me, but he paused midreach. *Wise.* I glared at his hand and he retracted it. "What do you want?"

"I thought we could get dinner. Sometime. Since I'm in the area."

"No."

"What the hell?" Seth raked a hand through his hair.

My heart softened slightly at his legitimate confusion. The Sky brothers weren't lacking in the beauty department, and Nate and Matt had brains to spare, but Seth . . .

Seth was either dense or so egomaniacal that he couldn't fathom being friend-zoned.

"I'm sorry, Seth. I just think it's better if we don't hang out."

"Why?" He glowered at the sidewalk. "Nate said you're going to the zoo with him in the spring. Why won't you hang out with me?"

I balked, momentarily speechless. Weird . . . I couldn't picture Nate sharing those plans.

"Uh, the zoo thing is tentative," I said. "Very tentative. And Seth, that's different. Nate is . . . Nate. Nate has a wife, kids . . ." I trailed off, looking meaningfully at Seth.

"So? Are you implying that I have ulterior motives?"

"Not implying anything."

"So what's the problem? What if I *do* have ulterior motives? You're gorgeous, you're funny and smart, and I want to take you out."

"It's not happening, Seth."

"Never?" He glared at me.

"Never. Sorry."

"Then we'll be friends. Let me take you to dinner. Bring a friend if you want."

I could see that Seth wasn't going to give up, and I was beginning to feel cruel. What could he really do to me over dinner? Nothing, except bore me or hit on me. Or both.

Besides, I didn't believe Seth really wanted me. To him, I was Matt's old flame, available yet unattainable, and my resistance was probably fueling his pursuit. Maybe if I gave in to a dull dinner, he'd give up, too.

"Dinner." I sighed. "Tomorrow night?"

His dark eyes lit up. "All right, tomorrow night."

"Meet me at Cherry Creek. Seven okay?"

"Seven is fine." Seth's face fell. "The mall?"

"Yeah. They have a nice food court. I'll meet you outside Macy's."

I bounded up the steps before Seth could object.

"Han, I am so *hot* for this guy." My sister fanned herself as she drove. "Like if I were a dude, I'd be *gay* for this guy. *That* hot."

"I don't think that's . . . quite how homosexuality works," I murmured. My hands twitched on my lap. I was fighting the urge to steady the wheel.

"Whatever, whatever." Chrissy turned up the music—Goldengrove, of course—and raised her voice to compensate. "Just let me work my magic! You have your—"

She glanced at me as we pulled up to the shopping center. I was wearing a loose turtleneck sweater dress, leggings, and boots. Nothing sexy about it.

"Okay, you have your frock going on there. I'm working this."

My sister gestured to her chest. Her tight leather jacket was unzipped enough to show a line of cleavage. She looked good, as
always. Her short hair was styled perfectly, her makeup flawless,
her clothes fit snugly.

We laughed as we climbed out of the car.

"I'd pay you to take this guy off my hands," I said. "He's creep-
ing on me hard. Which is weird, am I right?"

"Oh, super weird." Chrissy nodded vigorously. "I mean,
Matt—" She didn't hesitate over Matt's name. Not once had she
given me the pity eyes or the lingering hug, even though this was
our first time hanging out since the memorial. Thank God for my
sister. "Matt *just* happened, you know? That shit *just* went down.
It is way too sketchy for his brother to be hitting on you."

"Thank you. My thoughts exactly."

Except not my thoughts at all.

My thoughts were more like: Matt is still alive and if he finds
out Seth is after me, he will flip the fuck out and discard anonymity in favor of fratricide.

Chrissy and I strolled into the mall. We talked smack about
every other outfit we passed.

"I'll wear that when I'm reincarnated as a whale," Chrissy said.
I couldn't help but laugh. Okay, maybe this would be fun. Life at
work, the condo, and the cabin was getting insular. Besides, I
missed my sister. We got along well in spite of our differences—or
maybe in light of them—and she always managed to make me
smile.

Plus, when I told Chrissy I needed a buffer for dinner with the
lead singer of Goldengrove, nothing could hold her back. The
indie group was one of her favorites.

Seth and a bandmate were waiting for us outside Macy's.

My heart fluttered strangely at the sight of Seth. *It's because I
miss Matt,* I thought, *and looking at Seth is like looking at Matt.
Of course.*

I recognized the bandmate from my debauched night in New
Jersey. He was the drummer, or maybe the bass guitarist.

"You brought . . . your sister?" Seth smiled at Chrissy.

Seth wore a gray wool coat over a T-shirt and jeans. His hair was tied back in a low ponytail. He almost looked preppy, except his shirt had . . . a squirrel on it?

"Yeah, this is Christine. Christine, Seth Sky." I smirked. "Nice shirt."

"Thanks. Matt gave it to me."

Annnd now I felt like an ass.

I shuffled around to shake hands with the bandmate, whose name was Wiley. Wiley couldn't take his eyes off Chrissy. I doubt Chrissy noticed, though, because she couldn't take her eyes off Seth. Ugh, this already felt like a twisted double date.

Seth wasn't particularly attentive as we ambled through the food court and studied our options. Chrissy gushed about Gold-engrove and solicited a signature, and Seth made amicable noises. "Oh," he'd say, or, "I see, yeah."

A passel of teens recognized Seth and Wiley. I braced myself for confrontation—it was never pretty when fans closed in on Matt—but Seth was gracious and talkative. Huh. Why couldn't Matt be like that?

We ordered gyros from Renzios and Seth paid. I watched him out of the corner of my eye. Laconic smiles, slow graceful gestures, an edge of nervous energy.

Unable to get a word out of Seth, my sister turned her attention to Wiley. The two fell to chatting while Seth and I stuffed our faces in silence.

Cool. Friends, hanging out. This was what Seth wanted, right?

I peeked at him while we ate.

Damn, he looked sort of pitiful. He sat hunched over his tray, holding the sloppy gyro with both hands and gazing at the table. A bit of onion dangled from his shirt.

"Seth?" I tapped the edge of his tray.

He startled and then smiled. "Not bad food," he said, gesturing with the gyro.

"It's good." I nodded. "You okay?"

"Wiley and I are going shopping," Chrissy announced. I looked up to find Wiley and Chrissy crushed together, Wiley's tattooed arm around her waist. I narrowed my eyes. This was *not* our plan. Chrissy was supposed to save me from Seth, not go wandering off with random Wiley. I tried to convey that with my glare.

No dice.

"Call me when you're ready to go," she said. She gave a little wave.

Great . . .

I expected to find Seth smiling slyly at me, but he was staring at the table again.

"Seriously, are you okay, Seth?"

He finished his gyro with a big bite and washed it down with a swig of Coke.

"I'm a little bummed," he said at last. He sighed and sat back. I tried to meet his stare, but it was so intense, so penetrating, that I finally looked away. "I like you, Hannah. That night after the memorial was so fucking fun. And I got this . . . idea." He pressed a hand to his head as if the idea were an ache. "This idea that you'd go for me. You liked Matt and he was a dick—no offense, bro." Seth winked at the ceiling. "And you like Nate. So why—"

"Whoa, there. I *loved* Matt, yes. I like Nate as a friend, that's it."

"Fine, why can't I be a friend?"

I ground my teeth. Seth *would* drive the conversation into awkward land.

For the space of a minute, I pictured Nate's face—darkly handsome and dignified, always full of kindness—and then I pictured Matt. Gorgeous Matt . . . passionate, aloof.

"You're smiling," Seth said.

"Yeah." I looked him dead in the eye. "Thinking about Matt."

"Is it too soon? Is that the problem?"

I finished my gyro and piled our trays together.

"You're being pretty aggressive about this, Seth."

"I just want to know if I have a chance."

"I don't think you do."

"Why not?"

Because Matt is still alive.

I shrugged and crumpled my napkin.

"Okay," Seth persisted. "Do you think I'm attractive?"

I frowned at him. "Obviously you're attractive, Seth. I'm sure you're aware. If you need me to reinforce that fact, you've got some serious middle child syndrome going."

"Hey, maybe I do."

"Can we walk around?"

"Uh-huh . . ." Seth watched me as I discarded our trash. I felt his dark eyes on me.

Abruptly, Seth stood and stalked off.

I jogged to catch up.

"I hate the mall," he snapped. "It makes me tired and depressed. And you know what? It's fucking depressing and sad that you made me take you to dinner at the food court."

I studied the passing floor.

Yeah . . . I was starting to feel like an asshole for suggesting we dine at the food court. Except . . . "I didn't want you to get the wrong idea," I mumbled.

"Wrong idea not gotten, have no fear."

We moved aimlessly through the mall. We didn't go into any stores or talk at all, which suited me fine. I hate small talk.

After a while, Seth caught my hand.

"Hannah," he said, drawing me up short. "Let me try something. Let me just—"

His words ignited a memory—so vivid—and my cheeks flushed. I remembered Matt in my car, the first time he rode away from the cabin with me. Our heated kiss that turned into more. *Let me just . . . touch it, Hannah . . . let me put my mouth on it. Please . . .*

Seth's desperation sounded identical.

He pulled my body to his and hugged me. I thought he was going for a kiss, but no . . . just a hug? Or was he holding me? I stiffened in his arms. *Get a grip, Hannah. Hug Seth like you'd hug Nate.* Except Seth and Nate had nothing in common.

Hugging them had nothing in common . . .

I relaxed enough to wrap my arms around Seth's back. Oh, he

felt hunger-thin under his coat. Just like Matt—hard muscle and bone. Why didn't Seth have a girlfriend? Who took care of this wild boy? It could never be me. I had my own wild boy to take care of.

I gave Seth a gentle squeeze and heard him exhale.

"I miss him." He spoke into my hair. "Matt. Why did it happen this way?"

I swallowed a knot of guilt and laid my cheek against his chest. Seth pressed his hips to mine.

Shoppers parted around us, oblivious or annoyed.

Seth nudged me against a wall. My body bumped against his and I felt the unmistakable bulge of his arousal. I struggled, the friction making him twitch and expand. He gasped.

"Hannah, I—"

My pity turned to cold alarm.

"Get off me!"

With a violent shove, I launched myself out of Seth's grip. I sprinted into the crowd. I crashed into a stranger and bleated an apology.

"I'm sorry!" Seth called after me. "Hannah!"

I glanced wildly over my shoulder. Seth stared at me, his face ashen. I couldn't shake the sensation of him hardening against me. My panic. The serrated edge of adrenaline.

Seth wasn't chasing me, but I felt like he was. I kept running and looking back and colliding with shoppers.

And that terror—the thrill of it—*oh,* it almost felt good.

Chapter 26

MATT

I waited for Melanie at the end of the drive.

"The cabin is on your left," I told her. "It's your first left coming up the hill. You can't miss it, and anyway, I'll be standing at the end of the driveway."

I went out too early to wait.

I wasn't nervous or worried that Mel would bring a fleet of reporters. I should have been nervous and I should have been worried, but once I make up my mind about something, a steadiness comes to me like a cold needle in my arm.

I lit a cigarette and checked my watch. Mel lived in Iowa City. She packed and left yesterday, just hours after I called, and spent the night in Omaha. She called to say she was leaving Omaha around 9 A.M. my time. I Googled her route—an eight-and-a-half-hour drive to the cabin—which should put her on my doorstep at 5:30.

At 5:45 I was still standing in the cold, waiting. I'd smoked three cigarettes and was lighting a fourth when I heard tires on the snow. I walked onto the road to watch.

An electric blue Corolla crept up the hill toward me. I shielded my eyes against the headlights. It had to be Mel; after half an hour, not another car had come up the road.

She waved through the windshield—a thin wrist moving energetically.

I nodded and pointed to the driveway.

The sun sat at the edge of the mountains. Soon it would fall behind them. Excitement ghosted through me—this was when Hannah always arrived—and I tamped it down. This was *not* Hannah. This was Melanie, whom I'd invited to Colorado to chauffeur me around. "I can't drive," I explained, "but you can, and you need a job."

And you know my secret, and I know yours. That was the subtext of our arrangement.

Mel didn't require much coercing. After a few quick questions about logistics—"Where will I stay?" and "What happens when Hannah's around?"—she agreed.

She emerged from the car laughing.

First I saw her head. She had brilliant red hair, which she wore in a wavy bob. Her eyes were large and luminous, and looked larger for her small face. She was small all over. Petite shoulders, a slim torso, slender legs. A pixie.

She came bouncing over to me, the furred hood of her coat bobbing.

I stepped backward and nearly fell into a snowbank.

"This is the craziest thing I've ever done!" she shouted.

On the phone, Melanie gave an impression of polish and poise. Before me stood a girlish and excitable waif.

"Then I feel sorry for you," I murmured.

"Oh, stop it. What's the craziest thing *you've* ever done?"

I gave her a flat look. "Gee, Melanie, I dunno, that would be a close tie between acid and faking my own death."

She beamed up at me.

I frowned down at her. "Look, how old are you anyway?"

"Twenty-two." She arched a brow. "How old are you, old man?"

"Twenty-nine."

"Oh, dang." She giggled. "Climbing the hill, old sport."

Old sport? I cocked my head.

"Let me get your bag."

"Bags," she chimed.

Bags indeed. Two large, cheap suitcases and a duffel bag filled the trunk.

"Are you serious?" I hauled the suitcases to the front door. Mel brought the duffel. "I only need you for . . . a week or two, remember?"

Melanie hovered around the cabin. She ignored my remark and I dropped it. In truth, I had no idea how long I *needed* Mel, or how long I would want her around.

I paced behind the couch and watched her.

Unreal, to have another person in the cabin. And not Hannah, and not just any other person. The woman who published my book.

No, the girl who published my book.

She wore a fitted canvas jacket with fur trim, skinny jeans, and black Uggs. I really must not have lifted my head at the book signing, because Mel's face was a stranger's face.

At the moment, she was making a study of my desk. She smoothed a hand over my laptop, tapped the mouse, and then reached for my notebook.

"Don't touch it," I said quietly.

Melanie spun to face me. Her smile trembled and her voice faltered. "Sorry! So . . . curious about the writer's cave."

"The writer's cave?"

"Yeah. Haven't you heard that expression?"

"No." I walked around the couch and settled down, my ankle propped on my knee, eyes on Mel. I forced a small smile, which only seemed to exacerbate her nerves.

"Well, it's just a thing. Like, a thing people say." She gestured frenetically. "I know because I seriously *live* on the Internet. I have a blog. I blog about my hobbies—gardening, cooking, reading, dance. Anyway, the cave, uh, your writing space. Stupid jargon, basically it—"

I held up a hand. "I understand. Thank you."

Mel laughed too loud. She shifted her weight from foot to foot and avoided my stare.

"Are you hungry?" I said.

"No."

"Thirsty?"

"Nope nope nope."

"Suit yourself. There's food and drinks in the fridge." I pointed. "And the pantry. Cups are there, plates there. I won't cook for you, so make yourself at home."

Melanie nodded. She went to her duffel bag and began rummaging through it. I watched her with interest.

"Are you afraid to be here with me?" I said after a while. "You can stay at a hotel."

"No, I'm fine." She removed a book from her bag, then another, building a pile.

"Do your parents know you're out here?"

She snorted. "I'm twenty-two. I have an apartment with friends. My parents don't need to know everything I do anymore."

"You say twenty-two like that's old. You're a child to me."

"You're only seven years older." Melanie set the books on the coffee table, and I saw that they were . . . mine.

There was *Ten Thousand Nights* with its handsome jacket, and *Harm's Way, Mine Brook, The Silver Cord*, all in hardcover.

"You'll be surprised how much older you feel in seven years," I said. I leaned over the books and inspected them, smiling. "The gravity of living"—I flipped open *Mine Brook*—"increases exponentially."

Mel thrust a pen at me. I smirked and took it.

"You signed my paperbacks in Denver," she said, "and you didn't give me the time of day. I'm your biggest fan. So I'm trying again."

"Fair enough." In *Mine Brook*, I wrote: *For Melanie, my driver. M. PIERCE.*

"Sign your real name," she said.

I opened *Ten Thousand Nights* and scribbled: *For the persistent Melanie. W. PIERCE.*

"You're a dork."

"All right, all right." I laughed and rolled my eyes. I signed *The Silver Cord* and *Harm's Way* MATTHEW R. SKY JR.

Melanie traced her finger under the scrawl. "Junior," she said.

"Yes. Matthew was my father's name." I rose and moved away from the couch. "You can sit there, if you like. Before I forget—"

In the desk drawer was an envelope containing three thousand dollars, which I'd separated from my funds last night. I handed it to Mel. Her eyes widened at the feel of it; three thousand in fifties is quite a wad. "There's that. It's the amount I mentioned on the phone, and it should cover your travel expenses to and around here, and back to Iowa, with money to spare. If you stay on another week, I'll pay you again."

She fumbled with the envelope before shoving it in her duffel bag.

"You can count it," I said. I fetched a bottle of water from the fridge and set it on the coffee table. "Please drink that. You look pale."

"*You* look pale." She plopped onto the couch. "Your hair . . ."

"What about it?"

"It's so black. It makes you look a little pale."

"You're one to talk about hair color." I gestured to Mel's wild red locks. "That cannot humanly be natural."

She shrugged.

We stared at one another in a silent deadlock.

My God, a twenty-two-year-old. I wanted to kick myself. Had I known Mel was so young, I would never have invited her. It felt weird—wrong, almost—to have this girl at the cabin. I should keep my distance. Keep this as professional as possible.

I cleared my throat.

"I'm going to my room," I said. "Your room is down the hall to the left. Knock if you need anything." I checked my watch. "I was hoping to go to Denver tonight, but it's getting late and I'm sure you're tired of driving. We'll head down tomorrow."

"Sure thing." Mel began to unpack her duffel. I loitered and watched as she got out an iPad and a laptop and turned them on.

"What are you doing?"

"Making a hotspot." She grinned at me. "You know, so I—"

"I know what a fucking hotspot is. I mean *why?*"

"I have to update my blog."

"You can't blog about this!" I towered over Mel and glared at her laptop.

"Down, boy. I'm not blogging about *this*. I'm just writing about my trip."

"Typical." I threw up my hands. "Typical."

Melanie began to laugh, the sound high and fluting.

"What are you laughing at?" I snapped.

"If—if you could see yourself." She was breathless with laughter. "Oh, my gosh. You looked so mad just then, like you were going to attack my laptop." She gulped down another laugh. "Oh, wow. I'm sorry. Please don't have a heart attack."

"You know I trust you, Melanie." I stabbed a finger at her. "Don't fuck me over."

That chastened her. She frowned and looked at her feet.

I stalked toward the bedrooms, then doubled back to collect my notebook. I glanced around. "And don't . . . try anything funny. Don't make any trouble in here."

I closed the bedroom door behind me. I stood with my ear pressed against it.

No sound.

I stood like that for fifteen minutes. I couldn't shake the feeling that Mel had deceived me. She wasn't simply a fan of my writing. She had an online presence, some silly blog. If she wanted to out me as the author of *Night Owl*—and as being alive, for that matter—she had an audience ready to listen. Fuck.

Plus, she acted like a thirty-year-old on the phone. I'd been duped.

The smell of garlic drifted down the hall.

I stormed back out of my room.

Mel stood at the stove humming and doing salsa steps, her

hips swaying. I blinked. She'd removed her coat and wore a tight black sweater with a silver skull on the back.

"Stop dancing."

She whirled. A piece of scrambled egg flew from her spatula.

"Unless your name is Hannah, this is a no-ass-shaking zone."

I padded over to inspect Mel's cooking—a heap of scrambled eggs.

"Want some?" she said.

"No." I popped a piece of egg into my mouth. "Yes."

She made two plates. I pulled out a chair for Mel and took the opposite seat. As I was shoveling a forkful of eggs into my mouth, she said, "Do you mind if I say grace?"

I paused and regarded Mel from across the table. She held out her hand. After a space, I nodded and took it.

Her hand was tiny and feverishly hot.

For the first time in a long time, I lowered my head for prayer.

Mel began. "God is great, God is good. Let us thank Him for our food. Amen."

"Amen," I said, and I finally smiled.

Chapter 27

HANNAH

Chrissy dropped me off at the condo. We had a tense, silent ride home after I bawled her out for bailing on me. "Did something happen with Seth?" she said. I told her no. I told her it was the "principle of the matter."

My heart was still speeding.

I climbed the steps to my door and fit the key in the lock. I wondered how much longer Seth would be in town. He had a gig, he said. Singular. One gig. If I had to guess, it would happen tomorrow or Saturday.

So I needed to sneak into the agency by the back door tomorrow, get to the release party on Saturday, stay in on Sunday, and hope to hell that Seth was out of town by Tuesday.

Then I would spend the week watching *The Surrogate* destroy the bestseller list.

I smiled as I let myself into the condo. Yes, and then Friday would arrive and I would see Matt, and forget about all this confusion with Seth.

"You look happy."

I jumped and screamed, the sound somehow airless. *Oh,*

God. Oh, my God. There was a voice, a figure where none should be—a man in my condo—*this is happening, this is happening.*

All my instincts for self-preservation fled.

"Hannah, it's me."

My eyes adjusted marginally.

Matt stepped in front of a window and a streetlamp lit his profile.

I couldn't suppress my panic.

Matt . . . he shouldn't be here.

"It's me," he said again. "I didn't want to turn on any lights."

"How?" I said.

"I got a cab. Hannah, relax. I just got a cab. I had to see you."

I flattened myself against the wall. Adrenaline stormed through me and I laughed. God, I felt strange and wonderful. Terror mingled with desire, mingled with happiness.

Matt advanced, tugging me into his arms. I wriggled in his hold. Helplessly, I remembered the way Seth felt as he pressed me close—the way my struggling excited him.

Matt tilted his head. His eyes flashed in the dark.

I kissed him, my tongue lashing across his mouth.

"Do it," I whispered. "I want to fight it."

Understanding dawned on Matt's face. A smile moved his lips. My heart thumped, and I felt his beat harder against my chest.

"You remember our word?" he whispered.

I nodded. He meant our safe word, *peaches,* which I chose not long after we moved in together. Matt worried *peaches* might sound too much like *please,* but I wanted peaches, and so it was peaches.

Besides, I never needed the word. Not yet.

"Say it," he murmured.

"Peaches." I tried to pull out of his arms. They tightened around me and I gasped.

"Run away," he whispered in my ear. "Make this good for me, Hannah. Make me believe you don't want it. Fight me."

He gave me a push and I stumbled into the wall. My purse fell.

I was viscerally reminded of Seth's force, and of Nate with his black hair. *This hour is dreamlike,* Matt once said when I arrived at the cabin, *and nothing feels real in this light.* I understood as we faced off in the condo. Nothing feels real. The light goes out. We can be whatever we want to be.

I sprinted past Matt, my boots sliding on the hardwood.

The bitter taste of panic coated my tongue.

My night picked up where it left off at the mall. I was being chased. A stranger wanted me. He wanted to touch me in the most intimate way, and I wouldn't let him.

I flew into the office and locked the door. Papers rustled in the dark. I never worked in this room, never sat in this room. The memory of Matt lived here.

I crouched in a ball behind the desk, my breasts pressed into my knees.

And I waited.

In the silence, I heard the loud rush of my breath and hammering heart.

"Come out, come out," Matt called, "wherever you are."

His voice echoed eerily through the condo. His footfalls sounded in the hall.

I scooted under the desk.

He tried the knob—lightly at first, then harder, the brass rattling.

He pressed against the door. "In here, is it?"

Then came a long, weighted silence, and a *crack* like a shot. I yelped and scrambled out from under the desk. The door hung open at a slant. Matt stood in the frame rubbing his shoulder. When he saw me, his eyes widened.

I leapt past him.

He caught me, and the air burst out of my lungs. We went down struggling.

I didn't need to remember Matt telling me to fight him. I felt real fear—cold terror.

I twisted onto my stomach on the floor and scrabbled at the

wood, but I couldn't crawl away. Matt pinned me with his body. His strong legs locked against mine, and with one powerful hand he held down my neck. Air whistled through my windpipe.

"There you are," he crooned. "Ready for me now?"

I kicked and spat. I clawed at the arm holding me down. With his free hand, Matt yanked up my sweater dress. He squeezed my breast through the cup of my bra.

Unbidden desire wet my thong.

"No," I moaned, and a low thrill went through me. "Stop!"

"Your tits feel good," Matt growled in my ear.

He squeezed harder, fondling me with his hand trapped between my chest and the floor. He pushed up my bra and pinched my nipples.

I rasped.

Fuck, that felt good . . .

Matt's hand dove down the back of my leggings, between my legs, inside my thong. I squirmed furiously. I was practically humping the floor, slamming my ass against Matt and driving my hips into the wood, and the motion played right into his hands—literally.

He poised two fingers at my entrance; I jammed my sex onto them and cried out.

"Stop!" My voice was hoarse.

On some level, I knew that Jamie might hear us from her condo, but I didn't care. I screamed bloody murder while Matt laughed and fingered me.

He told me I must want it. He told me how wet I was.

I writhed on his fingers, trying to get away and succeeding only in stimulating myself.

The pressure of Matt's body lifted. I had a moment. A moment to move. I gave a great push. Matt's fingers, though, were hooked over my leggings and thong, and when I lunged forward, the fabric dragged down my thighs.

The cool air of the condo hit my bare ass. I moaned.

Matt pounced on me. He wound my hair around his hand and yanked.

The skin of my inner thighs was slippery with lust, and though I squeezed my legs together tight, I felt the head of Matt's cock pressing between them.

Damn . . . I wasn't the only one enjoying this.

I closed my eyes and panted. "Please. No . . ." God, but it felt good to say *no.* Why?

"Shhh," he whispered. "You see how hard I am? Now, where do you want it?"

Between my clenched thighs, Matt's cock felt larger than ever. It throbbed and I groaned. My arms were sore. I couldn't catch my breath.

If this were real, would I give up the fight? I felt exhausted, and Matt wasn't even winded. His superior strength overruled me.

"Where?" he taunted. He nudged his cock against my pussy and then up, toward my ass. My breath caught. "If you don't say your pussy, I'll put it in your ass."

"No, no . . ."

"Say it."

"My pussy," I whispered.

Matt penetrated me in one thrust. My body tightened, resisting the invasion, and my low, humiliated moan cut away when he wrapped a hand around my neck. My eyes rolled. My nostrils flared. Fuck . . . this felt amazing.

Matt moved against me ruthlessly, and he whispered *yes, yes . . . God, yes,* lost in his private ecstasy. I stopped struggling. I saw spots, white and yellow. Matt hadn't undressed; he'd only freed his cock. The zipper on his jeans scraped my thigh. Our bodies slapped together and thumped against the floor. I lapped at his palm. I was close, so close.

"It's over," he groaned. "Just lie here and take it. It's over baby, it's over."

He was right.

I came—a spasm that squeezed Matt's hardness, then pushed with equal force—and made a sticky mess on the floor. My pleasure was a throaty howl.

"Fuck!" he snarled. "*Ah*—I'm coming, Hannah, Hannah—" As

he sometimes liked to do, Matt pulled out and jerked off, and he came on my bottom.

I felt his pleasure dripping down my crack. It trickled over my swollen pussy.

We lay together on the floor collecting our wits.

I caressed Matt's face and he checked me over for scrapes.

A moment ago, he was convincing in his force. Now he was convincing in his gentle concern. I didn't ask myself which was the real Matt. People are light and dark.

"Who knew?" he murmured, kissing my throat. "You like it so rough, Hannah."

"I didn't know until today. Hey, you like it, too . . ."

"Mm, you noticed." He smiled and pulled me to my feet, rolling my leggings back up and smoothing my sweater back down. When he saw my wet spot on the floor, his smile turned to a satisfied smirk. "You *really* enjoyed it . . ."

"Is that horrible?"

"Not horrible. It wasn't real. It's not real." Matt tucked my head under his chin and stroked my hair. "It's a fantasy, and you trust me, don't you?"

I nodded. With the euphoria of orgasm still moving through me, it was easy to forget my troubles: Nate, Seth, and the fact that Matt had risked everything by taking a cab here.

"What we do in our bed is no one's business," he said.

"On our floor," I mumbled.

He laughed, the sound purring in his chest. "Yes, on our floor, too. Behind closed doors."

I grinned impishly. "Behind broken doors."

At that, we dissolved into laughter. We inspected the office door. One of the barrel hinges was loose, torn out of the frame. The mechanism inside the knob was busted.

"Oops." Matt jiggled the knob. His eyes were bright, his expression amused and apologetic. *Sheepish Matt . . . so fucking adorable.*

"Baby, did . . . did you use your shoulder?"

He glanced at me. "Mm. I was feeling manly. Should have used my foot . . ."

"Oh, sweetheart." I ruffled his hair.

"I'll fix it. Tomorrow or something." He took my hand and we went through the condo closing blinds. When we were sure no one could see in, I turned on a lamp in the living room. Laurence dashed back and forth in his hutch.

"He's excited to see you." I smiled.

"He's fat and he wants a treat." Matt fed raisins through the wire mesh.

More Matt adorableness: pretending he didn't love that rabbit to death.

I sat on the couch and watched Matt prowl around the condo. He glared at everything. He studied the plants and books, opened the kitchen cupboards, looked through the fridge.

"Feels good to be here," he announced.

"You look good here, Matt." I worried a pill on my sweater. "Like you belong here."

"Don't I look good everywhere?" At last, he returned to me. He wore a small self-deprecating smile. He knelt at my feet and pushed apart my knees. He rubbed my thighs and stared up at me. *Beautiful,* I thought. *Larger than life.* Matt filled the rooms of our condo with his anger and his electricity. Did everyone see that, or did I see it because I loved him?

I covered his hands with mine.

"Matt, did you seriously take a cab all the way out here?"

"Mm. Don't worry, Hannah." He produced a hat and sunglasses from his coat pocket. A scarf dangled around his neck. "I wore my disguise."

I sighed and laughed.

"I feel like a spy." He grinned.

Matt continued massaging my thighs, pushing my dress higher and higher. He looked good on his knees, and I was exhausted, so I let it go. If Matt wanted to take a cab from the cabin to Denver, I couldn't stop him. He couldn't be stopped.

The tempo of his hands changed. His expression sobered. Subtle changes I recognized.

I slid off the couch and onto the floor with him. I touched the front of his jeans. Beneath my fingers, his cock twitched and expanded. He exhaled softly.

"Hannah . . ."

I grasped a handful of his hair so that I could hold his head steady. I didn't want him hiding his face against my neck. I wanted to watch his eyes, his mouth.

His lips parted as I touched the shape of him. His arousal grew.

"Lift your shirt," I whispered.

Matt complied. In rare moments, he let me call the shots. He gathered his coat and T-shirt up his chest, and I leaned in to flick my tongue over his nipples.

His cock strained into my hand. Now I could grip it through his jeans and boxers, a taut prison of fabric. I handled him gently as I sucked on his nipple. He began to tremble, but he wouldn't ask me to stop. So proud. I knew how sensitive his nipples were. *Almost too sensitive,* he told me once. I bit down and pulled on his other nipple. He hissed. His cock tightened.

"H-Hannah. Take it out . . ."

"Look at it with me," I whispered. I tongued saliva over his nipples and lifted my head. His expression was tense—jaw clenched, brows knit, nostrils flared. He nodded and my fingernails scraped against his scalp. I wouldn't let him go. I wouldn't let him hide.

While Matt held his jacket, exposing his toned abs and chest, I undid his jeans and tugged at his boxers until his cock sprang free. He sighed again and closed his eyes. If he were given to blushing, I think he would have blushed then.

"Matt, I love it," I said. I palmed his smooth sac and he groaned. "Please, don't close your eyes. Look at it with me. I miss you. I miss this."

His eyelids lifted partway. He watched my hand and his erection, which stood out like a ramrod between us. The golden hair around the base was neatly trimmed. Here, even here, Matt was beautiful. The skin of his shaft was velvet, subtly veined, and thick and long. It ended in the sleek bell of his head, which leaked cum at the slightest attention.

I watched the fluid gather on his tip.

"Look," I said. I trailed my hand up his shaft to his head and rolled my thumb over it, smearing the cum. He trembled. I brought my thumb to my mouth and spread Matt's desire like gloss on my lips. I licked them clean while he watched.

Again, I gathered his cum on the pad of my finger. I rubbed it on his nipple and he moaned. "Hannah, enough."

I wanted to jack him off and watch him while I did it, but Matt wanted to be inside me again. My hold over him broke. He dropped his shirt and took my hand. He rose unsteadily.

Without a word, he led me to our bedroom.

Chapter 28

MATT

On Saturday evening, Hannah dressed in a black-and-white skirt suit for the release party. I tied a silk scarf around her neck to hide my love bites. We'd been in bed almost nonstop since my impromptu arrival, emerging only to bathe and eat.

And the sex was different—tinged with violence. Hannah struggled every time, and I fucked her hard while she begged me to stop. It gave me a terrible thrill.

"Why do you have to go so early?" I pulled her into my arms. "It's my book you're celebrating. I should have some say in this."

I kissed her neck and cupped her ass. She wriggled against my hands. *Such a tease.*

"Because," she said with a sigh, "I promised Pam I'd help set up, like I said. Several times."

"Let me look at your ass." I turned Hannah around and bit the back of her neck. I tucked her bottom against my groin. "You wouldn't leave me alone with a hard-on, would you?"

"I might." She grinned over her shoulder. "Lube's in the bed-side table."

"You're a bad bird."

We fooled around halfheartedly, and then Hannah left. I was instantly miserable.

I wandered the condo, trying to comprehend Hannah's life apart from me. Nothing looked different. There was her yoga mat, her exercise ball, a few manuscripts from work. The rooms were tidy. I found leftovers from various meals in the fridge.

I checked the wall safe. Everything was in order: the cash, her TracFone, the unit cards.

Hannah's life went on without me.

I peeked through the blinds at Denver by night. The shops were lit. I saw friends barhopping and heard car horns honking. People rushing to their Saturday evening plans.

And me with nothing to do, dead to everyone but Hannah. And Melanie . . . my "cab."

I called her.

" 'Sup, Cabin Fever? Hey, can I call you that?"

I sneered. The new nickname was too apropos.

"Checking in," I said.

"Uh-huh . . ."

"Mm, can you blame me? You're alone in a new city, twenty-two, prone to doing very illegal things on the Internet."

"And you're bored and lonely," Mel said.

"What? No." *Yes.*

"I know Hannah's at the release party. You told me, Matt."

"I'm not bored. I'm home on a Saturday night. I thought *you* might be bored."

"Sure." Mel chuckled. She was silent for a while, and then she clicked her tongue. "I'll pick you up in a few minutes, okay? I am pretty bored, come to think."

"I want to be back by eight." I think Mel knew she was doing me a favor, and I didn't care. "And don't meet me out front. I'll go out back."

"Fine."

"Fine." I hung up.

I killed time cleaning Laurence's hutch, then bundled up in

my coat, hat, scarf, and sunglasses, and slipped out of the complex by the back exit. Mel's Corolla idled at the corner.

I climbed in. "The color of this car, it's like a neon sign. Ridiculous." I was trying not to smile. The condo wasn't *home* anymore, not without Hannah, and it felt good to escape.

"Whoa, what happened to you?"

"Hm?" I adjusted my sunglasses. After wrestling with Hannah over the last two days, I looked a little worse for wear. She'd inadvertently elbowed my eye, purpling the orbit. A bruise darkened my jaw. Scratches lined my neck and I had hickies and other bruises all over my body. Hannah had a few marks, too, but no black eye, thank God. "Fight club," I mumbled.

"Tough love." Mel sighed. "Lucky girl."

"Drive."

"Okay, yeesh." She pulled away from the condo. "Wanna . . . watch TV? I've got HBO at the hotel. I have a deck of cards, too."

I glanced at Mel as she navigated Denver. She was a good driver, confident on unfamiliar roads. She didn't make one wrong turn during the two-hour drive from the cabin.

Tonight, she'd straightened her red hair. It was thick and glossy like shampoo commercial hair. She wore a tight puffy vest and a hooded sweater beneath, the hood fur-trimmed. Fur again. She owned a jacket with fur and furry boots.

"You like fur," I said.

"Profound observations from the late great author. So, the hotel?"

"No. I don't think we should . . . be in your hotel room."

"*Oookay.* Even though we're staying at the cabin together?"

"The cabin is different."

"Am I too tempting, Mr. Sky?" She flipped her hair. I snorted. "I'm kidding, kidding. I've seen Hannah. I know I've got no chance."

"I didn't realize you wanted a chance."

"Oh, please." Mel turned the wheel on a whim, taking us closer to the heart of Denver. "You're attractive, you're unmarried, you

have an actual brain, and you've got that whole"—she gestured—
"brooding artist thing going on. Do I need to spell it out for you?
Nine in ten women would want a chance."

"That's not true." I shifted on my seat. "And I don't have a
thing going on. You make it sound pretentious."

"You know what I mean."

"You're cute, Mel. You shouldn't have any trouble finding
someone. And even if circumstances were different—" I shook my
head. The lights of the city scrolled past, muted by my sunglasses.
"You're too young for me."

Melanie grew quiet.

A crowd crossed the street in front of us, friends laughing
and shouting.

I glanced at Mel. The excitement was gone from her face.

I meant it when I said Mel was cute—she was on par with
Hannah, at least—but the world is full of beautiful women, and
love, which starts as a feeling, always ends as a choice.

A familiar sign caught my eye, winking blue in the night. LOT
49, BAR AND LOUNGE.

I tapped the dash. "But you're not too young to drink," I said.

Ten minutes later, Mel and I sat in a private booth at the back of
the Lot. I still wore my winter regalia, which kept Mel giggling. I
even had on my sunglasses.

"You look ridiculous. Like, even more suspicious." Melanie
sipped her pint. She'd tried to order a rum and Coke, the drink of
drinkers who have no idea what they're doing, and I intervened
to order her a vanilla stout with a shot of blackberry whiskey.

I looked around and removed my shades.

"*Everyone* in Denver knows the story of M. Pierce," I whispered. "Plus, I mentioned this place in *Night Owl*. Can't be too
fucking careful."

"Hey, you wanted to come in here." She had foam on her upper lip. I gestured. "What, you like my mouth? Oh, my, Mr. Sky."

"Don't say my name!" I prodded her mouth with a napkin. "Did you even read *Night Owl,* or did you just publish it like a crazy person?"

"I read it." Melanie waggled her eyebrows. "This is where you saw the luscious Hannah for the first time."

"Ha. Luscious is right."

I relaxed as the minutes passed and slipped off my hat and shrugged out of my coat. The bar was warm and no one gave a damn about Mel and me. When I ordered another pint for her, the tender didn't look at me twice.

We chatted about Mel's blog, her unfinished four-year degree, and crappy temp jobs she'd taken in recent months. She'd worked in a concrete call center where she had to punch in and out for bathroom breaks. She'd taken surveys and picked up trash in parks.

"This is by far my best gig," she said.

I felt pretty fucking sorry for her then, and I wished she could keep on cashing in with *Night Owl.* Too bad.

Bob Dylan's "This Wheel's on Fire" started to play. I swayed to the ragged, honkytonk tune, and Melanie laughed at me.

"Let's dance." She grabbed my hand and hauled me out of the booth.

"No! Jesus. Not on the floor."

I held her hand and she spun. She teased her fingers up her side and sashayed over to me. I smirked and shook my head.

"You've got a Rita Hayworth thing going on," I said.

"High praise. You're not bad yourself, M."

"Yeah? My aunt forced us into lessons. I quit after a month."

I danced Mel in lazy circles by the booth. My training kicked in and I smiled at her as we moved. It felt good, and we danced through two more songs. Whenever Mel got close to me, she rubbed her slight body along mine. The gesture was subtle enough to be unconscious, though I couldn't be sure. The alcohol put a pretty glow on her face. Now and then, she leaned her cheek against my chest and sighed.

As we left the bar, I said, "Let me drive back to the condo."

Mel handed me her keys without hesitation. I raised a brow.

"You know I don't have a license on me, right?"

"Yeah." She shrugged. "You know Denver better than I do. Just don't get pulled over."

I checked the time as I got behind the wheel. It was 6:48. Hannah wouldn't be home until eight at the earliest.

The car rumbled under me and I sighed. "I miss driving."

"I bet."

"You mind?" I held up a cigarette. "Your buzz is making me jealous."

"Nope, but share it with me," she said.

"You can have your own."

"No, share it with me. I want to be able to say I shared a cigarette with M. Pierce."

"M. Pierce, that's not me." I smoked a bit of the cigarette and passed it to Mel.

"Okay, then I want to say"—she took a drag—"I shared a smoke with Matthew Sky."

"Not me either."

"Cal the demon?"

She passed it back. I tasted her minty lip gloss on the filter.

"Nah, not Cal. A demon, maybe."

"Cabin Fever!" She laughed.

I grinned and stepped on the gas, pushing the Corolla fast on an empty street.

Melanie was right; I knew Denver better than she did. Better than most. I knew how to cut corners, and where to get what. I knew the best restaurants, the coolest bookstores, the hottest clubs. But I was like a fugitive in Denver, and I had peace at the cabin. I needed peace. I needed Hannah. Why wouldn't she come away?

"Whatever trips your trigger," I said. I handed Mel the cigarette with a gesture that said, *Finish it.* "That's how it goes, right? You are who people decide you are."

I cruised around Denver for half an hour. Mel played Lorde and Banks and other artists I didn't recognize.

By seven thirty I was on the outskirts of the city. The road ahead drove straight into the prairie and the abrupt darkness. I slowed the car.

I felt a small, hot touch through the denim of my jeans, and I glanced down to see Mel's hand on my thigh. How long had it been there? It was time to turn back. I pulled over, the car crunching to a standstill on the gravelly roadside.

"What are you doing?" I murmured.

"What are *you* doing?" Mel said. Her fingers drifted up and brushed my cock. I seized her wrist. My body betrayed me; my shaft stirred beneath Mel's hand.

"Don't," I said. "You'll only regret it."

"How do you know you won't regret stopping me, Matt? Look at me . . ."

I humored Mel, inclining my head and rolling my eyes toward her. I still had a steely grip on her wrist. By now that grip must have been painful, but Mel moved her fingers anyway, exploring the shape of my arousal.

"Mm. *Stop.*" I hissed through clenched teeth. *She's drunk,* I thought, *and that's to blame.*

So what was to blame for my growing hard-on? I met Mel's gaze, and I cursed inwardly for putting myself in this position.

"You're saying stop," she whispered, "but your body . . ."

My stomach pitched. Sickening. So what if my dick was getting hard? Mel was assaulting me—I didn't fucking want this—and I wasn't about to take advantage of her.

I removed her hand carefully, though I wanted to fling it. I twisted away and adjusted my dick. *Fuck* . . . even my own touch burned, brushing over that stiff skin. *Calm the fuck down* . . .

"I know damn well what my body is doing," I snapped, too angry to feel embarrassed. "It's doing what it fucking should do when a pretty girl grabs my dick. And you're making a fool of yourself."

"Give me a chance," Mel pleaded.

"A chance for what? I'm with Hannah."

"I'm making a fool of myself for you." Melanie's voice became very small. I knew that if I looked at her, I would find her eyes imploring. I would pity her, and pity is dangerous. "I want you, Matt, and . . . I'd always regret it if I didn't try, okay? I'm sorry."

"You're sorry?" I laughed. "Perfect. You tried, and you failed. Are you happy now?"

"No. You don't see my point."

"What's your fucking point?" My dick was finally settling down. I exhaled roughly and glared at the night. A driving melody came from the speakers, and Banks sang something about love being a waiting game. Her sultry voice and the song's pounding rhythm weren't helping.

"My point is that I might be good for you. *I* might be the one for you, but you won't even consider me. I mean . . . why are you hiding in a cabin without Hannah? Why do you have to sneak into Denver to see her?" Mel's words tumbled out too fast; her speech sounded rehearsed. "It's because she won't run away with you, isn't it? But I would. I would do that for you happily, Matt. I really like . . . being around you. I don't need anything else."

A smirk twisted my lips. Mel barely knew me, and she thought she wanted me.

How immature . . .

How ridiculous.

And yet, as I glowered at the night, I considered the truth of her words. Hannah *wouldn't* run away with me. But Mel would, and this total darkness could swallow us now . . . tonight.

I suspended my irritation long enough to feel the night beckoning.

I heard a silvery click—Mel's seat belt unlocking—and then she was on top of me, straddling my lap.

"Melanie," I snarled, "get the fuck—"

Her mouth covered mine. Between layers of fabric, her small breasts pillowed against my chest. Her hand darted between my legs and my cock sprang back to life, straining into her palm. *Fucking Melanie! And fucking me!* Why was I reacting this way? I tore my mouth off hers, but a soft, unbidden moan slipped from me.

Mel took my moan for encouragement. She began to stroke me through my jeans, coaxing my arousal into a raging erection.

"Stop!" I shoved her, hard, and she spilled over the console and crumpled on her seat. I lurched out of the car and slammed the door. I stalked into the grass.

"Ah, fuck," I whispered. *"Fuck."*

A few yards from the car, I stopped. I kneaded my neck and struggled to relax. In the cold night, I felt a hundred degrees.

I took deep breaths, one after another, and stared up at the stars, zillions of glittering flecks visible in the prairie darkness. My God, I wanted to disappear. Disappear completely. I felt that I stood right at the edge of reality, or maybe I had walked off that edge. Maybe I had succeeding in dying after all.

The thought didn't frighten me.

My arousal cooled along with my anger, and I strode back to the car. I thought of Hannah, who was a woman and not a child. I remembered our violent passion over the last few days and how it fed this dark appetite of mine.

She satisfied me—completely.

With that thought in my heart, I opened Mel's door and dropped the keys on her lap. I climbed into the back of the car, buckled my seat belt, and closed my eyes.

"Drive me back to the condo," I said quietly. "That's all you're here to do, Mel. To drive. Don't forget it."

Chapter 29

HANNAH

'I was on my fifth glass of champagne when I saw Seth.

I don't know why I hit the bubbly so hard that night. Maybe it was because Pam kept calling me her assistant. I thought of myself as a lot more than Pam's assistant. Sure, I'd only worked at the agency for nine months, but I was already responding to queries, vetoing manuscripts, overseeing contract negotiations—doing the work of an associate agent, at least.

"This is my assistant," Pam said to a group of distinguished-looking ladies, and their eyes slid over me like a hand clears dust.

Assistant. Helper. Definitely not the future partner of Pamela Wing and Laura Granite.

And seriously, there was nothing to *do* at the party. No door prizes. No trivia. No reading. Just a bunch of literary types milling and getting toasted.

I let the crowd pinball me around. I caught snatches of gossip.

Seven figures, someone said.

Thought she was a shoo-in, said another.

James Frey waiting to happen. Short stories. No, they aren't on speaking terms.

No one was talking about Matt or *The Surrogate*. In fact, except for a table displaying the book and a picture of Matt, this could hardly be called his book event. More like Pam and Laura's excuse to hold a literary soiree.

Meanwhile, the man himself was hiding in my condo.

And I missed him. I should have stayed with him. Sweet, strange, broody Matt . . .

I found myself staring down at oysters on a bed of ice. The slippery-looking, discolored meat made me feel ill. The other snacks on the table were dwindling—toasted brioche with salmon, caprese canapés, focaccia cake, and a variety of tartlets.

"I wouldn't eat seafood in Colorado," said a voice too close to my ear.

I downed my drink and turned to face him. Seth.

My head spun—or the room spun. Oof . . . too much champagne.

I backed into the table. Seth caught me by the shoulder.

"Hannah, are you all right?"

"Get . . . away from me," I mumbled. "You are *sick* and *perverted* and third time's a . . . three strikes . . ." I set my glass on the table.

Three strikes and you're out, is what I was getting at. Seth had tried to kiss me in New Jersey. He had tried to dry-hump me at the mall. I wasn't giving him a chance for strike three.

"Just go away." I gestured.

"It was an accident," he said, his face pulling into a grieved expression. "I'm sorry . . ."

My vision focused and Seth loomed. For once, he looked elegant in a fitted dark suit. Alarm bells went off in my heart. *Run away. Danger.* His silky hair hung loose around his face, and I felt the most infuriating urge to run my fingers through it.

Seth wore the wild-child look too well . . .

"Whoa there," I slurred. "Fancying it up."

"Why are you drunk? Is someone bothering you?"

"Just you." I pointed at him and accidentally dug my finger

into his chest. I lurched back. Seth caught me before I took down the hors d'oeuvres table.

"I think you need to go home, Hannah. Did you drive?"

"Oh no, you don't." I stumbled on my heels. The alcohol seemed to hit me all at once. "Is this where you suavely offer to drive me home? Sketchbag." I snickered at my new word. *Sketch-ball + douche bag*?

"I'll call you a cab, if that's what you want. I won't let you drive like this."

"Miss Catalano. Fancy meeting you here."

I turned to see Aaron Snow approaching, his black hair and pale face unmistakable. The faintest scar showed where Seth had split his lip.

"Just the other most person I wanted to see," I mumbled.

Okay, Seth was right. I needed to get home. The reporter was here, and I could barely speak straight.

Aaron offered his hand. I shook it loosely.

At the cemetery, with his camera and his flailing, Aaron Snow had looked like a weasel. Tonight he looked more formidable. His suit matched Seth's in cut and color. He was clean, sober, and super alert.

"Back up, pal," Seth growled.

Aaron flicked a glance at Seth.

"I apologize for the scene at the memorial, Miss Catalano. I acted unspeakably."

I nodded numbly. All I could think was, *This serves me right for not checking the guest list*. Seth Sky *and* Aaron Snow were invited to the release party? Fucking hell . . .

"I decked you once, Snow. I'd love to do it again." Seth moved between Aaron and me.

"Would you please stop being . . . barbaric?" I said. "Mr. Snow, what do you want?"

"I want to share a theory with you. I'm putting together a new article for my paper."

"*No Stone Unturned*?" I laughed. "Not quite a paper yet, is it?"

"We have a print edition. You're right, though. Mostly we operate online."

"Must have a massive staff." My hand flew to my mouth. Wow, I was being an asshole.

"Can we talk in another room?" Aaron said.

"All ri—"

"*No,*" Seth said.

We all glared at one another.

"Then I'm coming," Seth added. "You're not going to be alone with this freak."

"Look who's talking," I muttered.

We moved into one of the libraries, which was more like a sitting room where Pam and Laura stored books by their authors. I left the door ajar.

Aaron went to the shelves and began hunting, and shortly he said, "Perfect, good."

Seth refused to sit. He stood by the table like a bodyguard, arms folded. Aaron and I settled across from one another.

"Okay, Mr. Snow." I gestured. "Wow me."

"Read the draft of my article. Here." Aaron pulled an iPad from his laptop bag, swiped at the screen, and pushed it over to me.

I kneaded my temples. *Focus, Hannah, focus . . .*

I squinted and began to read.

The title of the article jarred me wide awake.

M. Pierce, **Author of** *Night Owl*

"This is *not* true," I said. "Whatever you—"

"Keep reading." Aaron leafed through the books he'd retrieved from the shelf. They were Matt's books, including *The Surrogate.*

I kept reading.

New evidence suggests that *Night Owl,* a self-published erotic romance relating events in the life of Matthew Sky, was written and possibly published by Sky himself.

Since *Night Owl* appeared online in January 2014, readers

and critics have speculated about the identity of the author, who
uses the pen name W. Pierce.

Sky used the pen name M. Pierce throughout his career.

In a revealing interview with Wendy Haswell of Geneva,
New York, a woman named in *Night Owl* . . .

"Hannah, are you all right?" Seth touched my shoulder. I
shuddered.

As I read on, I saw that Wendy—the woman who transcribed
for Matt in Geneva, the woman at the farm—confirmed the details in *Night Owl* as truth.

And there was more. Aaron drew parallels between *Night
Owl* and Matt's other books. He established the time line of
events in *Night Owl*. He listed legitimate landmarks: Matt's apartment, our condominium, the Granite Wing Agency, the cabin in
Geneva, Lot 49.

The article was rhetoric, and each point built Aaron's un-
assailable thesis: that Matthew Sky, M. Pierce, wrote *Night Owl*.

And maybe that revelation wasn't a big deal, but the last lines
of the article were.

> This new information leaves readers wondering: Is *Night
> Owl* fiction or autobiography? Is Matthew Sky alive and pub-
> lishing under the pen name W. Pierce? Was Sky's ambiguous
> death a cover for his disappearance?
>
> *No Stone Unturned* continues to follow the . . .

I pushed the iPad away.

"And look at this," Aaron said, passing open books to me.
"Here, this phrase from *Night Owl,* it's repeated in *The Surrogate.*
Then here, in *Mine Brook*—"

"Stop." I covered my face. "I'm . . . I'm too dizzy for this."

Seth helped me stand and I let him. I needed the help.

And then, because I was drunk and desperate to throw Aaron
off the trail, I said, "You're wrong. You're wrong because *I* wrote
Night Owl. I wrote it, you dumb ass."

Aaron's eyes widened.

"What?" Seth looked equally stunned.

"I'll explain *later*," I hissed. "Let's go. Take me home."

At the door, I turned to take a parting shot. Aaron was smiling and calmly shelving Matt's books. I frowned. It didn't work. He didn't believe me. On the contrary, my rash statement seemed to have given him some private pleasure.

"And if you publish what I just told you, I'll sue your stupid magazine. I have a good lawyer." I swallowed. "And you better not publish that article either, because it's . . . er . . . defamation. Haven't you had enough of your stupid online magazines shut down? Give up."

Seth guided me out of the agency to my car. I slumped against the door. My heart was leaping in my chest. *Fuck.* I had to tell Matt what just happened. I had to get home.

"Drive me home," I said.

Seth didn't move. He stood on the sidewalk, hands in pockets and eyes narrowed.

"You lied to me," he said. "You told me you didn't write that book."

"Oh, get over it." I wanted to scream. "I didn't publish it, okay? I *wrote* it. It was stupid, silly, whatever. And yeah, it was kind of influenced by Matt's books. I never meant for it to get online. My e-mail was hacked. I . . . I e-mailed the story to myself. For backup."

Seth frowned. Zero belief in that frown.

"That's what happened." I groaned. "I didn't tell because it's embarrassing, okay? That story was meant for me and Matt and no one else. I don't care if you don't believe me, just drive me home or—or don't!" I threw a hand in the air. "I'll call a fucking cab."

I rummaged through my purse hysterically.

"Get in the car," Seth said. He snatched my keys.

Finally. Seth Sky doing something useful.

I gave drunken directions to the condo and Seth drove in silence. After a few wrong turns, we pulled into the lot.

He climbed out of the car with me.

"Wait—what are you doing?" I backed away, bumping into another car.

"Walking you to your door."

"No, no, no." I staggered away from Seth. "I appreciate the ride, but—"

"Would you quit your whining?" Seth seized my shoulders and hauled me toward the complex. I stumbled along.

I told Aaron Snow that I wrote *Night Owl*.

Matt was in my condo.

Seth was walking me to the door.

And I was too drunk to process the implications of all this. My mind stalled.

I started to laugh. Everything was so fucked-up. So many lies. A castle of lies. And Matt was its king, and I was the queen, holding together our elaborate deception.

"Darling, you're going to be feeling this tomorrow," Seth said. He helped me up the stairs to my door and unlocked it for me. My fine-motor skills were gone.

"Hey, so . . ." I blocked the doorway. "What—how much longer are you in town?"

"I'm leaving tomorrow. Our show was last night." Seth peered into the condo. "Hannah, did you leave candles burning in here?"

"Huh?" I turned. *Oh, shit.*

Matt was nowhere in sight, but he'd lit a dozen candles on the coffee table and several more in the kitchen. The prelude to a romantic evening, under any other circumstances.

"You're crazy. You could burn this whole fucking complex down."

"What's up . . . what's up with your tattoos anyway?" I braced my hands against the doorframe. Seth didn't seem to notice me grasping at straws. He kept looking into the semidarkness of the condo, then looking at me.

"Goldengrove is . . . from a poem. So is 'the penny world.' It's nothing." Seth narrowed his eyes. "It's about stuff we leave behind."

"Stuff?" My voice trembled. I wanted to slam the door in Seth's face, but I felt that if I lowered my arms, he would walk right into my condo.

"Yeah, stuff. Youth, innocence, ignorance. The best times, like—" He hesitated, his dark eyes fixing on my face. "Like when my parents were alive, and our family was normal."

"Normal but loaded." I laughed shakily. *Wow.* Inappropriate Comments 101.

"Hannah, did . . . did you do all this for me?" Seth nodded toward the candlelit living room. "Did you know I would be at the party tonight?"

"What? No. God, no."

"You did, didn't you? And that's why you're drunk. A little too much liquid courage, right?" Seth smiled, wonderment and disbelief on his face. "Hannah . . ."

He leaned down and crushed his lips to mine. The kiss stunned me to stillness—the heat and hunger of it. The loneliness behind it.

"Kiss me," he mumbled, pressing me into the condo with his body.

When Seth slid his tongue between my teeth, I bit down—hard.

"Fuck!" He reeled away.

I backed into a wall. *Oh, shit.* I could see the night cohering into Seth's deluded reality: I was the oversexed author of *Night Owl*, I was falling for him, and I was sending him signals with my drunken bumbling and candlelit condo. *Shit, shit . . .*

Seth cringed and touched his mouth.

"What . . . is going on here?" At the sound of Matt's voice—dry, measured, and low with rage—I collapsed. I slid down the wall as he materialized from the hallway. He looked like he could kill.

Seth blanched. His expression was horrible to see. First emptiness—a face devoid of emotion—unable or unwilling to comprehend. Then hurt and a flash of confusion. How could this be? Eyes wide, mouth open in fear. *Am I seeing things?*

Finally, anger and understanding. Seth's features resolved into a mask of hate.

"You son of a bitch," he said. His voice shook with emotion. "You son of a bitch."

Shadows darkened Matt's face. He looked around, as if there might be a fourth guest, and then between me and his brother.

"What is this?" he said. "Don't touch her. Don't you fucking touch her."

"Matt, it's nothing," I said. "Seth just—"

I don't know who moved first, though both men were on the edge of violence. Hands clenched. Jaws tight. Eyes wild.

Someone swung and they began to grapple. Matt got Seth around the middle and slammed him into a wall. A picture fell. Glass shattered. He hit Seth across the face once, twice, then Seth kicked and Matt fell. He kicked again, driving his foot into Matt's gut. Matt groaned.

Matt rose and they collided, huffing and shouting as the sickening thump of blows filled the room. "Stop it!" I screamed. "Stop it, stop!"

I scrambled to my feet and launched myself at the brothers. Between inebriation and the flashing candlelight, I couldn't see a damn thing. I hit hot muscle and tangled limbs.

"Stop!" I shrieked.

A fist plowed into my face. My head belted back. I heard a wheeze and a crunch like the sound of a broken accordion. White spots exploded before my eyes.

Someone said, "You hit her! You son of a bitch, you hit her!"

Another voice. "*You* hit her! You fucking hit her!"

I tried to protest, and then the world went black.

Chapter 30

MATT

I sat in the back of the Civic with Hannah on my lap.

"Little bird," I whispered, "wake up."

I stroked her hair and cradled her head. Shallow puffs of breath told me she was alive, but the muscles of her face were lax. Her breath hitched as the car went over a bump.

"Slow down," I spat.

"Fuck you," Seth said.

He was driving Hannah's car, the nearest vehicle at our disposal.

The tires squealed as he swung into the ER parking lot.

He leapt out of the car and opened my door.

"Give her to me," he said, reaching toward us.

"No, I'm taking her in. Get out of my way." I clutched Hannah's body.

"You're wasting time!"

"Go fuck yourself." I scooted along the seat with Hannah. "You're going to tell everyone I'm alive anyway. I'm taking her in."

Seth blocked the open door.

"I'm not saying jack shit about you being alive, Matt. I *wish* you were dead, all right? Why don't you fucking die for real and do me a favor? You think I'm going to tell Nate and Uncle and Aunt Ella you're alive and break their fucking hearts, you stupid shit? You've fucked with this family enough. *Be* dead, if that's what you fucking want. Give her to me!"

I hugged Hannah's warm body to my chest and nuzzled my nose into her hair.

Be dead, Seth said. *Die for real.*

An ambulance blew past us, wailing and flashing.

"Matt, for fuck's sake!" Seth crawled onto the backseat and clasped Hannah. I let her go.

Seth was going to keep my secret; I could see, even through his rage, that he was telling the truth. And it hurt that he wanted me gone for real, but I deserved it.

I snagged Seth's wrist as he backed out with Hannah.

Her head lolled over his arm. Her legs dangled.

"What happened . . . between you two?" I said.

Seth wouldn't look at me. After this, I knew he wouldn't speak to me.

"Nothing," he said. "She's devoted to you, God knows why."

He slammed the car door and carried Hannah into the ER.

I waited in the car all night. Seth had the keys, and anyway, I didn't want to go back to the condo. I wanted to wait. I wanted to be there for Hannah.

I curled up on the backseat and shivered as the night cooled.

Around midnight, I broke down and called Mel. I told her where I was—not why—and gave her directions. "Bring blankets," I said.

"Sure! Of course . . ."

A tense silence followed, and I was tempted to hang up. I didn't.

Mel and I had to fix things. I needed her, and what happened earlier—Mel coming on to me—was girlish infatuation fueled by alcohol.

And it felt insignificant now, with Hannah in the ER . . .

I winced.

Hannah . . .

"We're fine," I said abruptly. "What happened in the car—don't worry about it. We're okay, Mel. I can forget about it. Can you?"

"Yes. God, yes, I can. I've been kicking myself. Are you angry at me?"

"No, I—" *I channeled all my anger into beating my brother.* "I'm not angry. I'm cold."

Melanie showed up twenty minutes later with two fleece blankets from the dollar store.

"What are you doing here?" She sat next to me in the back of Hannah's Civic. She looked like a child in her fuzzy pajama pants printed with stars.

"Waiting. Thanks." I wrapped a blanket around my shoulders and draped the other over my lap. "Waiting for Hannah. She's inside with my brother."

"Oh . . . shit. Do I need to get lost?"

"Soon." I frowned. "Not yet. Seems like they're holding her overnight."

We sat in silence, watching the ambulances come and go from St. Luke's. Mel didn't ask for specifics, thank God. I wouldn't have told her. Either I hit Hannah or Seth hit Hannah, and maybe Hannah had a concussion. I scrubbed my face.

"Fuck," I whispered.

Mel rubbed my back. I tensed, then relaxed. The gesture was nothing but amicable.

"You need anything else? Food, smokes?"

I shook my head.

After a while, I said, "Saint Luke. Why do they have to make saints out of everything?"

Melanie chuckled.

"He was a doctor," I said. "Doctor Luke." And then, "I'll be buried in a Presbyterian cemetery. Did you know that? I'm tired enough to go there now." I could say that to Mel because she was young, and she wouldn't roll her eyes at me. She didn't.

After Mel left, I dozed, but sirens and the cold kept pulling me awake. I drifted in and out of strange dreams. Dreams of Hannah. Dreams of quiet earth.

Hannah and Seth emerged from St. Luke's as the sun rose.

Seth wheeled her out in a chair—my heart faltered—but as soon as they reached the sidewalk, Hannah stood and jogged toward the car.

I burst out of the car and ran to meet her. Seth hung back, watching us from the curb.

Hannah gestured for me to get back in the car, but there was no chance of that. If someone recognized me, fuck it. Nothing could stop me from going to her.

As I got closer, I saw a deep purple shiner under her left eye and a bluish bruise along her cheekbone. "Ah, goddamn it," I said. I wrapped my arms around her.

"Matt, you're so cold." She sniffled and hugged me. Her tears dropped onto my neck. "Did you spend the whole night out here?"

"It's fine, baby. I wanted to. My God, are you all right?"

"Yeah, it . . . was nothing. Too much champagne at the party. The punch put me down for the count, that's all. I'm fine, I promise. No concussion." She stroked my hair and I held her tight, my eyes locked on Seth. *Round two, brother?* I couldn't erase the image of Seth's mouth on Hannah's, his greedy hands pulling at her.

"He going to join us?" I said.

"I don't think so. He doesn't want to talk to you . . ." Hannah glanced back at Seth.

"Fine with me," I said, but I hesitated and watched my brother awhile. "You think he's going to tell anyone?"

"No, he won't tell. He's leaving today. He wants nothing to do with us."

"Good. He's got nothing to do with us."

After some moments, Seth turned and rolled the wheelchair back into the hospital.

That was the last time I saw him for quite a while.

Hannah let me drive the short distance back to our condo.

We were too stunned to speak, or too relieved. She leaned against the seat with her eyes closed and her hand in mine.

Near the condo, I said, "Hannah, what was going on between you and Seth?"

"I'll tell you inside," she said, and she did. We sat on the couch and I rubbed her back while she cuddled against me. She came clean about the night in New Jersey when Goldengrove played and Seth tried to kiss her onstage. She told me how they went to the mall and he held her, and how he appeared at the release party last night.

She told me, too, about Aaron Snow's article and his new online zine, *No Stone Unturned*. She explained his theory about me writing *Night Owl* and how and why she said she wrote it. "Seth was there," she said, "but I don't think he'll tell anyone, and I don't think Aaron is going to run the article. I sort of . . . threatened him."

I mulled over the new information.

"Mm, no matter," I said. "He can publish the story or not. No one will believe him. I doubt many people read his stuff, and those who do are fanatics. Seriously, I don't know what that guy would do without his lifelong boner for me."

"Start a zine about aliens?" Hannah giggled.

I laughed for the first time in too long.

"Sounds about right," I said.

Hannah didn't have an icepack in the freezer, so I filled a ziplock with cubes, wrapped a dish towel around it, and held it to her eye. She had a prescription for Vicodin but refused to fill it. "It makes me groggy," she said.

"Hey, you could always sell them."

"Matt!"

I laughed and shrugged. "It's what I would have done when I was younger."

"Yeah, but you were a bad boy."

"Mm. Hannah, I—" I bundled her up and carried her to the bedroom. "I'm so fucking sorry. I don't know . . . if it was me, or if it was Seth . . . who hit you. I was—I couldn't—"

"Don't." She touched my lips. It was one of her little gestures that I loved, the *be quiet, Matt* gesture. Her fingertips brushed my bruised eye. "Now we match. It was no one's fault."

"What are you going to tell people?"

"I dunno. I'll come up with something. I'm becoming an expert liar."

I set her on the sheets and undressed her. She didn't help except to lift her arms indolently and extend her legs while I peeled down her stockings. The black-and-white skirt she wore to the party . . . I'd hoped to take it off under different circumstances.

When Hannah was naked, I began to undress. She watched me with her lustrous eyes—her face calm and serious, her breasts rising and falling gently.

"I'm tired," I said.

My body ached after a night in the car. My mind couldn't hold another thought. I was dangerously weary, too tired to see all the angles, and I had a growing sense that Hannah and I would not get away with our lie.

Seth knew I was alive. Melanie knew. Aaron Snow suspected. There were too many unknowns. Too many people I couldn't control.

"I know." Hannah reached for me. "I am, too."

I stretched out alongside her and pulled the covers over us. I moved against her and sighed. *There.* I had one perfect thing in my life.

And though I said I was tired—too tired for sex—the warmth and softness of Hannah's body made me hard. Her pillows smelled sweet. Her nipples grazed my chest. She rolled away so that I could enter her from behind, and I held her close as I moved inside her.

Chapter 31

HANNAH

We woke in the afternoon and Matt ran a bath for me.

I offered to drive him back to the cabin, but he said he would take a cab. I knew he was antsy to go. Denver was a cage for him now, and he hated cages. Plus, *The Surrogate* hit stores Tuesday, which meant M. Pierce fever all over again.

Matt insisted on carrying me to the bathroom. I hugged his neck.

"Matt, you realize I can walk with a black eye, right?"

"I'll be the judge of that." He set me on the counter and I squeaked; the marble was frigid under my bare bottom. He dropped one of my bath bombs in the tub and watched it fizz and color the water purple.

Once before I had managed to convince Matt to use a bath bomb with me. It was called a "sex bomb" and it was supposed to "put us in the mood" with "exciting scents" and "natural pheromones." I grinned at the memory. As soon as Matt realized the bomb was coating his skin in sparkles, he leapt out of the tub ranting about "looking *Twilighty*" and "smelling like a girl."

"What're you grinning at?"

"You." I smiled. "And this bath, which is such a transparent effort to avoid saying good-bye. Sweet . . . but transparent."

Matt frowned and paced the small space of the bathroom. Ha! I was right. Matt planned to leave me in the tub and slip away.

My poor, adorable night owl—he really had issues with good-byes.

"No," he mumbled. "Maybe . . ."

"Can I induce you to stay a little longer?" I uncrossed my legs deliberately and spread them. Matt watched. He folded his arms and tilted his head.

"How does your cheek feel?"

"They're cold." I grinned.

"And you say I'm bad." He slid me off the sink and turned me. I watched our reflection through the patchy steam on the mirror. Matt—God, he was so tall, and the look on his face was arresting. He wanted me. I knew that look.

"Getting warmer now," I murmured, nudging my bottom against his groin. His cock stirred in his pants.

"Are you?" He spread my cheeks. He, too, watched our reflection. He lifted a hand to play with my breasts. His green eyes traveled between my face and my chest. "Such gorgeous tits, Hannah. So heavy." He lifted one and stroked his thumb over the nipple. I shivered. "You know I have to go, and maybe I shouldn't have come. But what if I hadn't?"

What if he hadn't . . . ?

For the first time, I imagined last night without Matt. Just Seth, forceful Seth, reading the signs all wrong. Kissing me. Grabbing me. The two of us in my condo.

I shook off the thought.

"I don't have time for what-ifs," I said.

Matt recognized his own words and laughed reluctantly.

"You . . ." He sighed. "You . . ." He bit my neck, then my shoulder. He leaned around to bite my breast. I felt him hardening rapidly against my ass.

I reached back to caress his bare sides and play with the band of his lounge pants. With our black-eyed reflections and love-marked bodies, we looked criminal. I found myself admiring us. We dodged a bullet last night. We were living on the verge of disaster.

And it excited me.

"You make me so hard, Hannah." Matt sank to his knees and bit my ass. He kissed it and licked it, groping the soft curves. I bent over the sink. "I'm going to fuck you," he said, "here—right here." He tapped the tight ring between my cheeks. "And you're going to get off with your fingers. I'm going to come in your ass. Understand?"

I heated instantly, a blush spreading over my face. *My . . . my ass.* Good Lord. How could Matt say that stuff with a straight face?

"Y-yeah," I whispered.

He rose and leaned against the towel rack. He slid his dick out of his pants and stroked it as he watched me.

"Get me ready," he said. "Get yourself ready, too."

I crouched and fumbled with the stuff under the sink. Spare toilet paper, Windex, razor cartridges. *Fuck, fuck, fuck . . . I used to have lube under here.*

I was already panting, and I heard Matt chuckle behind me.

"You look good down there, Hannah."

Finally, I found my small bottle of JO Premium.

I shuffled over to Matt, unable to meet his gaze. I wondered if I would ever feel confident in moments like this. My confidence—my sense of sexiness—seemed to come and go on a whim. And it was decidedly gone whenever Matt held the reins.

"Go on," he said. He pushed down his pants and kicked them aside. "I would tell you to look at me, but right now . . ." His strong hand cupped my cheek. "Right now, you're turning me on like this, with your blush . . . your lowered eyes. So shy sometimes, Hannah."

My hands shook as I squirted lube into my palm and began spreading it over Matt's shaft. He went on stroking my face and talking to me calmly. God, if only I could quit blushing and quaking like a mouse—but the way Matt drew attention to my nerves only made me more nervous. Maybe that was the point.

"In fact," he said, his voice thick with desire, "don't look at me this time. Keep your eyes lowered, and don't speak—unless you want me to stop."

I nodded. I spread the lube generously over Matt's cock, from base to tip, because I knew that daunting length had to go inside me.

"Mm . . . you're so good, Hannah. Now yourself. Turn around so I can watch."

I trembled with anticipation and arousal. I turned and began rubbing lube against my anus, willing the clenched muscle to relax.

"Inside," he prompted.

I swallowed. Right, inside.

I'd done this before, first on Matt's birthday and once after that. We didn't make a habit of it. It was a rare treat for both of us, and Matt insisted we exercise great caution.

I lubed up a finger and slowly pressed it into my backside. I kept my eyes lowered. Behind me, Matt moaned.

"I could get off just watching this," he whispered.

I could get off to you watching this.

I spread the lube inside and outside again, and I braced my hands on the sink. I gasped when I felt Matt's fingers between my legs.

"So wet," he murmured. "You love to do this for me. You love to do it for yourself."

He reached for the lube, his forearm moving on the periphery of my vision.

The little opening of the bottle pressed against my anus.

"I think you need more inside," Matt said. His tone was mocking. He squeezed the bottle and a thick strip of lubricant squirted into my bottom. I jerked. It was cold and felt so strange, and so . . .

"*Good,*" I moaned.

Matt's hand hit my ass with a slap. I yelped.

"That was for speaking. Now, Hannah, nod if you're ready."

I gave a little nod. God, was I ever ready.

He spread my cheeks and poised his head at my entrance. I inhaled and exhaled deep from my belly, bending forward and controlling my breath the way I did in yoga. My body relaxed by degrees. The aromatic bathwater and steamy, low-lit bathroom helped.

"Hannah, fuck . . ."

Oh, and hearing Matt's pleasure helped too. Before I knew what I was doing, my hand drifted between my legs and began circling my sex. I pushed back to meet his pressure. When his head popped into me, I groaned. *More.* I wanted to say it, but Matt wouldn't rush. He would scold me; he would say it's dangerous to rush. He might stop altogether.

As the minutes passed, Matt worked his thick cock in and out of my backside, tiny thrusts taking him gradually deeper. I fingered myself and teased my clit. Soon our moans were echoing around the bathroom.

When Matt noticed my hands working my sex, he went crazy.

"God, Hannah," he snarled, "already playing with yourself? Tell me . . . tell me you're my slut. Say it. Fuck, if you could see my dick in your ass . . ."

His member throbbed inside of me, the girth spreading me wide. It didn't hurt. *It shouldn't hurt,* Matt told me once, *and if it does, we'll never do it.*

I snuck a glance at Matt in the mirror. His head was lowered— eyes on my ass—face awash with pleasure. "I'm your slut," I whispered. The word came easily. *Slut.* Just for Matt. "Only yours, Matt. Only for you."

"My God. Fuck." He thrust into me and paused. I moaned to put him at ease, and he thrust again—and then again. The feel of him back there, in there, made me shake. "Watch . . . watch us." He turned me carefully and I grasped the towel bar. One hand lingered between my legs, teasing my clit. I was close, too close. If I wanted to come with Matt, I needed to slow down.

"Look," he growled.

In the mirror, I saw our bodies in profile. Matt's cock moved easily in and out of me. I looked . . . far gone. Eyes glazed, lips parted, features slack. Matt looked no better.

"Your ass, Hannah . . . it's so fucking good. So tight, God . . ."

He fucked me harder, faster, and his moans grew ragged. When he began to curse and tremble, insisting that he loved my tight ass and telling me how he needed to come in it, I pushed myself over the edge with him. I watched him the whole time. For once, I got to see his unadulterated pleasure—the way he fought it, and then gasped and arched and buried his cock in me. He squeezed my ass as he came and leaned over me.

I came with him, my spikes of pleasure peaking in a pulse of bliss.

I moaned his name shamelessly.

Afterward, Matt wrapped a hand around my neck and pulled my back flush with his chest. "How's that," he panted, his breath beating against my ear, "for a good-bye."

He put me in the tub. The warm lavender-colored water lapped at me. It smelled of blackberries and shimmered on my skin.

"I'll see you on Friday, won't I?" Matt said.

"Friday." I smiled at him and resisted the urge to wave. Even the accoutrements of good-bye seemed to bother him. I figured that had something to do with the loss of his parents, but I never asked. I hated saying good-bye to Matt, too, and the reasons didn't matter.

He closed the door and I listened to him moving through the condo.

After a while, I heard his voice. Calling the cab. Silence, then the condo door shutting.

I waited a moment in the water, and then I stepped out carefully and wrapped myself in Matt's bathrobe. I grinned as I crept through the condo. It would serve me right if he reappeared, but I wanted to watch him go.

I peeked through the blinds at the front of the condo. Huh. No taxi. Poor paranoid Matt, he probably told the guy to meet him out back.

I went to the bedroom and looked down from the window. *What the . . .*

Matt, wearing his coat but no sunglasses or hat, strolled up the alley toward a bright blue Corolla. He waved at the driver. The driver-side door popped open and a tiny redhead appeared. She gestured toward the back of the car and laughed. Matt laughed.

Who . . . ? What?

Panic and all the worst possibilities hit me. Matt has another lover. Matt met someone near the cabin. She knows who Matt is—or worse, she doesn't. Matt can be truly anonymous with her. She'll run away with him like I won't. *He's leaving me.*

How's that for a good-bye?

I dashed through the condo and down the complex stairs. I rushed barefoot out of the building. The cold stung at my damp skin.

"Hey!" I said as I rounded the corner.

I waved my arms and Matt's bathrobe flapped around me.

Matt and the redhead turned. His eyes widened and he went stock-still. Then he held up a hand and shook his head.

"What—" I slowed as I neared the car. "What's going on here?"

"Hannah. I didn't want you to worry. Let me explain. This is my driver."

The redhead stepped forward. She extended her hand and nodded.

"Alexis Stromgard," she said. "Mr. Callahan's private driver."

Private . . . driver? I blinked and took the girl's hand. She grasped my fingers in a curt shake and moved away. "Mr. Callahan, I'll take your bag."

Matt, still looking shell-shocked, handed his duffel bag to the girl. She carried it to the back of the car. I watched all this in a state of wonder. Something didn't *fit.* The car was too garish. The girl was too young.

"Come here." Matt steered me up the alley. When we were out of hearing range, he said, "Yes, okay, I lied about the cab."

"I can see that." I tightened the tie on his bathrobe. "Mr. Callahan?"

"She doesn't know who I am. It's just an alias I gave her. She's from out of state."

"Why did you lie?" My cheeks reddened with cold and embarrassment. And hurt. I thought Matt and I were past the lies. I thought we were partners in crime.

"Baby, I didn't want you to worry. I knew it might seem . . . risky, to hire a driver like this, and I didn't want you worrying about me blowing my cover, you know?" Matt squeezed my hand. "But it's actually safer, Hannah. She doesn't know who I am, and she . . . she's very discreet. Very professional. We signed paperwork and stuff."

I looked at my toes. "Where did you find her?"

"What?"

"How did you come into contact with her?"

"Well . . . I found her on Craigslist."

"Craigslist? Seriously?"

"Hannah, I have to go." Matt glanced around and put on his sunglasses. "Yes, Craigslist. She's very professional, like I said. I hired her for the weekend to bring me here, that's all. I couldn't stand the idea of a weekend without you. Is that so wrong?"

"So she's leaving?"

"Yes, she's driving me to the cabin. Are you angry with me?"

I shifted my feet on the cold, prickly pavement. "I'm not angry, Matt. I'm sad that you felt like you had to lie. I'm glad you came to Denver, though. I missed you."

Matt hugged me, squashing my damp body to his chest. He kissed the top of my head.

"Nice bathrobe," he murmured. "Now get inside before you freeze your cute little ass off, all right? I'm sorry. I love you. We'll talk soon."

I faked a smile and kissed Matt's cheek. I took one look at the blue car. The driver sat inside, her slight silhouette almost invisible.

She was cute—adorable, even—and that bothered me more than Matt's lie. *Very professional,* huh? I saw that laugh she shared with Matt before I charged out of the condo.

"I love you, too," I said. "And I want her gone by tomorrow."

Chapter 32

MATT

Melanie peeled out of Denver like a race car driver.

"That was some fucked-up shit!" she said above the music.

Fortunately, Mel's taste in music didn't bother me. All the same, I didn't feel like shouting. I turned down the volume and lit a cigarette.

I'd smoked more in the last month, I realized, than I had in all of 2013.

"Alexis Stromgard, huh?"

"Damn straight." Mel beamed. "Quick on my feet, right?"

"Mm." I smoked and looked out the window.

"You can thank me whenever the mood strikes you, Mr. Callahan."

"Thank you? Do you think I'm proud of that performance?" I scowled and turned away from Mel. "Maybe you have a future in fiction writing. You have to be a great liar to write fiction, a real historical revisionist."

"Hey, buddy, that lie saved your ass."

"It saved *your* ass," I hissed. "I could have fucking told her who you really are. I should have. You're the bitch who stole my work and published it."

Mel hit the brakes. I pitched forward and grabbed the dash.

"Get out of my car, you asshole."

"Drive." I stared at Mel and she stared at me. A car behind us laid on the horn, then pulled around and sped past.

Mel eased back into the traffic. She glared through the windshield.

"Sure, you could have told her that," she said, "and I could have told her that *you* put *Night Owl* online in the first place— and that you told me to keep selling it."

I smirked and flicked my cig out the window. I knew Mel was right, and I knew I was using her as a punching bag. I just felt so goddamn guilty.

"But I wouldn't threaten you with that," she went on, "because I'm not a douche bag. And if you call me a bitch again, I'm going to shove your three thousand bucks up your ass and kick you out of my car myself, all right?"

I smiled in spite of my unhappiness. Mel sure had a way with words.

"All right," I said, and that was that.

I didn't apologize and Mel didn't try to wring an apology out of me. It was horrible, more than I could make Mel understand, to lie to Hannah and to see someone else lying to Hannah. I promised myself that one day it would stop. One day, only honesty would exist between us. I wouldn't lie to protect Hannah. I wouldn't lie to protect myself. Only honesty . . .

It was dark by the time we reached Estes.

"I'd like to buy you an ice cream cone," I said.

"Excuse me?"

I dialed down the music again.

"I said I'd like to buy you an ice cream cone."

"You are . . . the weirdest person." Mel laughed.

"Pull over!" I snapped.

Mel jumped and swung into a metered parking spot. The street was desolate, the little tourist town dead in the middle of March. I put on my hat, scarf, and sunglasses. I paid the meter and we walked along the sidewalk.

"It's winter," Mel said in a quiet voice.

"Yes, and?" I scowled at the passing shops. Native American gifts, Colorado gifts, a bar, more gift shops, another bar. Half the stores were closed. "It's nearly spring."

"It's just . . . a little chilly for ice cream."

"I'm buying you an ice cream cone." I turned on Mel. I shook her shoulder—not hard, but firmly—and spoke in the calmest voice I could manage. "I'm buying you ice cream. One ice cream cone. If you don't want it, the offer is off the fucking table. Why can't you be happy?" I leaned in, my voice rising. "What my parents always bought me was one ice cream cone. And it was delicious. Why can't you fucking accept it?"

I squeezed my eyes shut. God, what was Mel's problem? Couldn't she see that I wanted to share something of myself? Always, when Mom and Dad took us to Cape May, they bought us saltwater taffy and one ice cream cone each. Then Dad would call us "the emperors of ice cream." The emperors. Me, Seth, and Nate.

"The emperors," I whispered.

"Matt . . . ?"

"What?"

"That . . . actually sounds great. Ice cream." Melanie smiled. "I'd like that."

A relieved smile broke out on my face. "Yes," I said. "Let's go."

We found a little ice cream parlor and Melanie chose a mint chip cone. I couldn't quit smiling as I paid.

"You don't want one?" she said.

"No, no. That's not how it works." We sat at a small round table and I watched Mel eat her ice cream. She looked genuinely happy. "How is it?"

"Great." She grinned.

When she finished, the last bite of waffle cone gone, I cleared my throat and said, "Hannah wants you to leave."

Melanie's grin dropped. "What?"

"Mm. She wants you gone. She doesn't want you driving me around."

"Wow." Mel chewed her cheek. "She didn't strike me as the insecure type."

"She's not insecure. She worries about me blowing my cover. She's in this, too, you know?"

"So am I. Do *you* want me to leave?"

I shrugged and made a noncommittal noise.

The answer was no, I didn't want Mel to leave, but I wouldn't give her that. She would read my answer wrong.

"What you did—" I paused, frowned, smoothed my hands over the table. "Melanie, you can't—" *You can't grab my dick, or hop on my lap, or try to kiss me. Ever again.*

God, how to say this?

I forced myself to look at her. Her eyes were wide, her face colorless. I smiled thinly.

It was hard to believe that this timid girl found the courage to grope me. Go big or go home, I guess. Or, in Mel's case, don't go home. I wanted Melanie to stay. My loneliness at the cabin was too absolute, and Mel's cheerful attitude made a good counterpoint to my gloom. And, most important, having a car at my disposal gave me a much-needed sense of control.

"Don't try anything stupid again," I said finally. I narrowed my eyes. "Understand?"

"Yes." Mel nodded vigorously. "I won't. I swear."

"Good. It should be enough for you to know that—" *That I wanted you. That my body came alive at your touch.* "That I want you for a friend, Melanie. A friend."

She drove me back to the cabin and I went straight to my desk. I told her I needed to be alone, so she closed herself in her room.

I wrote for several hours.

I wrote about Melanie's appearance in my life and the things that happened in Denver.

I wrote about Seth—exhaustive passages I would ultimately cut—and Hannah, of course, beautiful, clever Hannah.

No matter how I reached for her with my words, she slipped away. I had such ideas about her. If only I cast my net wide enough,

I might capture her in my language—but it was always too much or not enough. Then I laughed because she defied me. She defied me here, where it mattered most, on the page.

A storm came up the mountainside and mixed with my thoughts and my writing. The blue night turned black. Mel remained in her room and I walked through the cabin, my mind thundering. *It is not so important to be happy,* I realized, because I was satisfied and not happy. *It is only important to do what you were born to do.*

Mel didn't leave on Monday, and I said nothing about it.

She drove into town on Tuesday morning, bought groceries, and made us a breakfast of bacon, eggs, and Belgian waffles. I ate too much and had to lie on the couch.

From her bag, she produced a brand-new copy of *The Surrogate.*

"Really?" I laughed. It was release day, and I'd forgotten.

The book was larger than I had imagined—a Clancyesque monstrosity. I examined the jacket, spine, and flaps. I rolled my eyes at the author blurbs.

A chilling meditation on the human condition, said an author I disliked.

Still, here was *my* book, the sixth in my repertoire (counting *Night Owl*), and I smiled as I studied it. All was as I liked: Thick creamy paper, stylish drop caps, wide margins.

"Thank you, Mel," I mumbled belatedly. "Get a pen and I'll sign it for you."

Mel was clearing dishes. "For me? It's for you."

"I don't want my own book. What, do you think I'm going to reread it, or put it on the shelf and gaze proudly at it?" I chuckled. "No, but I appreciate this. My only author copy."

Mel brought me a pen. I wrote: *For Alexis Stromgard, a spirited private driver. MR. CALLAHAN, AKA THE SURROGATE, AKA MATTHEW ROBERT SKY JR.*

After my breakfast settled, I wrote. Melanie disappeared into her room. When I finished writing some hours later, she presciently reappeared. She trailed me outside and watched me split firewood. I let her have a try, but her toothpick arms couldn't heft the axe.

Wednesday followed suit, then Thursday. She scrammed while I wrote; she came around at dusk, just as I got begrudgingly lonesome.

"What've you been up to?" I'd say, and Mel would say blogging or reading or walking. Sometimes she left the cabin by the back door and drove off, and as I heard her car receding I thought, *Ah, there goes Mel, back to Iowa and I won't see her again.*

But she always returned.

We celebrated the first day of spring with an ambling walk through the woods. It was Thursday, so I said to Mel, "You really have to get lost this weekend."

"All right," she said.

I folded my arms and frowned at her. Sometimes, I felt she didn't take me seriously. Other times, she seemed intimidated by me.

"I'm serious," I said. "You can't be here. If Hannah sees you—"

"I got it, I got it. I'll find a motel."

"Good. And clean up after yourself. I can't have any trace of you here. Nothing in the bedroom, nothing anywhere. It needs to look like you were never here."

"I can do that. Lean down, will you?"

I sighed and leaned down. She put her hands in my hair and sifted through it like a primate, peering at my scalp.

"Your roots are showing. It looks hilariously bad."

I snorted. "Fine."

"And you really need a haircut, Matt. You're starting to look like a mountain man, minus the beard and flannel."

I stroked my smooth jaw. "I could grow a beard."

"Oh, please don't!" Mel laughed and I laughed with her.

"Buy me some black dye, then. And buy shears, while you're at it. Put it on my tab. And Mel . . ." I dropped the smile. Whenever

I showed Mel a little kindness, I instantly worried it was going to her head. "I'm serious about this weekend. I want you gone like you never existed."

"Yes, sir." She saluted.

I rolled my eyes and walked back toward the cabin.

Chapter 33

HANNAH

We're never going to get away with this.

The thought plagued me.

The thought? No, the knowledge. Matt's visit to Denver was like a revelation, and I saw our castle of lies crumbling.

My black eye resolved quickly. Pam, the epitome of professionalism (or the embodiment of indifference), didn't ask about it. She was in high spirits on Tuesday. *The Surrogate* was everywhere. She had a phone interview with the *Denver Post* at noon and a face-to-face with Gail Wieder of *Denver Buzz*, a morning talk show, on Wednesday.

"If only Matthew could see all this," Pam said. She avoided my gaze and my purple-yellow eye. "But he would have hated it, wouldn't he? The attention."

"Yeah." I sighed. *Poor Matt, fame is so rough.* I winced at my uncharitable thought. Jeez, where did that come from?

Maybe I was still upset about Alexis the private driver from Craigslist. I didn't care what Matt said; that business smelled funny.

But—the girl was gone. Out of state. Miles from Matt. I smiled and booted up my work computer. I'm not a jealous girlfriend, not really, but it didn't take a genius to see that the redhead wanted to put her paws all over my man.

Over my dead body.

On Friday, I wore a special springtime set of lingerie—a sheer floral bra from Fox & Rose and lacy crotchless panties—and I drove out to the cabin. Matt took me from the car to bed. *Mmm*, I loved having that effect on him.

"I'm crazy about things that don't hide you," he told me. "Things that show me your body—like this." He bit my nipple through my bra and pushed a finger into my sex. He fucked me while I wore the lingerie, and he made me say I wanted it and that I wore the panties so he could put it in me easily, and that I wanted it in me all the time—which I said with pleasure.

The warming weather seemed to revitalize Matt. He talked about his writing—in general terms, of course—and he was less broody, less prone to anger. Only once did he lapse into a mood that weekend. I made the mistake of mentioning the private driver, Alexis. I said, "You sent her packing, right?"

Matt frowned and said he wanted to write. Then he sat at his desk and doodled in his notebook for half an hour. Classic.

Apart from that, we had an idyllic weekend. The following weekend was the same, and then it was April. And despite my certainty that Matt's fake death and my lies were coming undone, I began to hope. To hope that we were in the clear.

A call from Nate changed all that.

It was the middle of the first week in April. Unseasonably warm wind blew through Denver. At work, I daydreamed too much about Matt. At home, I opened the windows and let the sweet breeze swirl through our condo. And I daydreamed about Matt. Matt beneath me, holding me close, pounding into me . . .

Or the two of us lying in bed, laughing . . . walking in the woods . . . watching the stars . . .

My cell rang and I rose lazily.

When I saw Nate's number, my good mood faded. But not entirely. I even smiled a little, because how could I really dread a call from Nate? He was so uniformly good to me, so mannered and gentle. I remembered his concerned face and dark eyes.

"Hey, Nate," I said. My voice sounded dreamy.

"Hannah." And Nate sounded truly happy, his voice radiant with warmth.

"I've missed you!" I flopped onto the couch. "Really. You're like the older brother I never had. That's how I feel." I'd had a large glass of wine when I got home from work, which made it easier to say those things—but it was how I felt.

"Well, I'm honored. And you're like the little sister I never had."

"Not that little." I laughed. "How old are you anyway?"

"Thirty-five. That puts, what, eight years between us?"

I counted on my fingers. "Seven in May. How do you know my age?"

"I have a dossier of Hannah facts. I keep up to date on these things." Nate chuckled. "No, Matt told me—in Geneva. He was very drunk at the time, mind you, and waxing on about how he wouldn't stop drinking until Hannah forgave him. So I said, tell me about this Hannah, and he said, she's twenty-seven but you wouldn't know it to look at her, she's always going to look young because she's full of light, and I'm never going to love anyone else."

I smiled and hugged a pillow. *Oh, Matt . . .* "What did you say?"

"I said, you're drunk, Matt, and I can see why the girl is half a country away, and twenty-seven is terrifically young to me, light or no light."

"Well, thirty-five is young too," I said. "*Terrifically* young."

"You're good to say so. You seem to be in a great mood, Hannah. I'm glad."

"I am; you're right. It's the weather. April's finicky in Colorado, blizzards or sunshine. It's sunshine right now."

"I know. I'm in town."

I sat up. "You are?"

"Yes. I said we ought to go to the zoo in the spring, didn't I? I'm here with Owen. But can you believe my own wife and daughter preferred New York to my company in Denver? Worse, they're out there with Seth. I wonder if I should be worried." Nate laughed.

"Seth?" My voice was airless. "New York?"

"Yes, didn't you hear? He finally signed a record deal. Goldengrove is off touring."

"Oh . . ."

"I thought he would have told you. He gave me to understand you two hit it off. Wasn't he in town for the release party?"

"For a gig," I said. "I saw him at the party, yes." I walked to a leaning mirror and watched the color return to my face. So, Seth was keeping his word. He was keeping our secret.

"Well, Hannah, what do you say?"

"Excuse me?"

"The zoo. You, me, and a very excitable nine-year-old."

"Uh, sure. Of course." I tried to sound cheerful. I couldn't see any way out of it, and once I regained my composure and my good mood, I might even enjoy it. As long as Nate didn't bring up Shapiro and *Night Owl* . . .

"Great. I'll pick you up at ten tomorrow?"

"It's Thursday. I've got work. Maybe I can—"

"No, no, I cleared that with Pam."

I gaped at my reflection. Cleared that with Pam?

"Nate! Would you please stop going over my head like that?"

"I don't know, Hannah. Old dog, new tricks. See you at ten."

I smiled and sighed. These incorrigible brothers. "See you at ten."

Nate held Owen's hand as we walked through the zoo.

"Let me see!" Owen shouted every several minutes. Nate, wearing an eternally patient expression, would release the boy's hand and watch like a hawk as Owen raced to this or that enclosure. Soon, Owen returned and reattached himself to Nate.

Owen quizzed me as we sat in the Wolf Pack Woods and waited to glimpse an arctic wolf. "Do you live by yourself?" he said. "Do you have a boyfriend? Do you rent your own house? Are you in love with someone?"

"Owen," Nate finally said, "stop being annoying. You don't ask questions like that."

"It's fine." I laughed.

The animals were lively in the cool morning. We spent at least an hour watching the hyenas, lions, and African wild dogs. The tigers made me think of Matt. To and fro they loped, their majestic coats rippling, their stares stoic and knowing.

"You like the tigers," Nate said. I smiled at him. How strange it had been, to see Nate observing the hawks in the aviary. Nate was so hawkish himself. That day, he wore his usual formal attire— dress slacks and a pale button-down shirt, no tie, his wool coat unbuttoned. I wondered if he owned a pair of jeans.

"Yeah." I rubbed the back of my neck. "I love the big cats."

"Are you going to ask me about the lawsuit, Hannah?"

I shook my head.

"I told Shapiro not to bother you about it," Nate said. "He hasn't, has he?"

"No."

"Good. I could tell it troubled you. It scared you off, didn't it? Something about the litigation is bothering you. Hannah, tell me." Nate came around, placing himself between me and the glass enclosure. His dark eyes implored me. "You can tell me."

"Are you *trying* to scare me off? I'd rather be home alone than talking about this."

Hurt flashed across Nate's face.

"I see," he said.

"What, is there some news? Something I should know?"

"Yes. Do you want to know?"

"We've hardly seen the animals." I turned away. "I want to see the birds. The tropical birds. Doesn't Owen want to ride the carousel? Tell me later, Nate. Before I go."

"Of course," Nate said, and we didn't speak about the lawsuit again as we walked around the zoo. Nate told me how Matt, in his days of drinking and petty crime, conspired to release a bunch of birds from their enclosure.

"He hated the zoo," Nate said. "Hated it. Would never go. And if anyone mentioned it around him?" He gave a low whistle. "Anyway, it was an enclosure much like this—" Nate gestured to the open habitat, a tropical replica. Birdsong filtered through the warm air and colorful, feathered bodies flickered among the plants. "Which looked like paradise to everyone, except Matt. All Matt saw was a lot of sad birds. He propped open the doors, and then—" Nate began to laugh. "Ah, Lord. Then he tried to shoo the birds out. But of course they didn't want to go! He terrified them and they flew all around screaming. He got so furious as they'd fly out and fly right back in."

I laughed at the image, which I could see clearly in my mind.

"You tell great stories," I said.

"Well, thank you. It looks like I've got an agent in my corner whenever I sit down to write my memoirs, hm?" He patted my shoulder.

"I wish." I sighed.

Nate coaxed me into a conversation about my job, and my dream and despair of becoming Pam's partner. It felt good, discussing it, and Nate was sympathetic and optimistic.

I dragged out the zoo visit as long as possible. *I just want to see the snakes,* I said, and then, *I really want to see the elephants.*

The truth? I didn't want to talk about the lawsuit.

Owen fell asleep in Nate's arms, and when that happened, I knew it was time to go. We walked back to Nate's rental car. He arranged Owen on the backseat and we sat up front.

"Too warm?" Nate said. "Not warm enough?"

"I'm fine. Go on. Tell me about the thing."

"We've had a sort of breakthrough, Hannah. I think you'll be interested." Nate kept his voice low; Owen was sound asleep. "You know we planned to subpoena the publisher's name after we filed the lawsuit, yes?"

I nodded.

"And then *Night Owl* was taken offline. The distributors should still have records. But"—Nate held up a finger and smiled—"Shapiro enlisted a tech guy to do some digging for us." Nate opened the glove compartment and withdrew several papers. "He searched the IP addresses associated with *Night Owl,* with the site where we believe it was originally posted and other sites that have duplicated or reviewed the book. The same IPs kept coming up."

"Nate, this jargon is lost on me."

"Bear with me. Our anonymous publisher is not Internet savvy. They did nothing to disguise the IP address, no proxy server, no domain privacy." Nate grinned like a boy detective. "Our tech guy followed the browsing history for the most prevalent IPs, and one stood out. The same IP is associated with this e-mail address"—he pointed to a page—"which is associated with a domain, which happens to be a blog, and which just *happened* to rave about *Night Owl* and advertises it. The same IP regularly searches the book, checks the book's ratings, et cetera. It's almost a certainty, Hannah. This is our girl."

Girl? I let out a tremulous breath. Nate passed the papers to me.

The first page showed a jumble of text, strings of numbers and ICANN data, none of which made sense to me.

The second page was a printout of the blog melaniereads. com. There was a black-and-white banner image with a few male torsos and the words *Melanie Reads* in pink. The subheading read: *Recipes, reviews of sexy books, dance stuff, and everything else Mel loves!*

I skimmed the *Night Owl* review. It raved about the hot sex and "unputdownable" nature of the book. I sighed.

"I hate to tell you this, Nate, but reviews like this are all over the Internet."

"Yes, but *not* by users who also have accounts at the Mystic Tavern, the site where—"

"I know, I know."

"And not by users who check the book's rank on the best-seller list dozens of times a day, Hannah. This is the one."

I shuffled to the next page and stopped. This is the one. *Who is the one?* I stared at the printout of Melanie's profile. "Impossible," I whispered.

"She looks so young, I know."

I began to laugh. The sound was hysterical and unstoppable. Melanie. Alexis Stromgard. Matt's "private driver" stared at me from the page. There was her unmistakable hair, the short red waves surrounding her face. She grinned at me like she'd grinned at Matt while I watched from the bedroom window.

"Hannah?"

My laughter rose and rose, and then it stopped. I felt nauseous.

"She's just . . . so young," I stammered. No—what did this mean? It couldn't be a coincidence. The girl who published *Night Owl* couldn't work as a private driver for hire on Craigslist and just happen to be working for Matt.

Matt lied to me. Again.

Matt knew who she was and he lied to me.

All this time, he knew who put *Night Owl* online. While I dodged Shapiro and Nate and Aaron Snow. While I lied for him, he lied to me.

Questions swarmed my mind. I covered my mouth and pressed my forehead against the car window. Tears threatened, stinging in my eyes.

"Hannah, please. Talk to me." Nate touched my shoulder. He always touched my shoulder, my elbow, somewhere chaste and safe. After a moment, his hand slid to the middle of my back. "I shouldn't have brought this up. It makes you miserable. God, I'm so insensitive."

Nate loosened the papers from my hand and shoved them back in the glove box.

"I'm fine," I mumbled.

"No, you aren't. I can't imagine how horrible it's been for you—this book circulating—after everything that happened. Forget this, please. Look at me."

I swiped my coat sleeve across my face and turned to Nate. I almost started to cry again when I saw his worried gaze.

"Do you seriously"—I sniffled—"think she wrote it?"

"I think she published it. Did she write it? Maybe not. She's legally liable for distributing it, though—and more so if it's not her own work. But that doesn't matter, Hannah." Nate tilted my chin up. I flinched at the touch. His long, elegant hand was exactly like Matt's, but his eyes were far kinder. Why didn't guys like Nate ever fall for me? "The lawsuit, I can see how much it bothers you. If you wanted me to drop it, you only ever had to ask."

Nate's words settled on me slowly.

He would drop the lawsuit for me, which Matt and I wanted all along.

"No," I said. I buckled my seat belt and steadied my breath. "I don't want you to drop it, Nate. I want you to ruin that girl's life. And I want a drink."

Nate was staying in the Chancellor's Suite at the Hotel Teatro.

"I have a bottle in the room," he told me, which turned out to be two bottles—Johnnie Walker Quest and Balvenie. (And "the room" turned out to be three rooms—a bedroom, boardroom, and living room—with wood-paneled walls, European furniture, a table for ten, and a limestone fireplace. Damn.)

"Too early for this?" He lifted the Balvenie. "I like to bring something nice when I travel. I'd rather not be at the mercy of wet bars, if you know what I mean."

Nate seemed altogether comfortable with me in his hotel room, maybe because Owen was present. After Nate carried him up, Owen went straight to the bedroom. I heard the TV.

I checked my watch. "It's past noon. A good time for a drink."

"Agreed, Miss Catalano. Single malt or blend?"

I blushed. Scotch whiskey was all Greek to me.

"Whatever you're having," I said. I draped my coat over the couch and sat, my fingers fidgeting on the damask fabric.

"Single malt, then. The Quest was a gift." Nate smiled and poured a small amount of alcohol into two tulip-shaped glasses. "Did you know I have friends in Denver? Old college friends. I've had a chance to visit with them this week." He brought the glass to me and sat near the arm of the couch, putting a few feet between us.

I tried not to frown at the tiny amount of booze. I wanted to get drunk. Seriously drunk. I wanted to turn off my brain and stop picturing Matt and Melanie and wondering what the hell I should do about Matt's latest lie. Or lies. What else was Matt hiding? Were Melanie and Matt in cahoots, publishing *Night Owl* together? Were they fucking? Had he even sent her away?

I shuddered.

I wanted to shoot my drink, but I glanced at Nate and followed his lead. He gave his glass a swirl, gazed at the film of scotch, and then brought it to his nose and inhaled. I did the same.

Nate lowered the glass, lifted it again, smelled the booze. I sighed and copied him. The second whiff of whiskey was lighter. A complex, peaty aroma filled my nostrils. "Tastes even better," Nate murmured. I flinched. He was grinning at me.

"Ugh. Nate, I have no idea what I'm doing."

He chuckled. "I can tell. What do you smell?"

"Wood . . ." I sniffed at my glass again. "Smoke? A little . . . fruitiness."

"Very good. Have a taste."

We sipped our scotch. The mellow flavor filled my mouth and went down like silk.

"And enjoy the finish," Nate said. He smiled and leaned into his corner of the couch. He watched me with obvious enjoyment. "This visit with you has been by far my most pleasant in Denver." When he took another sip, I took another sip.

I didn't have the guts to tell Nate that I wanted to get drunk off his expensive scotch, but he refilled our glasses twice, and by my third glass I was feeling good. Thoughts of Matt and Melanie drifted off on an amber river. I felt happy and warm in Nate's company, and he was all good-natured smiles and easy conversation.

Owen wandered out of the bedroom to announce that he was watching *The Crow*. Nate, obviously ignorant of the dark cult classic, said, "Fine, just keep the volume down."

Nate moved constantly when he spoke. He leaned back with his laughter and motioned as he explained things, his animated body so graceful. I watched him in a daze. Early afternoon turned to midafternoon, and mid to late. We each had a fourth glass of scotch.

That day reminded me vividly of my early days with Matt—when he took me to a restaurant in Boulder, and when he visited my family on the Fourth of July. Matt, like Nate, was a natural gentleman in public. I missed that side of him. He denied me that side of him—any side of him—with his insistence on anonymity, his lies, his obsession with writing.

Nate's voice broke into my reverie.

"Being with you reminds me of Matt," he said.

I looked up into Nate's face.

"That's funny. Being with you reminds me of him, too. I was just thinking of him."

"Were you?" Nate tilted his head. Black hair flopped across his brow and his dark eyes roamed my face. "About what in particular?"

"About how he loved to write," I said. "How he loved to write more than anything."

"He loved you, Hannah. He loved *you* more than anything. Don't you know that?"

"No," I said, "I don't know that."

"You must know that, though. He loved you. Are you falling out of love with him now that he's gone? You can't do that." Nate touched my arm. "You can't be angry with him for leaving. He's the golden boy, you see? We always forgive him."

Forgive him?

The cold finger of presentiment ran up my spine.

"You know," I whispered.

Nate held my gaze without flinching.

"You know. You *know* . . ." I searched Nate's face for confirmation of the fact—but his calm stare *was* confirmation. My world tilted on its little axis.

Confusion struggled over Nate's expression, and then he said very softly, "I'm my brother's keeper, Hannah."

I staggered off the couch and fell. Nate moved to help me, but I scrambled away from his hands. "Don't touch me!" I said. "You knew. All this time. You knew he was alive. You lied to your own parents. You—"

"They're not my parents," he murmured.

I gripped the arm of the couch and pulled myself to my feet. I had the sense of falling, as if the world were rushing past at great speed.

Could this be?

Nate's tearful eyes before the memorial, his offer of his portion of Matt's inheritance, even his showing up in Denver to watch over me—it was all part of an elaborate act.

"Oh, my God." I covered my mouth.

"Steady now, Hannah."

"Why couldn't I know? Why couldn't you tell me? Why couldn't he tell me?"

"This was the way he wanted it." Nate hesitated. Even now, he was reluctant to betray Matt. "It had to be believable, down to the last detail. But Matt needed money to live on. My job was simply to . . . ensure that you received his inheritance."

Nate's *job*.

The word pierced me.

Nate . . . so generous, so good, so thoughtful . . . was only doing Matt's bidding when he offered me Matt's money. And Matt was only ensuring he retained control over his money. Matt planned all this without telling me, letting me believe we were the closest of coconspirators.

But I was not instrumental in Matt's plan. I was incidental to it. A footnote.

I stumbled away from Nate and clutched my purse.

"Have you talked to him?" I said.

"No. We've had no means of communication." Nate wrung his hands. "Can you tell me how he is, please? Hannah, I've had no idea. It wasn't until I called you last month and you said you were at the cabin . . . that I knew things had gone as planned."

I yanked on my coat and headed for the door.

"No! I'm not going to tell you how he is. You can both go to hell. I feel so ridiculous, Nate. What was the point of this?"

Nate dragged a hand through his hair. He looked flustered, less dignified than I'd ever seen him. "Hannah—"

I went out before he could answer, and I slammed the door behind me.

Chapter 34

MATT

Hannah didn't show on Friday. Our light—the last light of day—came and went. I called her prepaid cell and got no answer. I waited for her at the end of the drive.

I called again and again, though finally I got a grip and put my phone in my pocket.

After all, what if someone else had her cell? What if someone was visiting the condo?

As I walked back to the cabin, I envisioned Hannah's car in a ditch. I envisioned her at St. Luke's with postconcussive syndrome. I envisioned Seth returning to terrorize her.

Fuck.

"Where are you, bird?" I said into the silence of the cabin.

I'd sent Melanie away, as usual. She was going on four weeks in my service, and before she left for her motel that weekend I gave her a fourth envelope of three thousand dollars.

Maybe that explained why Mel kept coming back—not out of loyalty or interest, but because twelve thousand bucks in four weeks is damn good earnings.

I decided that Hannah was merely late and I resolved to wait for her. My panic waxed and waned as the hours passed. *Hannah is fine. Hannah is in trouble. Hannah is busy. Hannah is lying in a ditch. Hannah is out with friends. Hannah is in the hospital.*

I ran Google searches for Denver accidents, car crashes between Denver and the mountains, Hannah Catalano. I tried her cell a few more times. I swore and paced.

Morning light paled the sky.

I called Melanie, who picked up just as her cell was going to voice mail.

"Matt." She coughed. "Six . . . six o'clock. *Whyyy?*"

"Hannah never arrived. Do you understand? She isn't here."

"Well . . . I'm sorry, Matt."

"You're sorry? What the hell could be happening? She comes *every* weekend, every Friday at the same time. When she couldn't make it, she called. Something is wrong."

"Did you try her cell?"

"Obviously!" I wrapped a throw around my shoulders, stuck my feet in boots, and yanked open the deck door. I lit a cigarette. So much for April's warmth; a cold snap brought a new sheet of snow to the mountains. "Yes. Yes, I called her. I called her a few dozen times."

"Okay, chill. Let's think. Are you okay? Have you been up all night?"

"Do I sound okay? What do you think?" I kicked a clod of snow. It went soaring through the deck rails and broke into glittering pieces. "I'm freaking out. I don't know what to do. She could be sick. She could be dead. I can't calm down enough to figure out what to do."

"There's nothing you can do, Matt, short of having me drive you to Denver so you can check up on her. And that's not tenable."

"Not tenable," I repeated.

Mel was using her mature phone voice, that deceptive tone I first heard in February, and right now I appreciated it. Right now, I could almost believe we were peers and that she might shed some light on my dilemma.

"Yeah. Because what if we go there and she comes here and . . .

you know. Or what if we go there and she sees me? Then you're really in trouble."

"Right. So I do nothing?"

"You try to relax and stay positive. Try to get some sleep, too."

"That's not happening," I said.

"Do you want me to come over?"

"No, God. What if she shows up? You stay put."

"All right. I'm sure she'll call. And I'm here if you need me, Matt."

I thanked Mel and said I would keep her up to date. Nothing had changed, but the call served its purpose. I felt a shade calmer.

I tried writing, failed at that, stared at the TV for a while, and finally lay in bed. Fatigue and anxiety make a bad pair. I drowsed and woke depressed, my chest tight with unease.

I was still in bed at noon when my cell rang. I came fully awake in an instant and answered without looking at the caller.

"Hannah," I said.

"Yeah."

"God, it's you." I threw back the quilt and stumbled out of bed. "Are you okay?"

"No." She paused, and then repeated firmly, "No."

My stomach started to churn.

"What the hell is going on? I've been worried. Where are you?"

"Well, Matt, I know your little *private driver* published *Night Owl*. And I know Nate was in on your fake death, and that's why he offered me your money. All part of your plan, huh?" Hannah's voice shook.

I shook, too—an irrepressible tremor starting in my hands and working down my arms. Fuck. *Fuck.* She knew.

"Hannah, let me explain—"

"No!" Her shriek pierced my ear. "You always have an excuse. I don't understand—why—why you would keep me in the dark—"

"I didn't ask Melanie to publish *Night Owl*. Listen to me." I collapsed into an armchair and wiped a clammy hand across my brow. "She—well, I—" The facts scattered. How much did Hannah know? What should I explain? And how did she even find out? "Let me—"

"No! No, no, *no*. I don't care, Matt. I've known since yesterday. I spent the night trying to calm down, and I can't." Hannah laughed miserably. "God. Our relationship started with lies. I don't know why I thought you'd changed. Is she still there? Is Melanie still *driving* you around?"

I opened and closed my mouth. I thought if I spoke, I might throw up.

Finally I whispered, "Yeah."

"Of course. Are you fucking her?"

My thoughts flashed to the nighttime drive in Denver and Mel's hand on my thigh, then on my dick. Revulsion rolled through me. "No."

"Well, I wish I could believe you," Hannah said.

I gripped my skull and felt the thick nausea that comes with anxiety. Oh, yes, this was familiar. I lied to Hannah and she caught me in the act. I should have known better, but I never learned, and I wondered at myself as I waited for Hannah to say more. Why did I always do the worst things? Why did I always arrange my life so that it was on the brink of collapse?

The answer came to me as if it had only been waiting for the question.

Because happiness is useless to me. Because I need agony and heat in my life.

I swallowed. My saliva was bitter.

"I thought the book would bring you back to me," I said. "Say something."

"The book? What do you mean?"

"*Night Owl.* I posted it . . ." I rose and began to pace, cutting back and forth across the room. Surely Hannah would understand that everything I had done, I did to bring her closer to me. "I posted it on that site. The Mystic Tavern. And Melanie, she just . . . found it and published it. Do you understand? I had no idea, but I wanted—"

"Then how . . . do you know her?" Anger rippled through Hannah's voice. She sounded raw, on the brink of screaming or tears. "And why the fuck did you put the book online?"

"I didn't know her. I found her on the forum. Doesn't matter. I called her . . ." I waved my hand. God, nothing was coming out right. None of this really mattered. The only thing that mattered was that . . . "I did it for *us*," I hissed. "The book. I wanted everyone to know about us. I thought if you understood how it felt, when the whole world can see the most private parts of your life, that you'd finally get how it is for me, Hannah . . . and that you'd leave all that behind."

Hannah said nothing.

I stopped pacing and listened to the fast, heavy beat of my heart.

"Hannah?"

She giggled. I smiled uneasily, one corner of my mouth quirking up.

"You see?" I said. "I missed you so much. When I got out here, I realized I couldn't—"

"You really are insane," she whispered.

I realized I couldn't live without you.

"What?" I steadied myself against the wall.

"Yeah. You're fucking crazy. You . . . you put *Night Owl* online . . . and let some stranger publish it . . . to make my life hell? To make me so uncomfortable that I . . . would abandon my life and come live in the fucking woods with you like a fucking crazy person?" Hannah's voice rose hysterically. "*Fuck* you, Matt Sky. Fuck you!"

"No. No, Hannah. Listen—" I shook my head.

"*You* listen." Hannah's quavering voice grew clear and diamond hard. "This is over."

"What? I—"

"This. Is. Over. We. Are. Over."

Above the sound of my booming heart, I missed the click of Hannah ending our call. I kept talking, my voice insistent and panicked. Angry. Then pleading. "It is *not* over! What do you mean, over? You don't get to say that. I love you. You don't understand . . ."

I panted in the silence. Jesus—she couldn't be serious.

"Hannah? Hannah?"

I looked at my phone. She was gone.

My thumb hovered over the Send button, and then I lowered my cell. I knew this game. I would call; the call would go to voice mail. I would leave messages; she would delete them.

We'd been here before, and because of my lies.

Happiness is useless to me.

I focused on controlling my breathing, in and out, slowing my heart rate.

I slipped my phone into my pocket and flattened my hands against the wall.

I pressed my forehead to the wall, too, and stood entirely still.

And then I wound my arm back and slammed my fist into the wall—once, twice, harder each time—until I heard a low crack and felt the pain.

Chapter 35

HANNAH

I turned off my TracFone. I turned off my iPhone, too.

I unplugged the condo landline, shut down my laptop, and sat on the couch.

The couch Matt bought.

I gazed around the living room, and everywhere my eyes landed I saw something Matt had purchased . . . for us. A steady static buzz filled my mind.

Right now, I knew, he was calling and calling and calling. Or making lists. Or drinking. Or maybe driving off into the sunset with Melanie.

Or hell, maybe he was already conspiring with Nate to bribe me into forgiving him—which wasn't happening. Not this time.

I scrubbed my face and hugged my legs to my chest, forehead on knees. *There.* Somehow, that tight, defensive posture would protect me.

My mind skipped over the last nine months, a stone touching memory. I thought of Matt at his best: watching me compulsively, smiling when I caught him staring, or looming over me in bed, moving with his trademark hunger and intensity. Hair wild. Skin gleaming.

His handsome face. His complicated heart.

And then I thought of Matt at his worst: drunk in New York, unable to meet my eyes, or hiding in our condo, disgusted by the world's curiosity. Paranoid. Angry. Duplicitous. And now . . . shamelessly admitting that he put *Night Owl* online in a twisted effort to manipulate me.

Memory stopped, and I sank.

Tears threatened, hot with anger, and fear tightened around my heart. Matt . . . my Matt. *No!* Not my Matt. A liar. Always lying. Always hurting me to get what he wanted, even when I was the thing he wanted.

Despite my balled-up barricade of limbs, I began to tremble. Blindly, I felt for the nearest pillow and buried my face in it. Ribs of corduroy pressed back. I swear, that pillow smelled like Matt. A dry sob escaped me, and I screamed—the sound ugly and hoarse. It was over. *We* were over. I gave myself up to the rending panic of separation, the heart clinging to what it knows—*Matt*—and then I dropped the pillow and shuffled into the kitchen.

Painful hiccups constricted my throat.

But at least I wasn't a crying, snotty mess. Sadness could wait until later. Right now, I needed anger.

After a few false starts, I wrote a note on our magnetic memo pad.

> *Matt,*
> *Fool me once, shame on you. Fool me twice, shame on me. I tried to get close to you. I tried to know you. But you never let me in. You're the lord of lies.*
> *Don't try to find me. Like I said—we're over.*
> *Hannah*

I reread the note, then tore it from the pad and left it on the kitchen counter.

Like I said—we're over.

The words became a rhythm, driving me forward.

If Matt wasn't losing his mind right now, he was on his way here. I had two hours tops.

We're over. I dragged my suitcase out of the closet. *It's over.* I began to pack, grabbing clothes and toiletries. *We're over.* My laptop, my purse, work-related papers. *It's over.*

I took nothing Matt had given me. I took only what I needed.

A wide-eyed Laurence watched me dash through the condo.

When my suitcase was full, I plunked it down by the door, my car keys jangling in my hand. Ready to go. My heart thudded crazily. A sweat-soaked curl stuck to my temple. In my head, the voice of reason said: *Get out! Get away from this unhealthy situation. Get away from this unhealthy man. Matthew Sky.*

"Matt," I whispered, and his name summoned the memory of him, tall and moody, demanding, passionate, green eyed. My own personal monster of jealousy. I winced. Another girl might have found Matt's devotion compelling—he was willing to do anything to have me—but it frightened me. *He* frightened me.

I had called him the lord of lies, and that title seemed more and more appropriate.

"Good-bye," I said. The word slipped off my tongue, into our quiet condo, which held our hundreds of memories. *Please,* I thought, *let me go this time.* And even as I issued that silent plea, I knew he wouldn't. How could I make him let me go?

My heart hurt—that tight, ironic pain localized in the chest.

I fished a pen out of my purse and walked back to the kitchen counter.

I knew how to make Matt let me go, and it was terrible.

I had to hurt him. I had to lie. I had to get on his level, and make him know this pain.

My hand shook above the note on the counter. After all these lies, what was one more? I swallowed, and then I scribbled a line at the bottom of the page:

P.S. I slept with Seth.

Chapter 36

MATT

Mel followed me through the cabin as I packed.

I didn't have much—just a duffel bag of clothes and toiletries, a few books, my laptop, and my writing supplies. I moved the perishable food to the freezer. I made my bed.

In my mind, I said good-bye to each room.

The master bathroom where I fucked Hannah in the tub.

The bedroom where we made love all night.

The guest bedroom, which I considered "Mel's room."

The cellar where I hid Kevin's broken chair.

Good-bye.

I lingered in the open main room, the kitchen and living room with its many windows. Afternoon sunlight lay along the floor. It glanced off the counters and gleamed on my desk, which was not really my desk.

But it had been my desk, as much as anything belongs to anyone. I sat there and did good work. And when I needed a break . . .

I walked out onto the deck. Mel lurked, my petite shadow.

"Your hand," she whispered.

I glanced at my hand. Something was broken; I'd made sure of that. Maybe a knuckle. Maybe one of those long fine bones between the joints. Nate would know, though I didn't particularly care. I just wanted the pain—hard and real and punishing.

A pain to keep me in the present moment.

A pain to keep me from losing it, because losing it is the easy way out.

"It feels fine," I lied.

I adjusted the bandage around my palm. It was Mel's handiwork, a bulky mess of gauze and medical tape. I'd called Mel as soon as I got off the phone with Hannah. I said we needed to get to Denver—*now*—and then I started packing with one hand, swearing every time my swollen knuckles grazed a wall.

By the time Mel arrived, my hand was puffy and wine red.

"You're sad," Mel insisted, her small voice bringing me back to reality.

I shrugged. It seemed like a good sign that I wasn't manic with urgency, and it also seemed like a bad sign. Like I was resigned. Like I was going back to Denver the way people return to a burnt home—not to salvage it, but to wade through the wreckage and suffer.

This. Is. Over. We. Are. Over.

"Not sad, Mel. Just saying my good-byes."

I looked to the mountains, which were magnificent with snow and sunlight. They were horrible, too, because I almost died there. *Good-bye.* Good-bye to the aching silence and this white, unembellished peace. The incredible wind. The night full of coyotes, their ululating cries like laughter, and owls calling in the dark. Good-bye.

Melanie joined me at the railing.

That day, she wore her boots with fur flaps and her fur-trimmed canvas jacket.

"I thought you were scared of good-byes," she said.

"I'm not scared of them. Why are you so happy? Don't you know what this means?"

"I'm not happy." She hunkered into her jacket. "I'm . . . accepting, I guess. I knew you couldn't pay me to keep you company forever."

I smirked and turned to really look at Melanie. Silly girl.

"I paid you to drive me," I said. "The company, I hope, was free of charge."

She smiled. "Yeah. It was."

"Mm . . . I thought so." Because we would be parting ways soon and there would be nothing more between us, I slid my fingers into Mel's hair. The red mop felt as I'd imagined: heavy and glossy. She laughed while I fluffed her hair, but I could see her disappointment.

"This is all I get, huh?" She rolled her eyes up toward my hand.

"Yes."

"You won't kiss me?"

"No."

"How about a hug?"

I tilted my head, frowned, and then I pulled her little body to mine. She wrapped her arms around my waist. She felt smaller than she looked. Fragile. "Listen, Mel. After you drop me off, I want you to go home. You understand that?"

"Yeah." She buried her face in my coat.

"No more of this. Don't come back to the cabin; it'll be locked. Don't stay in Denver. Go home. Do you have all your things?"

"Yeah."

"Good. Hannah knows you published *Night Owl*. I think my brother knows, too."

Mel flinched in my arms. Her head shot up. "He does?"

"Yes. Just listen to me, Mel." I gripped her shoulder, my bandaged hand hanging uselessly at my side. "If anyone calls or e-mails you about the book, you don't speak to them. Soon it will be over. And remember, I told you to put *Night Owl* up for sale."

Mel's brow creased. "No, you d—"

"Yes," I said, "I did. Are you not hearing me? I contacted you online in January. I didn't reveal my identity to you, but I gave you a link to my story on the Mystic Tavern and I gave you permission to publish it as an e-book, and so you did. I told you to keep the earnings, which you did. You've done nothing illegal, and you didn't know I was Matthew Sky. We never met."

"Why?" Mel said.

"Do you want my brother to sue you? He just might, Mel, even if he knows I wrote the book. What I told you is your story. Tell it to me."

Mel looked at her feet. God, what a child she was. She only saw me erasing her from my life. She didn't see that I was protecting her.

"You . . . contacted me online—"

"Not me," I snapped. "A stranger. Via the forum. Start again."

"Okay, okay. A stranger contacted me on the forum. Gave me a link to the story and told me to publish it and keep the money, so I did."

"There's my Alexis Stromgard." I forced a smile, which felt thin and defeated. "Oh, and I told you what pen name to use. I told you to use W. Pierce, didn't I?"

Mel nodded. I paused, considering her face.

"Why did you use W. Pierce, anyway?"

"I wanted to give you some credit," she said. "I *knew* you wrote it, Matt. I just knew it; I could tell. And so I knew you had to be alive. I wanted to get your attention."

I laughed suddenly, although I wasn't happy. She wanted to get my attention?

"Well, Melanie vanden Dries." I gave her a kiss on the cheek. "That you did."

Every bump in the road sent a pulse of pain through my hand.

Mel kept glancing at me—I felt her anxious stare—but I watched the passing scenery.

Mel didn't play music. I barely let myself think. If I thought, after all, my mind ran in circles. *Why am I even going to Denver? It's over with Hannah, and I should have stayed at the cabin. I need a new plan. I need . . .*

What?

The winding mountain road cut through one-street towns, and soon we were on the highway and I felt the unavoidable pull of the city. I slouched in my seat. Exit ramps and neighborhoods went zinging past. The world that wanted to stare into this car, and into my life.

Soon it would get its wish.

About half an hour from Denver, I dialed Nate on my prepaid cell.

We hadn't spoken in months. I'd decided we should avoid contact after I staged my death—but that didn't matter now.

Several long rings sounded on the line.

Then, my brother's voice. "Hello?"

"Nate, it's me."

"Oh . . ." He went quiet. I knew emotion had a hand around his throat.

"It's good to hear your voice, Nate."

"Matt. How are you?"

"I'm all right. Don't worry, I'm all right."

I heard a muffled, choked sob. God, it really fucked me up when Nate cried. I turned away from Mel as best I could and lowered my voice.

"It's okay," I said. "I'm coming back to Denver, okay? It's over."

"Thank God. Can I see you?"

Nate told me he was in Denver then. "Checking up on Hannah," he explained, and he talked about Hannah in his hotel room and their argument and her departure. I ground my teeth as I listened. Nausea roiled in the pit of my stomach. *Of course,* I thought. *This is how Hannah found out about Melanie. Nate's lawsuit. Nate's involvement in my phony death. All of it.*

"Matt?"

"I'm here. Sorry." I leaned my head against the window and exhaled a patch of fog. It was too late to get upset with my brother. Everything was crumbling. "I'd like to see you, yes."

"She guessed . . . about me. I couldn't say no. She looked me right in the eye and told me I knew. I'm sorry . . ."

"Don't be, Nate. Don't worry about it. I should have told her from the start."

"I've got Owen with me. Meet me in the hallway?"

"Yeah, sure." I eyed my bandaged hand. "And hey, I could use your orthopedic skills, if you've got the time."

"What happened? What's going on?"

"It's no big deal. A minor accident. I'll be there in twenty minutes or so."

Nate said good-bye and I ended the call.

"Problems?" said Mel.

"No." I swiped her phone from the console and changed our destination to the Hotel Teatro. "Slight change of plans, that's all."

Melanie dropped me off in front of the hotel.

There was no parking on the street, so I told her to circle back in fifteen minutes.

I knew my way around the Hotel Teatro. The concierge barely glanced at me as I headed to the elevator.

I rode up alone to the Chancellor's Suite, and when I stepped into the hallway, I saw Nate in front of the door. He stood with his head inclined toward it, probably listening for Owen, but when he saw me he came running.

"There you are," he called.

We clasped one another in a hug. Nate kissed my neck and thanked God. I clung to him with one arm.

"Brother," I said, and I squeezed him with all my might.

"How are you? God, look at you. Look at this." He ruffled my hair.

"I know." I smiled bleakly. "Disguise, you know?"

"Sure. Of course." He patted my cheek.

We held on to one another, and Nate's eyes shone with tears, and my voice kept catching with emotion. The last year had been so mad. I regretted dragging Nate into my messes, but he couldn't be kept out. He came willingly, forcefully. He'd been that way since we were boys.

"I can't stay long," I said. "Gotta find Hannah."

Nate drew back, held me at arm's length, and scrutinized me. His eyes paused on my bandaged hand, continued down my legs, then tracked back up to my face. Searching for signs of damage, physical or mental. Always the doctor.

And I closed my eyes, because looking at Nate then felt too much like looking at Dad. He knelt to study my hand, and memories drowned me. Dad's dark head bent over my boyhood scrapes. Dad laughing, scolding me, smoothing a Band-Aid across my leg. Or Mom with her heavy auburn hair and delicate body, saying good-bye before they left for Brazil.

I don't remember my parents. Another lie I told Hannah.

Nate chuckled, the sound jarring with my thoughts.

"I don't want to leave Owen alone much longer myself," he said. "Don't want him barging out here, you know? But let's take a quick look at this hand."

Nate unwound the tape around my knuckles. I didn't open my eyes. I felt dull pain and a small dislocated sensation, and then a sharp flash of hurt as Nate applied pressure.

"Fuck!" My eyes flew open.

"Okay, it's okay." Nate smiled up at me. I gave him an anguished look, because every fucking thing hurt. Memory hurt, my heart hurt, my hand hurt, and I needed to get to Hannah. "It feels like you've got a boxer's fracture. I won't ask how this happened"—his eyes narrowed—"though I think I know. The good news is, it doesn't feel too displaced. You'll need X-rays. I'm going to buddy tape it, but don't use this hand until you see a doctor."

"I am seeing a doctor," I muttered, and Nate ignored me.

He reused the medical tape to bind my middle and ring fingers.

"Best I can do for now. I'm not going to offer you pain meds."

"Don't want any," I said. "How's Hannah?"

"I don't know, Matt. I saw her on Thursday. She left angry, like I said . . ."

"I need you to drop the lawsuit."

Nate's head came up. His face clouded with confusion. "She told you about that?"

"Of course. *I* wrote *Night Owl.* I wrote it. That girl who published it—Melanie—she did it because I asked her to. You can't bring charges against her. It was my doing."

"What?" Nate's voice was breathless.

"I can't explain it all now. Please, will you let it go?"

"Matt, of course . . . I . . ."

My words were a blow to Nate, I could see that. He reeled and touched the wall. And God, I felt like a criminal. All these months he'd been pursuing *Night Owl,* imagining he was doing me a favor, and probably focusing on the case in lieu of worrying about me. Now I yanked it out from under him.

"I'm sorry, Nate. I should have told you. I didn't want to risk the contact, but I should have . . . told Hannah, and had her tell you. Something, I don't know."

"It's . . ." Nate paced the narrow width of the hall. "I had no idea. It's nothing like your other books, it's—"

"Vulgar," I murmured.

"That, too." He rolled his eyes. "How could you publish such a thing? Did you spare one thought for Hannah?" Nate turned on me, his gaze hardening. "You didn't even change her damn name. How could you?"

He took a swift step toward me and I moved to meet him. We bristled in silence, glaring into one another's eyes.

"It's *my* book. *Our* story. Don't tell me what I should have done or shouldn't have written. It's my writing, Nate."

"Oh, you and your precious writing."

"What about it?" I got in Nate's face. There was a time when Nate could beat me handily, but we were older now and equals. "I love Hannah. She knows I love her."

"Does she?" Nate's temper defused with a sigh. He backed down, and I backed down. He turned away. "Go see about it. I'll call Shapiro tomorrow."

"Don't be angry with me." I moved around to look at Nate. "You can't be."

He smirked and shook his head slowly. "Don't I know it, brother."

"I have to go, Nate. We'll talk soon. Thank you. Thank you for everything."

We embraced again.

"How do you plan to come back to life?" Nate said.

"I don't know. With a bang?" I nudged him. "Nah, but really . . . I'll contact Pam. If she doesn't kill me or drop me, she'll help me negotiate something with the press. She has all these"—I waved a hand—"connections. I'll tell you, though, it's going to be fucking painful."

Nate nodded and smiled at me. So much emotion had boiled over in that hallway, it was hard to believe he was smiling again.

"You better get back to your boy," I said.

We shook hands and Nate grasped my arm.

"And you get back to your girl," he said.

I didn't want to wait for the elevator; I didn't want to watch Nate walk off. I took the stairs down to the lobby. As I breezed through the opulent space—white marble walls, high ceilings with gilt molding—my fingers went for the hat and sunglasses in my coat pocket.

I stopped my hand. *No, no more of that.*

I walked out into the bustle of Fourteenth Street. I searched for Mel's bright blue car. People pushed around me. A show must have just ended at the arts center or opera house.

Before long, I heard a silvery giggle and a gasp float over from a group of women.

"It *is*!" one said, elbowing her companion.

"You're crazy," said another. "Stop staring."

I glanced at them.

The bold one, the slender woman who spoke first, approached me.

"You're M. Pierce," she said. She pointed at me with her cigarette. "I know it's you. I saw a thing about you in the *Post.*"

"In the flesh," I said. I shook her hand and she laughed giddily.

"You're *terrible*!"

"Quite."

Mel's car came around the corner. I excused myself and gestured for Mel to roll down the window. I leaned in. "Hey, kid."

"You look smug," Mel said. The noise on Fourteenth Street was outrageous. We shouted to one another.

"Well, I'm going to see Hannah. Going to fix everything. And it feels good to be alive. Pass me my duffel bag, will you?" I pointed to the bag at the foot of the passenger seat.

Mel wedged it out the window. I slung the strap over my shoulder.

"You're going," she said.

"We're just a few blocks from here. I thought I'd walk."

Melanie nodded and fluffed her hair. "Fine, get going."

"Mel, it's been real." I held on to the edge of the window. "Look at me."

She glared at me with bleary eyes. "It's been surreal, Matt."

I unzipped my bag and pulled out my notebook. I tossed it into the car.

"My next book," I said. "It's not complete, but you can review it for your blog, huh? Or put it all over the Internet, right? Mail it back to me."

I couldn't get a smile out of Mel. She hugged the notebook and drove away with big tears slipping down her cheeks. I turned and headed up Fourteenth Street. The crowd seemed to be moving against me, which made me laugh. People smiled as I passed. Everyone was in a great mood because it was spring and tomorrow was still the weekend.

Now and then, I heard my names in the crowd. *Matthew Sky. M. Pierce.*

I let the people get a good look at my face, which is just another mask for the heart.

I remembered what I said to Mel when we shared a smoke in her car.

That's how it goes, right? You are who people decide you are.

So let them talk. Let the rumors fly.

Around four, I reached our street and jogged toward the condo. I felt good—hopeful, warmed by the April sun—and I knew I shouldn't feel so good. Not an hour ago, I was sick with worry. Dangerous . . . these changeable moods.

As I bounded up the complex steps and let myself into our condo, I remembered Mom and Dad again, and I remembered

Nate inspecting my hand, and the day felt full of consequence and significance. I dropped my duffel in the doorway. I scanned the kitchen and living room. Silence. No sign of Hannah.

Unease prickled through my blood.

Without checking the other rooms, I suddenly knew she was gone. I saw signs of a hasty departure: The cupboard hanging open, Laurence's hay dish newly filled, an uncapped pen on the counter. And a note.

I walked into the kitchen and read the note.

I reached the last line—*P.S. I slept with Seth*—and nodded slowly, my hand rising to my mouth. Of course. Seth and Hannah. Of course.

She wanted me to know that we were really over.

She told me the truth to help me let go.

It was a kindness, really.

And tomorrow, and the next day, there would be time for me to be strong. Time for me to handle this like an adult.

But for now—I sat on the kitchen floor and cried like a child.

Chapter 37

HANNAH

"Yeah, the three cheese." My sister squinted, chewing her gum with a loud snapping sound. "And pepperoni, sausage, um . . . onions?" She gave me a thumbs-up. I gave her a thumbs-down. "Nix that, no onions."

Chrissy went on talking into her cell, and I turned my attention to the TV.

My head felt stuffed with cotton. Too many gin and tonics.

On the screen, a couple kissed and music swelled. Roaming hands. Grasping and grinding. I changed the channel.

"Misery food successfully ordered," Chrissy announced. "What are we watching?"

"Nothing." I shut off the TV. "But you know—" My voice slurred. "Thank God for hotels. Even cheap hotels." I waved the remote like a wand. "Just the necessities, right? You've got your . . . scoliosis-inducing bed." I slapped the mattress. "TV. Crappy coffeemaker. And let's not forget . . ." I groped at the bedside table drawer. "The good old Book of Mormon."

Chrissy scooted closer to me on the bed.

She smiled uneasily and glanced around my room—Econo Lodge, downtown Denver, eighty dollars per night—where I'd been staying for the past three weeks. I refused to run home and hide. I refused to repeat last summer. This time, I had money saved and didn't need to lean on my parents. I also didn't want Matt to find me, if he was even looking.

P.S. I slept with Seth.

I winced and shook my head.

No, he probably wasn't looking.

"Have you been back to work?" Chrissy said.

"Nope." I sipped my drink and eyed Chrissy over the glass. She'd been keeping me company some nights—or checking up on me. No one else knew that I'd broken up with Matt, but everyone else knew Matt was alive.

The day I moved out of our condo, the Internet exploded with M. Pierce news:

Unstable author back from the dead.

Did anyone believe he was gone?

More publicity stunts from M. Pierce.

I didn't read those stories or watch the news.

I kept expecting a phone call from Nate, but it never came.

I took a week of vacation from work, called in sick the following week, and was rapidly running out of excuses to avoid the agency. But Pam didn't call or e-mail. Dead air.

"I'm going to," I said. "Probably, um, on Monday." *If I still have a job.*

"Great. You need a wake-up call?"

I rolled my eyes. "What I need is for our pizza to get here."

"Your pizza, Han. I've got a date." Chrissy hopped off the bed and stretched like a cat. A tight black skirt inched up her thighs. Her lashes were spiky with mascara and a stud glinted on her nostril. Huh. She did look more dressed up than usual, which I'd failed to notice in my gin and tonic haze.

I glanced down at my sweatpants.

A surge of self-pity went straight to my eyes and I blinked quickly, looking away.

"A date. Cool."

"Yup. Working, dating, showering . . . things people do in the land of the living."

I glared at my sister and she arched a brow. Maybe this was why I reached out to Chrissy and no one else. Because I knew Chrissy wouldn't let me wallow.

"I guess I should . . . grab a shower," I murmured.

"Probably, yeah." My sister preened in front of the bureau mirror. She fluffed her thick short hair and checked out her ass. Looking at her, I felt grimier by the moment. When had I last shaved, washed my face, moisturized? "Then you can get dressed and come with me."

"Excuse me? I'm not feeling that ambitious, Chrissy."

"It's not a *date* date, okay? You won't be third-wheeling it. I'm—" My sister paused and sniffed, still studying her reflection. All the vanity I lacked, Chrissy possessed. "I'm just going to hang out with Wiley and the band guys," she said hurriedly.

"Wiley and the . . ." My mouth fell open. The band guys?

Goldengrove.

Seth.

Unwelcome memories rushed over me. Seth Sky driving his Bentley, sneering and staring into the dark. Bringing me a little plate of food in Nate's basement. Barging through my condo doorway, his hungry tongue in my mouth.

And then . . . standing beside my hospital bed, holding my hand as I coasted in and out of consciousness. All night.

"Yeah, I'm totally a groupie now." Chrissy laughed.

I bit my lip and searched for words. Clearly, Chrissy had no idea about my brief and sordid history with Seth. And to be honest, I had no idea about it, either.

A few weeks ago, Matt Sky was my lover, Nate Sky was my friend, and Seth Sky was my enemy. But now? Now I envisioned Matt and Nate together, closing ranks. How had I missed the deceit in Nate's smile and the lie in Matt's gaze?

And Seth, who seemed so unwelcome before, now stood clearly in my mind's eye. Vulnerable. Honest. A casualty of Matt's game.

I slid my drink onto the bedside table, ice jostling in the glass. "Isn't *Goldengrove* in New York?" I managed.

"They were. Like, a few weeks ago. They're on tour—got here yesterday. Wiley called me." Chrissy grinned and buffed her nails on her shirt. "So I'm crashing their suite at the Four Seasons, which is, like, five minutes from here."

Five minutes from here, and about five steps from the Hotel Teatro.

But Nate should be back in New Jersey by now, unless he stuck around to take care of Matt. If Matt needed taking care of. If Matt was going crazy like he did last year.

I huffed and pushed myself off the bed. Why did I even care?

"Fine," I said. "I'll go."

"You will?" Chrissy danced over and prodded me toward the bathroom. "Awesome. You grab a shower; I'll cancel the grease pie."

Twenty minutes later, my sister and I strolled arm in arm along Fourteenth Street. It was busy for a Thursday, car horns and voices ricocheting in the April night.

I was still buzzed, or still drunk. The city lights blurred beautifully.

"This might be the worst idea ever," I said as we walked.

I kept mentally reviewing my last encounter with Seth—when he wheeled me out of St. Luke's, down the long antiseptic hospital halls.

At the time, I had wondered if he was angry or hurt . . . or still in shock. And finally he'd said, "Why are you with him?"

He stopped pushing my wheelchair and I swallowed noisily.

"I love him."

Seth came around and crouched in front of me, resting his hands on my knees. Hands like Matt's, strong and elegant. A face pale with fatigue.

"Do you?" he said. "Or did he force you into this? Matt is a master manipulator, Hannah. And you're not a cruel person, I can tell. *Now* I understand why you were so high-strung at the memorial. You didn't want to do any of this, did you? The lying. The sneaking around."

My eyes misted—I get emotional at the worst times—and I glowered at my lap.

"Please, just take me to my car."

"Hannah . . ." Seth's fingers tensed on my knees.

"Are you going to tell anyone? I mean . . . that he's alive."

Seth's expression darkened. He rose and resumed pushing my chair. "He disgusts me, but I'm not going to tell."

"Do I disgust you?" *I should.* I was right there with Matt, lying and scheming.

But Seth had only laughed.

"You? No, Hannah. I feel sorry for you. He's got you right where he wants you. Fucking incredible, really." I peeked up at Seth, who stared ahead abstractedly. "He's always been that way. I've seen it my whole life." Seth's sneer faded, and he looked momentarily awed. "He draws people in without even trying. Puts them under a spell. And then he does what he always does—lies or disappears—and you break on the rocks you were too dazed to see."

You break on the rocks . . .

A master manipulator.

Chrissy pulled me to a stop outside the Four Seasons. She tucked a damp curl behind my ear and thumbed away an eyeliner smudge. I'd let Chrissy do my makeup and pick my outfit—a short denim skirt, moccasin boots, and a loose, striped boat-neck top.

I actually looked cute, and I felt human for the first time in weeks.

"It'll be fun," Chrissy said. "And if not, we'll leave. No harm, no foul. You okay?"

I nodded. *No.*

"Cool. Wiley said Seth's been asking about you."

"He has?"

Chrissy took my hand and led me into the hotel, through the modern, well-appointed lobby. Every surface burned with a high shine.

"Yeah. Just, like, wondering if you're okay and stuff. Because, you know . . ." She shook her head. "Matt's a psycho, basically. I mean, I still can't *believe* he faked that shit. I'm so glad you had the guts to leave him. He is truly fucking crazy."

"Yeah . . ." My stomach seesawed.

We rode the elevator to the thirteenth floor and Chrissy read off room numbers in the hall. She stopped and knocked on a door. I closed my eyes.

Through the wall, I heard the low pulse of music.

Click.

A breath of air. The door opening.

Wiley's voice.

"Baby," he said, "there you are." Chrissy's hand slipped out of mine, but not before she dragged me into the room. Warmer air. The smell of alcohol and sweet smoke. An unfamiliar song— hypnotic and grinding, electronic.

I opened my eyes to a dim room.

My pupils adjusted, taking in the suite. The only light came from the cityscape, filtering in through wraparound windows. A film of smoke clouded the air.

Two guys I didn't recognize and three overdressed girls sat around a coffee table with drinks and playing cards. One of the girls eyed me. Her stare was steely, her mouth a blot of lipstick. I wanted to run.

"Oh, there's Seth," said Chrissy. She bumped my hip and I stumbled forward.

In the corner, in the shadow of a thick curtain, Seth slouched in an armchair.

He wore the same deadened expression I had seen on his face at the condo the night he realized Matt was alive.

I padded across the room.

Seth's eyes met mine and registered no surprise.

When I reached him, he leaned forward and licked a white dusting from his finger.

"Hannah," he said.

His hair was tied back, one loose piece lying against his cheek. He was barefoot and looked vaguely bohemian in torn jeans and a halfway-unbuttoned shirt.

I processed the scene slowly. Seth licking his finger. A porcelain plate on the table. A pile of snowy powder and two thick lines beside it.

"Oh," I said, plopping onto a chair. Something greater than gravity pressed me into my seat. I *wanted* to be there, talking to Seth. I wanted the past nine months to make sense.

"No big deal," Seth murmured. He shrugged and smiled miserably at me. "I'm not like Matt. Just a party."

"Yeah, sure." I tried not to stare at the cocaine. I'd only seen this stuff in movies.

"Help yourself."

"Are you guys allowed to smoke in here? I mean—"

Seth touched my bare knee.

"No big deal," he repeated calmly. "The hotel staff won't bother us."

I met his dark, devastatingly careless stare, and I nodded.

"Hi," I mumbled.

"Hi."

The rest of the room diminished. Seth and I sat in our corner of the universe, unhappy, silent, studying one another.

After a while, he took a key card from his pocket and began thinning the ridges of coke. He bent over the table and sniffed away a line, then slid the plate toward me.

"I've been drinking a little," I said, as if that would excuse me, and I pressed one nostril shut and inhaled a thread-thin line.

Maybe I didn't need an excuse.

Or maybe Seth and I had the same excuse.

Matt.

"First time doing that?" Seth said.

"Yeah." I sniffed and looked around. No one was watching. Almost immediately, excess energy fizzled up my spine, effervescing in my brain. I smiled. "Weird . . ."

"But good, yeah?"

"Uh-huh. I think so." A muscle jumped in my leg. I bounced my foot to the music.

"Great, then no worries." Seth stood, rubbed his face, sat. He ran his fingers up and down his thighs. Whenever we looked at one another, our eyes locked a little longer than necessary.

We spoke simultaneously, our voices colliding.

"Congrats on your record deal," I said, and Seth said, "Come to my room."

We laughed.

I studied my feet.

"Come to my room, Hannah."

"Sure," I said. "We can't talk in here anyway."

Seth took my hand and led me through the suite. We passed the girls playing cards and I smiled at them. Now, somehow, I belonged in this smoke-filled room.

We turned into a bedroom off the suite and Seth shut and locked the door. The clack of the bolt resounded in my brain.

"Better," he said.

The room smelled like clean linen. I saw fake flowers on a glass table, a neatly made king-size bed, and the city beyond a vast window.

I said, "You're really living the rock star dream, huh?"

"What do you mean?" Seth held on to my hand. A frisson of fear passed through me—I was alone again with this unpredictable man—and I watched him guardedly. From the next room, Lana Del Rey's new song started to play. *Boy blue,* she sang in her sultry voice.

"I mean nice hotels, drugs, girls."

Seth flashed a smile, feral in the dark.

"Whatever," he said. "Everyone gives in eventually."

He stepped closer and I instinctively stepped back, bumping into the wall.

"Have you been okay, Hannah?"

"Yeah, I'm okay." Another lie. "Just figuring myself out. I left

Matt." I said it offhandedly, but the words hung between us. *I left Matt, and here I am.*

"You all right for money?" Seth said.

I blinked, then glared at his half-lit face. The city lights played along his features, his jaw rough with stubble, his liquid dark eyes.

"I am *fine* for money," I said. "I am not some victim here, Seth. You should know that. Or is that how you still see me—as a pawn in Matt's game?"

My heart punched against my ribs.

Seth raised a brow and stepped closer still, his hips touching mine. I could lift my leg, drive my knee into his groin, and he'd be walking crooked for days. But I didn't.

"What do you think you are, Hannah, a player in his game? The queen to his king?" He lowered his head so that his mouth hovered beside my ear. He smelled like winter, smoky and masculine. "No, I'll tell you what you are." His breath whispered along my neck. He pressed against my thigh and I felt the hard length of his dick. "You're a class A drug."

I shuddered and shook off Seth's hand, but instead of fleeing, I grasped his hips.

"Hannah," he growled lowly.

Lana sang *move baby.* The music vibrated through the wall, strumming my blood.

Everyone gives in eventually.

I bent my clean-shaven leg, silky soft, until my knee slid under Seth's shirt and rubbed over his flank. I pressed my calf against the small of his back and tugged him closer.

"God," he said, grinding his erection against my thigh. "You're strong . . ."

Strong? I felt ephemeral, suspended outside of the scene.

P.S. I slept with Seth.

I wrote it to force Matt to get over me.

Now I was doing it to force myself to get over him.

Seth didn't kiss me, but he took what he wanted. He squeezed my breasts through my shirt, hiked up my skirt, and kneaded my ass. Everything was different . . . from being with Matt. Seth was rangier. Sharper angles. Cocaine fueled.

I simply held on to him and breathed.

When he undid his jeans and freed his cock, the thick weight of it resting against my stomach, I looked down.

My lips twitched, but I managed to keep my expression neutral.

A Prince Albert piercing crowned Seth's tip, the silver barbell shining in the dark.

My eyes lifted—and I met Seth's sly smile.

"What?" he said.

I shook my head. "Nothing . . ."

Seth pulled my hand to his dick. My fingertips brushed the overheated skin and he sighed. Tentatively, I touched the piercing— cool and weighted—and watched the ripple effect of pleasure on Seth's face. Eyelids drifting down. Lips parting.

This is power, I thought, *touching a man like this.*

And then I knew what I wanted to do.

I wrapped my fingers around his shaft. He hardened fully in my hold. I began to stroke him, my gaze moving between his arousal and his face, and he watched some unspecified point on the wall. God only knows what cocktail of substances Seth took that night. He looked delirious. As I jerked him up and down, faster, reaching into his jeans to rub his balls, he braced his fore-arms against the wall and began to thrust into my grip.

We stood so close. The serpentine movement of his body hyp-notized me. If I stopped . . . we would fuck. I would undress him and see those curling tattoos on his sides. We would kiss and say things we didn't mean. Counterfeit intimacy.

"Sweet girl," Seth whispered.

His cock thickened in my grip. I wrapped my fingers tight around his girth and head, and I let him buck into my hand until he came. He was curiously silent. Warm fluid surged across my palm. An expression like pain flickered on his face, primal and stunned, and then it was over.

The drumming of my heart filled my body.

Seth tucked himself away, zipped his jeans, and turned toward the window. I moved automatically to the bathroom and washed my hands in the dark.

When I stepped out, my skirt straightened, I found Seth seated on the edge of the bed. A few more pieces of hair had come loose from his ponytail. He looked beautiful, and fallen, like Lucifer. He lit a cigarette and smoked vapidly, his eyes on the floor.

"I'm pretty fucking high," he said after a while.

"I'm kind of wired, too."

"I knew it would be this way, if I hooked up with you." He sucked in a lungful of smoke. "So I just let myself go."

"Hey, don't even worry about it."

Seth chuckled. "I'm not worried about it." He lifted his head, looked at me, and I felt nothing. Not aroused. Not embarrassed or coy. Nothing.

I knew if I thought about Matt, though, and how much this would have hurt him, I would fall to my knees.

The heart always knows what the mind refuses to accept.

My heart knew that I would be holding a torch for Matt forever.

"Stick around and I'll make you come," Seth said, but his voice was defeated, as if he already knew my answer.

I went to him and tucked a piece of hair behind his ear. I touched his cheek and frowned.

"I'm sorry," I whispered, and left him smoking on the bed.

I let myself out of the room and found Chrissy. I told her that I wanted to walk back to my hotel, and then I did, feeling less and less alive with each step.

Chapter 38

MATT

One foot in front of the other. The rhythmic slap of my sneakers on pavement. The streetlights passing in long yellow ellipses.

And my breath coming faster and faster.

Calves burning, arms aching, my heart outpacing my stride.

As if I could outrun the pain.

But maybe I could. When I ran like this—dead runs late at night—I left behind the nauseating unease of Hannah's absence. I stopped picturing Hannah and Seth together, and I stopped trying to work out the logistics of their romance.

I reached the point of exhaustion, and then I pushed myself harder. And when my limbs felt numb and my chest seemed ready to explode, I smiled.

Here we go, I thought, *I'm going to collapse.*

Except I never collapsed, and the effort left me feeling juvenile and stupid.

A streak of sweat ran into my eye, salt stinging.

I slowed to a jog and pushed back my hair. *Everything's going to be okay,* I told myself. Then I imagined Hannah touching my face and saying, "Everything's going to be okay."

She left three weeks ago.

This wasn't getting any more okay.

I passed the Hard Rock Cafe and a little Italian place and re-alized dimly that I was about to cross Fourteenth. I stopped. In the city lights and nighttime traffic ahead, I saw someone like Hannah walking. A trick of the mind, no doubt. I refused to give in to irrationality.

I turned and sprinted back to the condo.

I had one new voice mail from Nate. I checked the time—ten for me, midnight for him—and returned his call.

"Why aren't you asleep?" I said as soon as he answered.

"It's not that late. How are you doing?"

"Fine. I was running." I sat at the kitchen island and fiddled with the AlumaFoam splint on the counter. I'd removed it to run. I barely wore it, in fact, preferring the pain in my hand.

"Running at night?" Nate said.

"Yeah. Running at night, not drinking, not drugging, not call-ing Hannah, not stalking her sister, not driving by her parents' house. Anything else you need to know?" I felt instantly cruel for snapping at Nate, who loved me beyond reason.

Nate, of course, laughed good-naturedly.

"That about covers it," he said. "You get some sleep, Matt. I'll talk to you tomorrow."

"Yeah. You, too."

I ended the call and took a quick shower. I ran the water cold.

Afterward, as I dried myself and dressed, I considered calling my old therapist, Mike. He would prescribe something to get me out of my head, and he would help me understand this dual anger and longing for Hannah.

Anger. *She fucking cheated on me. With my fucking brother.*

Longing. *I miss her so fucking much.*

Fuck.

I dismissed the idea quickly. I didn't need Mike to hold my fucking hand.

I went out on the balcony for a smoke.

Denver was alive and alight. As I ashed my cigarette onto the street below, I glimpsed a flash from a parked car. I smirked and waved.

The car window slid down and a camera protruded. I smoked listlessly while the photographer got a few more shots. Then the car door opened and a familiar figure stepped under the street-light: Aaron Snow. I would have recognized him anywhere.

I gave another little wave. He beckoned. I held up a finger— *give me a moment*—and put out my cigarette. I left the condo quietly and lit another smoke as I stepped outside.

"Matt Sky." Snow advanced. "Aaron Snow with *No Stone Unturned.*" His eyes were bright. He looked no older than I was, maybe even a little younger. He offered a hand.

"Hello there, Snow." I shook his hand. "Would you like a smoke?"

"Ah—" He lowered his camera. "Could I?"

"Of course." I passed the pack and lighter to him. As Snow lit his cigarette, I noticed his hands were shaking. "It's all right," I said. "You know, I wasn't myself last year."

Snow puffed on his cigarette and coughed.

How strange, to be having civil words with Aaron Snow. In his articles and his pursuit of me, he gave an impression of cunning. Now he looked like a lost boy.

"I know," he said. "I'm sorry; you've caught me off guard by coming down."

"Caught myself off guard. Let's sit." I walked to the back of the condo and took a seat on one of the steps. Snow perched beside me. Waves of nervous energy came off him. "Calm down, would you? You're making me anxious."

Snow couldn't meet my eyes. Improbably, I felt sorry for him, and now that I didn't hate and fear him, I thought I understood him. He was a young journalist trying to make his way. M. Pierce presented a puzzle and Snow solved it. Then Matthew Sky disappeared: a new puzzle for Snow's able mind. "You're quite a journalist," I said.

"Why did you come back now?"

"Off the record?"

"Of course," he said.

"A girl." I glanced up at my bedroom window, which was dark. The whole condo was dark. I should have moved out, but I stayed in that place full of things I bought to make Hannah happy. Now it was like an abandoned circus—all color and ornament, no laughter, no life.

And here I was, speaking calmly with the reporter Aaron Snow—not because I was lonely, but because I had no fight left in me. Snow seemed to sense it. We watched one another through the dark, and he appeared defeated rather than elated.

"A girl," he said. "I guess there's always a girl."

"I suppose so." I turned on the stair to face Snow. "Don't you have more questions?"

"Many," he said. "On the record now?"

I nodded. "On the record."

Snow got his bearings and began to ask about my disappearance. Where did I stay? Was my "death" a publicity stunt, a warped promotion for *The Surrogate*? Did I have a breakdown?

And he asked about *Night Owl*. Did I write it? When did I write it? Did I publish it? Other papers had asked and printed the answers to these questions, but Snow seemed to want personal satisfaction. He wanted the whole truth, which I would never tell.

I fed him the story about Melanie—how I found her online and compelled her to publish *Night Owl* on my behalf. It wasn't news. Pam had already arranged phone interviews with the *Denver Post,* the *Los Angeles Times,* and the *New York Times.* Everyone knew what I'd done, and why, and everyone believed I orchestrated it alone.

I was no longer hiding and running.

I was simply lying on the tracks, waiting for the next stray train to take me out.

After three cigarettes and a parade of questions, I said, "Look, I've got to go."

"Can I get a picture?"

"Sure."

I remained seated on the stairs—it seemed fitting—and Snow

crouched on the pavement to get a good angle. "Do I look like a writer?" I said.

He laughed. "You do. Can I have a formal interview sometime?"

"Mm. But don't run this story tomorrow, Snow. Let me chat with Pam first."

"Your agent."

"That's right." We walked back around the condo together.

"I'm surprised she kept you on."

"Are you?" I smiled and we shook hands. Snow seemed very young then, and guileless.

As I was heading for the door, he said, "Hannah Catalano is the girl, right?"

I turned sharply.

"Back off," I growled, and Snow recoiled.

My anger faded as fast as it flared, but it stunned me. That fire. That fight I thought I'd lost.

Chapter 39

HANNAH

On Monday morning, I fortified my nerves with a smart outfit—a taupe square-neck pencil dress, nylons, and black heels—and marched into the Granite Wing Agency.

Yes, I took a week of vacation. And a week of sick leave. And another unexplained personal week. But I deserved it, which Pam would understand.

I shuffled up the winding stone stairs to the third floor. At the landing, I closed my eyes and took a deep breath, and then I opened my eyes and stepped toward . . . *Matt.*

I teetered on my heels.

He walked briskly toward the staircase, his hand gliding along the balcony railing. He appeared unaware of me—for now.

Relief flooded my system at the sight of him. He was doing okay. He was sober and sane . . . and ridiculously gorgeous in dark jeans and a fitted black T-shirt.

Ugh, I wanted to slap myself. *Anger. You are angry with him. Green-eyed liar.*

Matt's gaze focused on me, finally. His face paled and he twisted away like he might turn to stone if he looked too long. And I stared at his back, which I had touched a hundred times.

Yes—I smoothed my hand up his spine months ago in a storage room in Flight of Ideas.

Before all this craziness.

When he was mine, and I was his.

Matt visibly regained control. He tousled his hair, cleared his throat, and turned to face me. "Hannah," he said. "It's great to see you."

Great to see me? Matt stared at the wall beyond me—easy for him, because he towered over me. I fought the urge to grip his jaw and force him to look me in the eye.

He was clean shaven, another good sign. I studied the fine golden hair on his forearms, the veins atop his hands, and the soft, comfortable-looking flip-flops he wore.

"You look good," he said, still staring at a point above my head.

"So do you," I whispered.

His eyes lit up briefly and sought mine, then swerved away. God . . . my heart hurt. This poor beautiful fucked-up boy—I'd made him feel undesirable, made him doubt his incredible magnetism, with my stupid lie about Seth.

He draws people in without even trying. Puts them under a spell . . .

Seth was right about that.

"I need to go," Matt said. "Things to do."

He moved past me and I wanted to scream. *Things . . . like what?* Microwave dinners to make? Tears swarmed my eyes. *Fuck.* I was *not* becoming one of those weepy women.

I leaned against the railing and let him go. His sandals went slapping down the stairs behind me, the sound fading rapidly. I watched him cross the lobby far below. Black hair that should be blond. Broad shoulders I used to grip as he rode me. Not my Matt anymore.

Something less than Hannah proceeded to Pamela Wing's office.

I knocked and she called, "Come in."

I opened the door.

"Well, Hannah," Pam said, not rising from her desk. She shifted her glasses down her nose and gazed at me over the frame. "Good to finally see you."

My thoughts remained with Matt. How perfect that black shirt looked with his black hair. The subtle tawny tone to his skin. He'd gotten sun.

"Ms. Wing, I—"

Pam lifted a hand.

"No explanation needed," she said, "but you will never do this again. I, too, have a personal life, Hannah. We all do. Personal struggles do not entitle us to shirk responsibility."

I straightened my back. "I understand. Thank you."

"And Matthew Sky is my client," she went on. "Will this be a conflict?"

"No." I shook my head hastily.

"Did you know he was alive?" Pam's shrewd eyes narrowed.

"No." *Yes.* But I couldn't dispute the story Matt told the papers. He wanted to take the fall alone. "I only found out when he showed up at the condo. I . . . moved out."

I chewed my lip while Pam digested my lie.

"Smart girl," she said. "He's absolutely insane. Absolutely."

"Are you going to drop him?"

I held my breath.

Pam's brassy laughter filled the office.

"Drop him? Please, Hannah. I think his little cult following tripled in light of this stunt. Americans love their deranged artists. I could almost kiss him, if I weren't so furious."

I waited for Pam to say more. I wanted to hear *why* she was furious: because she missed Matt, because she'd grieved for him, because she loved him, in her way.

Matt and Pam never said that, though. They refused to acknowledge any feelings for one another. *She's a shark,* said Matt. *He's insane,* said Pam. But together, they were almost like family, and I envied their closeness.

"At any rate," Pam said, "you have a lot of catching up to do."

I know a Pam Wing dismissal when I hear it. I nodded and

moved toward my office, but Pam spoke again as I reached the door.

"Ah, speaking of Matthew—he's scheduled to appear on the *Denver Buzz* in May. May fourteenth. Gail made a special opening for him."

I tried to picture Matt surviving a major talk show, and I felt a fierce, reflexive protectiveness. *Leave him alone.*

"Great," I said. "That'll be invaluable exposure for him."

"Yes, exactly. We chatted about it this morning. I've e-mailed you his talking points, and I need those on index cards by the end of the day. He'll pick them up tomorrow."

"Sure. Of course." I thought about Matt saying he had *things to do,* and I knew he was lying. Pretending he had a life outside of his writing. "I . . . still have a key to our mailbox at the condo, actually." I made my voice indifferent. "I could drop them off tonight."

"Even better," Pam said.

I left work at seven thirty.

I could have spent another hour in my office—I was way behind—but I wanted to catch Matt when he came down to check the mail. An ambush. I needed to see him again.

I drove to the complex and let myself into the lobby, which was quiet and smelled of linoleum. For twenty minutes, I dawdled by the wall of mailboxes. I jingled my keys and paced.

Ideally, Matt would find me here, as if we met coincidentally the moment I entered the lobby. Better than Matt finding me opening his mailbox. If this was still his mailbox. What if he'd moved out? God, he probably moved out. Or maybe he'd already checked the mail.

Maybe. What-if. So many possibilities.

I wiggled the mailbox key into the lock on box seven.

I tapped the packet of index cards against my thigh.

The longer I waited for Matt, the more miserable I felt, because I couldn't remember the simplest details of his routine. When he picked up the mail. When he ate dinner or worked out.

And I wanted to know those things.

I wanted to forgive him and be his little bird, but I'd alienated him completely with my lie about Seth. Then, to make matters worse, I went ahead and hooked up with Seth.

God, what had I done?

With a whimper, I wrenched open the mailbox.

A small voice in the back of my head reminded me that tampering with mail is a federal crime. I almost laughed. It would serve me right, ending up in court for this.

I flipped through Matt's mail without removing it from the box. Okay, he still lived here. He had two bills, a book of coupons, the latest issue of *Poetry* magazine, and a padded manila envelope. I pinched the corner of the package and slid it out enough to read the return address.

My eyes didn't get past the sender name: *Melanie vanden Dries*.

A chill rippled through me.

What in the actual fuck?

My propriety—and any concern for legality—vanished. I yanked the envelope from the mailbox and tore it open. Bubble padding snapped in the silence.

The package contained a marble composition book and a letter. *They're keeping in touch. Matt and Melanie. Lovers. Of course. Of course!*

I shook open the letter with unsteady hands.

Dear Mr. Sky,

Thank you so much for the opportunity to review LAST LIGHT. Unfortunately, after carefully reviewing your material, I've determined that this particular project isn't the right fit for me. I wish you all the best in your publishing endeavors.

Sincerely,
Melanie vanden Dries (:

P.S. I bet you haven't gotten a letter like this in a while. Keeping you humble, Mr. Sky.

258 | M. Pierce

My brow furrowed.

Again, I thought, *What the fuck? Is this some kind of inside joke?*

I slumped onto the ground, clutching the notebook. I felt sure that what I was about to read would break my heart—and I was right, as it turns out.

I flipped open the cover.

On the first page, I recognized Matt's unambiguous handwriting. Black ink. Slanting letters crammed together. The words pressed hard into the paper:

December is the cruelest month to die in . . .

Chapter 40

MATT

I ran right up to the complex, holding on to that heart-stopping sensation until the last moment. I unlocked the lobby door and jogged in. My sneakers squeaked on the linoleum.

I almost missed her.

She made no sound, only sat crumpled below the mailboxes.

A torn yellow envelope lay across her lap, and on top of that, my notebook.

I breathed deep and fast. Acid burned in my legs and sweat poured down my face. I barely heard my voice above my heart.

"Hannah . . ."

Red puffiness rimmed her eyes.

As I got closer, I saw tear tracks on her cheeks.

"For . . . the talk show," she mumbled. She thrust a bundle of index cards up at me.

"Ah." I wiped my hand on my shirt, which was plastered to my torso. My basketball shorts were sweat soaked, too. "These must be . . . my talking points?"

I scanned the scene, starting to understand. Hannah brought the notecards to my mailbox. She still had a key. Maybe she meant to return the key.

She opened the box, saw Melanie's envelope, and . . .

"You read it," I said. "My new book."

"Some of it. I skimmed the whole thing."

I watched her fight a wave of emotion—she was beautiful, strong and proud—and she lifted her head in a simple gesture of defiance.

"Take the cards," she whispered.

I shook my head.

"You bring them up. I'm covered in sweat." I turned and headed to the stairs, listening for Hannah behind me. I can't say what I felt—I don't know. Was it anger, anticipation, gladness? Tonight, my little bird flew home.

When I opened our door, she stood behind me.

I flicked on a light in the kitchen.

I'd put away Hannah's good-bye note—thank God—and kept the place clean. I'd changed nothing in her absence, though the pantry contained chips and ramen instead of real food.

I brushed my finger splint from the counter into a drawer. No point explaining about that.

What now?

Hannah placed my mail and the index cards on the island. I wanted to touch her—to lift her dress—and then I thought about Seth and felt ill.

"I'm glad you read it," I said. "Now you know."

"What do I know?" She lingered by the counter.

That I love you, I thought, *and that I didn't sleep with Mel, and how everything slid out of control.* But all I said was, "I need a shower. I won't be long. Stay if you want."

I left her standing in the kitchen.

And I knew she'd be gone when I got back.

Chapter 41

HANNAH

Matt disappeared around the corner and soon I heard water jolting the old pipes. Jeez, he was dripping sweat. He never ran like that when we were together.

I drifted through the kitchen and living room. I trailed my fingers over Matt's marble notebook. *Last Light.* It was a sequel to *Night Owl.* More of our story. And what a story it was.

Why didn't he tell me about it?

I spent a moment in front of the hallway mirror, blew my nose and dried my eyes, and then I settled on the couch. Laurence watched my benignly.

If Matt's story was true, and I believed it was, then he never slept with Mel. He also spared me the harrowing details of his fall and the mountain lion attack.

And, though I hated to admit it, reading Matt's version of events helped me understand why he put *Night Owl* online—just a little. I still thought it was wrong, but at least I understood.

I stared into space until I heard the whine of our bedroom door.

Oh . . .

Matt was getting dressed.

I could walk into that room right now and find him peeling off his towel, naked, clean . . .

"You're still here."

I started. Heat rushed to my cheeks when I laid eyes on him. Good Lord. His towel-dried hair spiked in every direction. His handsome face was somber, eyes glowing. Dark lounge pants and a T-shirt clung perfectly to his stunning body.

For fuck's sake—this was exactly why I shouldn't be around him. He had this infuriating mind-melting effect on me.

I stared at my knees.

"Yeah," I said. "Still here." *Still working up the courage to tell you that I lied about sleeping with Seth . . . and then gave him a hand job.*

Matt's quiet chuckle sounded behind me. I glanced over my shoulder. He stood in the kitchen, leaning against the counter, shuffling through the index cards I'd prepared. His gaze flickered to me and I lowered my eyes. Fucking *fuck*. What the hell was going on here? Somehow, within the space of three weeks, I had reverted to Hannah Who Cannot Speak Much Less Think Around Matt Sky.

And I was supposed to be angry with him.

And he should really be angry with me.

Instead, he seemed quietly grateful for my presence.

"These are too much. Pam wants me to quote Thoreau?" He laughed. "It's quite simple, Gail. 'I went to the woods because I wished to live deliberately.'"

"Yeah, Pam is . . . kind of funny."

"Mm, kind of."

I listened to the *flip, flip* of the cards in Matt's hands. The sound stopped, and he padded around the couch to stand before me.

"Look at me, Hannah."

I gazed up at him. This close, I could see the deep emerald tone in his eyes and smell the subtle spice of his soap.

"What did you think of my new book?" he prompted.

"Um . . ." My fingers knotted on my lap. "It's a lot to process

right now. You probably have no idea how weird it is . . . to read
about yourself in a book. In so much detail."

"No, I don't." A trace of amusement glimmered in Matt's
eyes—*what the hell could he find humorous right now?*—but he
looked dead serious in the next moment. "I'm sorry I keep writing
about you. I keep thinking about you. I'm obsessed with you."

I inhaled swiftly.

I'm obsessed with you. Words that should frighten me. But
Matt spoke with a calm honesty that undercut my fear.

I gave a minute nod.

"Okay," I whispered.

"Okay?"

"Yeah . . . okay."

He touched my cheek. I tipped my face into the cradle of his
hand.

"Do you still find me attractive?" he said.

"Matt . . ." My voice broke. His question chipped at my heart.
And the look on his face—that disarming mixture of cockiness
and vulnerability. I reached for him. "God, you know I do."

He climbed onto the couch, straddled my lap, and took my
face between his hands.

This was simple.

We were good at this.

And selfishly, I needed this—to remember the difference between intimacy for pleasure and intimacy for love.

Matt, on the other hand, probably needed some affirmation
of his desirability.

He kissed me and I made a soft sound of pleasure.

He tilted his head to seal our lips. His tongue moved in and
out of my mouth, and soon he matched that suggestive rhythm
with his body.

He groaned when I sucked on his tongue.

I held his hips as he rocked against me. I parted my legs, my
dress riding up, so that Matt's hardness found the soft spot he
wanted. We ground together. I did all the little things that drove
him crazy. I slipped my hands under his shirt and tweaked his

nipples. I raked my nails through his hair, down the back of his neck. I dug my fingers into his tight ass.

"Take it out," he gasped against my mouth. Always so bossy.

"You take it out." I licked his jaw.

He fumbled with the knot on his pants. While I sucked on his neck, he guided my hand to his cock. Rock hard. I pumped it a few times, moving the skin over his rigid erection.

He tried to lift my dress, but I pushed away his hands.

"Hannah, please."

"Not yet." I leaned back into the couch. "I want to watch you. Let me watch . . ."

Matt's sadness was gone, replaced by frustration and confusion. I nudged him off my lap. I couldn't have moved him if he didn't want to move, but he yielded. Maybe he felt guilty about all the lies. Maybe he was too horny to complain.

"On the floor," I whispered. I watched him with wide eyes. Would he go along with my idle fantasy? Matt loved to see me desperate for him; I loved to see him desperate for me. We weren't so different in our desires.

Matt hesitated, glaring at me. I fluttered my eyelashes. *Please?*

"Fine," he said. He slid off the couch and knelt on the floor, his cock in his hand. My breath quickened as I looked at him. *Perfect.* Matt hadn't even taken off his pants. His hair still smelled like shampoo. He looked disheveled and delicious, a fantasy incarnate.

He stared at me as he jerked off. Sometimes his eyes strayed over my body—my legs in nylons, heels on my feet—and sometimes he glanced down at his cock, but most of the time he held my gaze. He didn't say much. He was trying to keep it together, I could tell.

He began to pant, his arm and hand moving faster. I licked my lips. If I had Matt's boldness, I would have told him that this was so erotic for me. *This.* My lover in his raw need. My pussy swelled in my tight thong, the sensitive skin tingling.

Matt's lips parted. He twitched with pleasure.

"Fuck." He sighed.

Cum oozed from his tip. I listened to the sound of his lust, the sound of him working his own body furiously.

"Don't cover it," I said. "I . . . I want to . . ." A wave of heat reddened my face. "I want to watch you come. On yourself . . ."

Matt moaned. He was too lost to pleasure to glower at me now. He stripped off his T-shirt and sprawled on his back. I stood over him, staring down. My jaw dropped. Why was this so hot? I clenched my hands to keep from touching myself.

Matt writhed on the floor. One hand caressed his sac while the other jerked up and down his shaft, twisting from base to head and back.

"God, oh God," he moaned, and I knew he was going to come. The first thick spurt of cum hit his chest, another spattered along his stomach, and finally it oozed down his cock to his fingers. He hissed and cursed and said *God, fuck, fuck,* his eyes closed.

I swayed on my feet.

My thong was soaked.

Matt's eyes drifted open. He relaxed against the hardwood, his chest heaving.

"How wet," he asked between ragged breaths, "are you—after that, Hannah? Are you happy?"

I touched my cheek. I felt feverish with arousal.

"Get down here," he snarled. "Get out of your clothes. Come ride my face."

Matt crooked his finger and beckoned. I wriggled out of my nylons and thong and practically fell on top of him. *Fuck.* How could I feel brazen enough to ask Matt to jerk off on the floor, and in the same moment too paralyzed with embarrassment to put my sex on his face?

"Dress . . . too," he said, slowly catching his breath.

I lifted off my dress and unclasped my bra. I tossed the garments aside, and then I hovered awkwardly over Matt as he stared at my tits.

"Come here." Lust strained his voice. His eyes were dusky. "Come on. I want this. Don't hold back, Hannah. Do your best . . ."

I trembled as I crawled up Matt's body.

I planted my knees on either side of his head and lowered the apex of my thighs to his lips. *Fuck . . .* this felt right and wrong and so hot. And I wanted it.

I quietly appreciated yoga as I sank, my legs flexing easily to bring my sex to Matt's mouth. The contact sent shivers through me. My damp body . . . his warm breath and lips. I moved cautiously—did he seriously want me to suffocate him?—but Matt seized my buttocks and forced my pussy against his mouth.

"Matt!" I groaned.

He moaned against my cunt. His tongue lashed out, tasting the soaked seam of my body and delving in and out of me. He sucked on my clit and bit my lips, tugging, savoring my desire. He made the most indecent sounds.

Pleasure warmed me from my abdomen outward. I curled my fingers against the floorboards and the blush staining my cheeks burned hotter. With Matt's mouth devouring my pussy, I kept getting wetter. I couldn't stop. I *tried* to stop, because it was embarrassing—the amount of arousal oozing from me and coating Matt's lips and tongue.

But Matt didn't care. Or rather, he loved it. He lapped at me and licked it away; he sucked on me and made me wet again. Delight crackled up my nerves and sent signals like fireworks to my brain.

"Oh, God . . . Matt," I moaned. "Matt . . . *Matt.*"

That boy loved to hear his name on my lips. He moaned in response, his voice vibrating over my clit, and I gasped. "Fuck, Matt!"

Another answering moan, muffled in the soft petals of my sex.

His strong hands encouraged me to move. He drove me up and down, rubbing my body over his lips, down to his chin, up to his nose. I shook violently. *Oh . . .* I was making a mess on my lover's face, I could feel it.

I dared a look at Matt. My breasts swayed above the floor, and beyond them I saw the top of Matt's head. Even in this, he couldn't stay still. He leaned away from the floor. He pressed his mouth into my body intimately, buried his face, gasped for air.

My hips wanted to roll against his mouth, but I held back. Why?

I want this, Matt said. *Don't hold back. Do your best . . .*

Matt always wanted me to abandon reason—in sex as well as in life. That's what he did. Why couldn't I? He lived without fear of what others thought. I lived like a normal person, in my self-imposed restraint. But Matt was free, I knew, and I was not, and the double edge of his freedom was his incredible instinctive selfishness.

I swayed my hips, bucking against his face. He slapped my ass. The swift sting heightened my pleasure. I thrust again and he hit me again. When I began to move on my own, he released my bottom. God, I probably had bruises, he gripped me so hard. And fuck, I loved that. I loved his fierce need.

I watched Matt as I drove my sex over his mouth. Sticky streaks covered his skin. He licked and sucked when he could, but mostly he let me work my rhythm. I understood then what he wanted me to do. He wanted me to bring myself to orgasm like this.

I didn't miss a beat as I moved. Why should I? So often during sex, Matt forced his erection into my mouth—and I gagged on it with joy. His desire and my degradation were white-hot pleasure for us both. My desire and his degradation were the same.

In the groove of Matt's mouth, I found a spot to rub my clit. I rode him steadily, my thighs tense as I applied pressure. He stopped spanking me. His hands rested against my sides and his noises quieted. I threw back my head, blood rushing to it, and the colors of the condo swirled kaleidoscopically. All for me—this crazy décor. Our small, safe, happy place.

I closed my eyes and searched for my pleasure.

When the roll of my hips grew tiny and frantic, Matt plunged his tongue into me. He fucked me with it as I came.

I moaned, my voice a hoarse cry, and I rubbed out the whole of my pleasure against his mouth, and it was fire and heaven all over again. That garden where only he took me.

Chapter 42

MATT

We lay together on the floor, sticky and breathless.

"Are you cold?" Hannah whispered.

With her sweet breath blowing across my ear, her body draped over mine, I almost believed we were all right.

"You know I am," I said, because I always get cold after I come, and she hugged me.

She doted on me for a while—rubbed my sides, kissed my collarbone, and feathered her fingers through my hair—and then she sat up and the spell snapped.

We weren't all right.

I wiped my face and chest with my T-shirt. I retied my pants.

Hannah swayed as she struggled back into her panties and dress. I watched, detached, rather than reaching to steady her.

My hand ached. Fortunately, Hannah hadn't noticed me favoring the left.

I retrieved a hoodie from the bedroom and returned to find her standing by the door, her expression inscrutable. *Don't leave,* I thought, though I felt so confused. Warring emotions. Loneliness for Hannah. Brittle anger when I remembered Seth.

"I'm sorry," she said. She plucked her keys out of her purse. "We probably shouldn't have done that. It confuses everything."

I folded my arms. "I enjoyed it."

"Yeah . . ." She trailed off. Her gaze danced along the floor, pausing where I'd knelt. "Um. Your keys." She freed our condo and mailbox keys and held them out to me.

I closed her fingers around the keys. "Keep them."

"Matt—"

"Just keep them. Where are you staying?"

"At a hotel. Alone."

"Move back in. We don't have to have sex. I'll sleep on the couch."

"Yeah, because we have so much restraint." Her gaze loitered on the floor. I could see her deciding that what just happened was a mistake. *Fuck.* It wasn't a mistake.

"Tell me what happened with Seth," I said.

Hannah blanched, her eyes growing wide.

"Tell me," I insisted. "If you don't, I'll keep imagining the worst, and the worst is—"

"I didn't sleep with him. I didn't. I never cheated on you. After I left you, though—" Hannah hesitated, and I stared at her mouth, unable to comprehend. *She lied to me? She didn't sleep with him. This is good news. But it feels bad.* "Matt, it's fucking impossible to explain. I was drunk. I gave him a hand job. That's all."

Instantly, the image materialized. Sickening. Hannah's hand on my brother.

I went for my cigarettes, which were on the coffee table.

"Fine," I said.

"Fine? You're angry."

"Yeah, fucking sue me." I turned away from Hannah. "Of course I am."

"It was a onetime thing, Matt. It was a mistake. I was drunk . . . I was messed up. How can you be angry now, when you thought I slept with him before? God, you make no sense."

I glared at the wall, seething.

"He took advantage of you," I hissed.

"No. *I* took advantage of *him*." Hannah's voice hardened. "And I did it because I was trying to get over you, okay? And I never will, and I know that now."

"Oh?" I laughed. "Now you know, is that right?" I rounded on her. I wanted to look her in the eye, let her see my hurt and anger. "All it took to clarify your feelings for me . . . was giving my brother a hand job?" I smiled venomously. "How convenient. Tell me, did you also have to blow Nate, or was handling Seth enough to—"

The flat of her hand struck my cheek, hard. My head whipped aside with the force of the slap. *Fuck.* I was asking for that.

The sting came belatedly, pain sizzling to the surface of my skin.

"Hey, fuck you," Hannah growled. "At least I wasn't buying drinks for some ditzy little girl, letting her feel me up by the side of the road—"

"Oh, get off it. Don't you fucking start in on my writing."

"Ha! Your writing. Is that even writing, or is that just transcribing your fucked-up life?"

"You wouldn't know the difference, Hannah. You're not a fucking writer—and you don't know a goddamn thing about it."

"God, you're so conceited! You don't have the fucking patent on pain, Matt." She shoved my chest. "You don't get to play the tortured genius card every time you fuck up."

Part of me—a small, remote part—admired Hannah even as we squared off. Dear fucking God, she was beautiful. She was alive in her anger, her eyes illuminated, her body electric. She gave no ground, took no excuses. She saw straight through me.

Magnificent.

We ran out of angry words, and Hannah left spontaneously. The emptiness of the condo echoed around me. Nate made his nightly call; I lied and told him I was fine. The living room smelled of sex and Hannah's perfume.

I killed the lights, smoked on the balcony, and thought about her.

Afterward, I sent her an e-mail.

My thoughts crystallized instantly into words—no brooding and backspacing.

Subject: (no subject)
Sender: Matthew R. Sky Jr.
Date: Monday, April 28, 2014
Time: 10:15 PM
Hannah,
Do you know the story of the Garden of Eden?
God banishes Adam and Eve from the garden, and he blocks the gates forever with angels and a sword of fire.
You're that sword—I swear.
Tonight I said things I didn't mean. You did, too.
But you know the truth. You'll never be happy without me. Come home.
Matt

I sat in the office waiting for her reply, which came within minutes.

Subject: Re: (no subject)
Sender: Hannah Catalano
Date: Monday, April 28, 2014
Time: 10:21 PM
Matt—
You're so poetic when you want to be. Are you manipulating me, or are you a hopeless romantic? I can never tell. This is what I get for falling in love with an artist. You don't see the difference between fiction and reality. Everything is your story.
I need a few days to think.
Hannah

"A few days to think" turned into a week, which passed in a colorless procession.

May arrived with warm, blustery mornings and the sort of

cool spring evenings that would have been heaven with Hannah—
and that were hollow without her.

I wrote and read and ran.

I seemed to fantasize nonstop.

When I slept, I dreamed I was still in the mountains—
surrounded by silence and thin air—and the search parties called
for me in the dark. *Matthew Sky! M. Pierce!*

Unfamiliar voices ringing through the woods.

I ran, of course, and they never found me.

Chapter 43

HANNAH

On May 7, I turned twenty-eight.

I drove to my parents' house, where Mom, Dad, Chrissy, and Jay threw a party for me. I felt like a kid. A kid with no friends.

Still, I could see that it made Mom happy, so I went through the motions. They all pitched in on an Amazon gift card, and we ate sushi and drank Red Stripe.

After the cake, Chrissy and I sat on the deck. I stargazed and she smoked a cigarette.

"So," I said. "You and Wiley."

"Me and Wiley." She sighed dreamily.

"Be careful, Chris. Those guys are into some serious stuff."

"You mean coke?" My sister smiled at me. Chrissy probably came into contact with drugs all the time, but I felt obligated to warn her. Older sister habits die hard.

"Yeah," I said, "and who knows what else? Just—"

"I'll be careful. Don't worry."

We sat in silence for a while. Chrissy smoked a second cigarette, and when she finished it, she said, "Han, I gotta show you something."

She led me into the house and down to my old room in the

basement, which now served as a storage room for junk. How depressing.

"Here." She toed a large box. It had been opened. "Dad was going to throw it out, because . . . he honestly thinks Matt is insane and dangerous, but . . ."

Matt? I knelt by the box. It was addressed to me at my parents' house. He must have assumed I moved home. I glanced at the return address. *PoshTots . . . ?*

"Hey, isn't this like . . . a high-end kids' store?"

"Pretty much," Chrissy said.

She perched on a stool while I peered into the box. A gift note lay on top of a mountain of Styrofoam peanuts.

Sweet Bird—Happy birthday. I didn't know where to send this. I hope you get it. Just a little something. I love you. Matt

I sifted through the packing material. My fingertips bumped into velvety fabric, and I withdrew a . . . plush rabbit?

Button eyes dimpled its small face.

"There's like twenty of them in there," Chrissy murmured.

She was right. I found more rabbits in the box, each made with unique fabric, as well as ducks, elephants, squirrels, pigs, owls, and turtles. "Over two-freaking-thousand dollars in stuffed animals," Chrissy informed me. "I Googled that shit."

I sat cross-legged on the carpet with my little menagerie surrounding me.

"Chris, I better give him a call."

She nodded and slipped out, closing the door behind her.

I found Matt in my contacts—we were back to using our real phones—and hit send.

He answered a few seconds into the first ring.

"Birds," he said. "Happy birthday."

"Hey. Thanks."

"Twenty-eight, huh?"

"That's right." I picked at one of the plush owls.

"Did you get the animal friends I sent?"

He was in a good mood, I could tell. Sweet warm voice, no cynicism in it, probably smiling, probably because I'd called. My toes curled instinctively. I loved happy Matt . . .

And the last Matt I saw was definitely not happy.

"Yeah," I said. *Yeah, leave it to you to give me the most ridiculously cute and whimsical birthday gift ever and make me feel like a child in the best possible way. Damn it.* "They're . . . great. Adorable. I don't know what to say, I mean . . . thank you."

"You could invite me over."

"Hm?" I sat up straighter. "Uh, it's pretty late."

"So what? I'm a night owl, remember?"

"How could I forget. Matt, I just . . . don't think you should come over. It's my first time home in a while. And my father might castrate you."

"Dang . . ."

"Yeah. He thinks you're crazy. You can probably see his point of view, right? The stuff last year in Geneva, now faking your death. You're not every father's ideal—"

"I won't knock," Matt said. "I'll park down the street and walk."

"No, Matt. I don't think—"

"Great. I'll meet you out back. By the hammock? Gimme ten minutes."

"Hello? Matt? I am saying don't come over. Are you—"

Click.

"Matt? Hello?"

I blinked at my phone. *That son of a bitch . . .*

I wrote a text.

Stubborn night owl. I'll meet you in the backyard.

I grinned when I hit Send. Hm, this was fun.

Fifteen minutes later, I crept through the basement to the patio door. Chrissy must have gone to her room, and Mom and Dad were sleeping—I hoped. Jay was gaming. He didn't look at me as I passed the computer. Only Daisy, our ten-year-old springer spaniel, showed an interest in my mission. She snuffled around my feet and whined as I peered through the glass.

I could just make out the pale cords of the hammock in the dark. I cleaned my glasses and looked again. It seemed to be swaying gently.

I let myself out, not Daisy, and strolled toward the back of the yard. Spring wind rushed through the trees. The stars looked like little sockets of fire, and I felt slightly displaced, which is what spring nights do to me.

I glanced back at the house. Lights out, good . . .

"Hello, little bird."

I froze.

Matt lay in the hammock, arms folded behind his head, legs crossed at the ankles. He wore a T-shirt and pale torn jeans. I knew those jeans. I knew how they hung low around his hips. His hair was disheveled. He smiled at me.

In two words, he looked *fucking edible.*

"The last time you came out of your house for me, all furtively, I mean, you were wearing some tiny"—he gestured at me—"tiny things, under a big old housecoat. Such a powerful memory for me, Hannah. Mm . . . when I remember that, I—"

"Okay, okay." I laughed reluctantly. "I think I know where you're going with that."

"Come keep me company."

My feet carried me closer to the hammock. "I've been thinking, you know, and—*Matt!*" I shrieked as his arm snaked around me. He yanked me onto his body. The hammock swayed perilously. From inside, Daisy sounded the alarm—three throaty old-dog barks. I giggled and she went quiet. "You're a jerk."

"You wouldn't have come out here if you were really angry with me." Matt tucked my body against his. His hands traveled over me, remembering me in their greedy way. "Mm, Hannah bird. I'm lonely for you. I bet you called to check up on me. Afraid I'll drink?"

"Should I be?"

"Should I drink? Will that make you come take care of me? I like when you dote on me."

Matt's hands made a persuasive case. He stroked my back again and again, the pressure and pace of his palms sensual. I pillowed my head on his chest. I breathed in the scent of his body wash. Oh, freshly showered Matt . . . fuck me . . .

No! Ugh. What the hell?

"No drinking," I said. "Of course no drinking. That's not a joke."

"I know, I know." Matt sighed. His hands were under my shirt, rubbing my sides. My toes curled and uncurled. "I'm kidding. Contrary to popular belief, I take my sobriety very seriously. So what were you saying—something about thinking?"

I trailed my fingers over Matt's neck. I remembered last July and how we lay in this hammock, and how Matt kissed me against a big cottonwood. That same longing existed between us, not at all diminished. Was it because we stayed apart so much? Would our passion fade if we stopped all this stupidity and attempted a real, durable relationship?

"I was thinking, I have a stipulation."

"Fancy," Matt murmured.

"If I move back in, you have to start seeing Mike again. Regularly. Or another therapist, I don't care."

Matt's arms stilled. "Why? I'm fine now."

"No, you're not. You think you can keep me in the dark, but you can't. The way you lie to me . . . it's a problem. It's like a chronic problem. Your lists? The way you flip out when you can't control something? What about the fact that you can't say good-bye? Look, everyone has issues, Matt. Everyone could benefit from a professional, objective opinion—"

"Fine."

I lifted my head. "Fine?"

"Fine. I'll see Mike. Whatever. Come home."

I kissed his chest. "Not yet."

There were other, darker things I wanted Matt to open up about—his anger, the loss of his parents, and that mysterious suicide attempt in college—but not tonight. Tonight I missed him, and I needed this peace and sweetness to help me forget our screaming match at the condo.

"Hannah?"

"Mm?" I looked up at him.

"Did Nate try anything funny with you? You know, did he—"

I touched his lips. "No, he would never." My mind wandered back to the Hotel Teatro. I pictured Nate's friendly smile, then the glint of wickedness in his grin as he watched me swirl my scotch. "He's so loyal to you," I whispered.

"We're loyal to each other," Matt said. His voice was sad.

I snuggled against his body and kissed his neck. It was easy to fall into those small gestures of comfort. Matt's hands resumed their roaming, and soon he was pulling my body against his in a way that said, *I want to fuck.*

"Oh, no you don't." I giggled.

"Hm?" He squeezed my ass.

Fuck, though . . . that felt good. I wiggled my hips against his. He sighed. "Hannah, I miss you . . ."

"Your dick misses me." I rubbed his flank. God, I loved his body. Was this his game—driving over here to seduce me in the hammock? Hilarious, and artless.

"That, too." Matt laughed. "Come home . . . I only need you all night . . . every night . . ."

"Tempting." I kissed his jaw.

"Or here? Here is fine, too. Motion of the hammock and all." Matt was half laughing, half serious—and he looked good like that. His strong, lean frame moved restively under mine. His hand slid between my legs, touching my sex through denim. He sighed when he felt that soft, plump skin. "God, Hannah . . ."

I squirmed on top of him. I should break away. Go inside. Sex wasn't conducive to rethinking our relationship. Right? He touched me there again and my body responded, rubbing along his. My nipples stiffened against his chest.

"Always," he whispered. "You feel it, too, don't you? You always want me. I always want you. We belong together, Hannah."

His fingers dug into my bottom and I squeaked. It hurt just enough to feel good. I rocked against Matt. He sat up halfway, vying for control. Trying to get on top of me. In the hammock. And we went over together, tangled, grasping at each other.

Matt managed a quick *"fuck!"* and I yelped as the hammock dumped us on the grass.

"Ack!" I landed on Matt's hard body. Matt landed on the hard ground. My arm was up his shirt and his hand was down the back of my jeans.

He rolled me over and pinned me to the grass, grinning.

"Gotcha."

"Matt, not here. Not right—"

As swiftly as he'd overturned me, he stood and pulled me to my feet.

"Then out here." He tugged me deeper into the yard. Deeper into the dark.

An unexpected wave of giddiness made me giggle.

He glanced over his shoulder and smiled, his handsome face veiled in shadow. A perfect half-moon hung in the sky, casting coin-sized spots of light through the leaves. That light moved over his body and he was beautiful, and he was mine.

He released my hand and started to undo his fly, the humor fading from his face.

My blood turned to magma. Thick, slow, scalding.

I mirrored Matt, unbuttoning my jeans. Our zippers sounded loud in the silence.

We moved together clumsily, hands fumbling in the dark. I touched his cock and he sighed, thrusting into my grip. *Nothing like Seth,* I realized. I remembered the nihilism of Seth's suite at the Four Seasons—people drinking and drugging and coming without feeling—and my heart quickened. That meant nothing. This meant everything.

We kissed. Matt guided me down onto the grass.

"Hannah," he whispered. "You know I need this . . ."

Without ceremony, he settled over me—and slid inside me, the flared head of his cock stretching me wide. *Ah*—that moment—I arched under him.

"God, baby," I gasped.

"Fuck, yeah," Matt answered, driving his length home. Such rich satisfaction in his voice. He touched me deep inside. I raked my nails down his back.

"Heaven," he said, and he moved over me. Filling me, emptying me. I flexed my body to meet his thrusts. "Not yet, no," Matt panted whenever he felt me nearing the edge. Then he slowed and I slowed, and we started that exquisite rising spiral all over again.

"I want to be with you," he whispered in my ear. "You're soaked for me . . ."

I caressed his silky hair and rubbed his back when he began to move more urgently. This wasn't our usual sex—rough and dirty and torturous. This was about love and mutual need, and my heart burned as hot as my pleasure.

I wrapped my legs around Matt's waist. His jeans rubbed along my inner thighs, his abdomen grinding over my clit. This time, we didn't slow down.

We gazed at one another in a state of wonder.

"Need this." He mouthed the words again.

I fisted my hands in his hair.

My climax came as a slow shock, mounting in intensity until I was shaking, and I felt Matt coming inside me. Is anything more intimate?

I watched ecstasy unfold on his face against a backdrop of leaves and nighttime sky. It was, inadvertently, the most romantic sex of my life, and afterward we clung to one another.

Only then did the full weight of relief settle on me. *Matt is going to live like a normal person. He's in Denver, not hiding, and he wants a life with me. A life we can actually share.*

We could really make a go of it now.

And if we failed? At least we tried.

I felt, too, the darkness of the last four and a half months—

Matt at the cabin, me in Denver, lies and secrets. Worries. Quick calls. Lonely nights.

No more.

No more waiting and wondering about the future. No more living with one foot in the real world and one foot in Matt's world. No more choosing between the two.

But I had been willing to give up a normal romance to be with Matt, because I loved him. Now he was willing to give up his sanctuary to be with me, because he loved me.

He loved me.

My happiness eased into soft, uncontrollable sobs. Matt held me close.

"It's all right," he said. "It's all right now, little bird."

His quiet voice went on and on in the dark.

Chapter 44

MATT

After the night Hannah cried, I assumed she would come home. She didn't. She "still needed to think," she said, and she "might have more stipulations."

On Friday afternoon, I met with Pam and Gail Wieder of *Denver Buzz*. Gail showed me around the set, thanked me for agreeing to appear, and briefly reviewed the program. Afterward, Pam and the staff talked me through a pile of paperwork.

"I need you here at seven on Wednesday," Pam said. "Here. I'm not going to hold your hand, Matthew. Call me when you arrive. We'll go over everything, they might want to do a little makeup, then we'll rehearse some more and—"

"Makeup?" I sneered.

"This is TV, Matthew. Don't be naïve. Also"—she glanced at my gray shirt—"no gray. And no crazy prints. Wear something solid, bold, a rich color that won't wash out under the light. No red and no white. Do you have blue? Well, of course you do. Wear blue."

Pam went on talking as we left the building. She gestured officiously as she spoke, tapping my shoulder for emphasis.

I stared at the pavement. The gray day suited my mood. Where was Hannah?

"Your job this weekend is to memorize the talking points. Hit your points. Less is more. You're conveying a message. And do *not* ramble."

"Hannah . . . you think she'll watch the show?"

Pam sniffed. "Not sure, Matthew. Not relevant."

"Mm. Sorry." I leaned against my Lexus.

"Any *relevant* questions? I need to get to the office."

"Will Knopf publish *Night Owl*?"

Pam laughed and began looking for her keys. "Knopf will publish anything you write, but you can't be serious. Haven't you already—" She cut herself short.

I knew where she was going.

Hadn't I already damaged my relationship enough?

"Hannah's a good deal more open-minded than you know, Pam. And she's a bit of a writer herself. You better watch out; you might find yourself in a book."

I opened my car door and lingered, waiting for Pam's riposte.

Pam rattled her car keys.

"Duly noted, Matthew, though you forget that I already am in a book. A certain W. Pierce refers to me as 'the shark.' My, my."

I grinned and climbed into my car.

Back at the condo, I lay on the couch and struggled to memorize my stupid talking points. I found myself concentrating on Hannah's handwriting—cute, bubbly cursive.

Hunger scraped at my stomach. I felt light-headed, depressed. I called Hannah and the call went to voice mail. "Leave a message!" she chirped.

I cleared my throat.

"Hey there, birdy bird. I'm just . . . hanging out at the condo. Not doing anything really. I wanted to say . . ." *To say what? Come home, I'm getting badly depressed?* "Uh, the cards. Thank you again . . . for the index cards. I've been memorizing them. Yeah, that . . . thing is on Wednesday. The *Buzz*. Talk show thing. So, wish me luck. Anyway . . . call me sometime."

Hannah didn't call.

I slept away the weekend, which is what I do when I feel bad, and I marked off days on the calendar. Four weeks since she moved out.

What did this mean? When was she coming back?

On Wednesday morning, I woke with the idea to e-mail Hannah a piece of our collaborative story. I hadn't thought about the story—*really* thought about it—for months. We simply left our characters on the road to Seagate, an imaginary port city in an imaginary world.

I smiled as I remembered. Hannah and I began with Lana and Cal. Their attraction was our attraction. Their adventure was our adventure. How could we let it go?

I showered fast and pulled on boxers and a blue cashmere sweater. Blue for Pam. I sat at my desk and sifted through e-mails until I found the last story installment.

Oh, right . . . Lana and Cal were camping by a river . . . bathing together.

I reread my last paragraphs, then Hannah's last paragraphs. Cal was washing Lana's skin. I described the water—cold and silver like mercury—and sidestepped much description of Cal's body. I noted a tattoo along the tops of his shoulders. I wrote that his hair was *long and corn yellow, his eyes shining and orange. Cal: a strange creature from the borderlands of reality.*

Hannah, too, shied away from the details of Lana's body. *Cal captivated Lana,* she wrote. *She barely breathed as he rinsed the soap from her skin.*

The scene was suspended before intimacy.

And I, who wrote *Night Owl* and sex scene after sex scene, felt suddenly anxious about writing sex with Hannah. What the hell?

I typed a few sentences. I deleted them. I couldn't access Cal's mind.

Defeated, I moved Cal out of the river. He dried himself and lay naked on his bedroll. Summer wind washed through the field. I felt that night as if I were lying in it—I saw the starry darkness Cal saw—and then the words came.

He called to Lana with his hundred voices.

I e-mailed the paragraph to Hannah. My phone began to ring. It was Pam.

"Where are you?" she said.

I checked the time. *Fuck.* It was 7:45 and I was sitting at my desk in a sweater and boxers, my hair dripping wet.

"Traffic!" I said. "Be there in five."

I ended the call. I used one of Hannah's old hair dryers on high. My black hair stood in every direction. *Shit shit shit.* I yanked on dress slacks and grabbed my index cards.

"C-commodity. My privacy is not a consumable commodity." I rehearsed lines as I sprinted to my car. "The woods . . . to live deliberately. Fuck."

I gunned it to the studio.

A team of staff met me at the door. A man with a headset said, "He's here, on in ten."

They ushered me into a wardrobe room and began combing my hair and powdering my face. I blinked and twitched. How weird, all these hands picking at me.

My cell rang again. It was Pam—again.

The wardrobe people kept fussing as I took the call.

"Matthew, did you miss the rundown with staff? What the hell?"

"Traffic, remember?" Someone turned on a bright lamp and I winced.

Last Friday, the studio was quiet and still. This morning, it was chaos. People everywhere, screens and cameras, wires, endless chatter.

"Okay, it doesn't matter." Pam sighed in my ear. "Remember, Gail is going to go off script; that's how talk shows work. Breezy, casual—then *bam,* a really probing question. Keep it light. Laugh. You aren't stressed. You have nothing to apologize for. Are you stressed?"

"Nothing to apologize for," I mumbled. I dropped my index cards. They went in every direction. Hannah's cute handwriting all over the floor. I dove after them. One of the wardrobe people continued messing with my hair. I flailed. "Enough! Get the fuck off me!"

When I got back up, I saw Hannah.

She wore a short spring green dress and heels . . . and the silver owl bracelet I gave her at the cabin. My mouth dropped open. She laughed.

God, she looked so cool, so calm and lovely.

Pam was in my ear. "Matthew! What happened? Matthew!"

I covered the receiver and walked to Hannah.

"It's Pam," I said. "She's going DEFCON one."

Hannah slipped the phone from my hand. "I'm here," she said to Pam. "Yes. I know. Yes. We have to go. Thanks, Pam. We will. I will." She ended the call.

I raised a brow. "Please teach me that skill."

"We have to go. We have two minutes."

"We?"

Hannah took my shoulder and guided me through the studio. People hurried past us. The air seemed to vibrate with energy.

"Yes, I'm going on with you," Hannah said.

"Does Gail know? Does Pam know?"

Hannah smoothed back my hair. Her face was tranquil and kind.

"They know," she said. "It was very last-minute. Don't worry, I'll stick to our story about everything. Trust me." She smiled. "I got index cards, too."

I held Hannah's face and focused on her eyes. The manic vibe of the studio was getting under my skin, and I couldn't lose it here, now. I drank in Hannah's calm.

"You forgive me?" I said. "Come home. Please come back."

"I will, Matt."

"Today. Say today."

"All right, today." She touched my cheek. "Do we have room for all my animal friends?"

I laughed and kissed her warm brow. I wanted to pick her up and spin her around.

"I have another stipulation," she said.

"Anything."

"Keep writing with me . . ."

"Of course." I brushed my thumb over her bottom lip. "Always."

"On in two," a man called.

I peered around the corner at the set. White light illuminated everything: the dark wood floor, the colored panels along the back wall, and a cream-colored couch and armchair. Because of the light, I think, and because of the darkness and chaos backstage, the set looked like heaven. Gail sat forward in the armchair. Her red-brown curls shone.

The light flooded over the audience—mostly women.

"And we're live in three—" A voice sounded through the studio. "Two—"

The canned intro for *Denver Buzz* played from speakers I couldn't see. Cameras panned over the audience. The people clapped and smiled, and Gail stood and strolled across the set. She gave the crowd a confident nod.

Then the crowd quieted and she began to speak.

"Today's guest is a very talented young man who's created a sensation here in Denver and around the nation with his shocking disappearance and, now, his reappearance."

My heart boomed in my ears. Hannah rose to her tiptoes and whispered in my ear. "And one more stipulation, Matt."

"This is his first-ever television appearance," Gail said. "He's agreed to talk openly with me about his life, work, and recent decisions that have stunned many fans."

I mouthed a word at Hannah. *What?*

"Marry me," she said.

Her cool voice, her hot breath, transported me right out of the studio.

I stood there staring at her, holding on to her, breathless and motionless. *Marry me.*

Gail's voice grew louder. She circled back toward her chair. "Please welcome Matthew Sky and Hannah Catalano."

The crowd clapped.

Cameras swiveled on the set.

Hannah took my hand, and we walked out into that light.

To be continued . . .

Dear Reader,

Here we are again, at the end of a book together. This is a good place to be. I hope you enjoyed Last Light *and that you'll enjoy the final installment of the Night Owl Trilogy,* After Dark.

One of the best ways to support an author is by leaving reviews, and I hope you will consider doing that for me. I read all my reviews and I appreciate the feedback.

You can connect with me online at www.mpiercefiction .com and www.facebook.com/MPierceAuthor. Be sure to join the Night Owl Facebook group, where I get to know my readers.

Thanks for your continued support.

M. Pierce

Acknowledgments

Thanks to Jennifer Weis, Betsy Lerner, Sylvan Creekmore, and my team at SMP.

For invaluable encouragement and support, thanks to Lisa Jones Maurer, Kayti McGee, Laurelin Paige, Naomi Walker, and the tireless admins of the Night Owl Facebook group: Jennifer, Michele, and Deborah.

Thanks to the inimitable book bloggers, Maryse of *Maryse's Book Blog;* Gitte, Jenny, and Sian of *Totally Booked;* Aestas of *Aestas Book Blog;* Lisa and Milasy of the *Rock Stars of Romance;* Angie and Kyleigh of *Smut Book Club;* and countless others who have helped spread the word about my books. I wish I could name you all. It's an honor to work with you.

For talking me off the ledge, thanks to Leah Hotcakes Raeder, Tarah, Sheri, Angie, Kiki, Paula, Aimee, and Jen. (I'll bring the rope.)

Many thanks to the friends I have made during this journey— you know who you are—and much love to my readers, to you above all, always.